TARGET

RICKY BLACK

CONTENTS

Chapter One	1
Chapter Two	14
Chapter Three	23
Chapter Four	31
Chapter Five	46
Chapter Six	60
Chapter Seven	70
Chapter Eight	80
Chapter Nine	92
Chapter Ten	104
Chapter Eleven	110
Chapter Twelve	118
Chapter Thirteen	128
Chapter Fourteen	137
Chapter Fifteen	145
Chapter Sixteen	155
Chapter Seventeen	163
Chapter Eighteen	178
Chapter Nineteen	192
Chapter Twenty	200
Chapter Twenty-One	211
Chapter Twenty-Two	221
Chapter Twenty-Three	236
Epilogue	248
Did you enjoy the read?	251
Target Part 2 Preview	253
Prologue	255
Read Blood and Business	257
Also by Ricky Black	259
About Ricky Black	261

CHAPTER ONE
WEDNESDAY 31 JULY, 2013

LAMONT JONES STOOD OUTSIDE A ROOM, listening to two men discuss killing him.

'Del, he's a problem,' the first voice kept saying. It belonged to a man named Ricky Reagan.

'He's pure profit,' a second, more accented voice replied. This one belonged to Delroy Williams, a kingpin on the streets of Leeds. 'Do you realise what we make from *Teflon*?'

'He's too big. Everyone wants to buy more from his people than ours.'

'We control his supply. That means they're still buying from us. We control him.'

'Teflon's sneaky. You think he'll be satisfied behind you? He wants your crown.'

'He does? Or you do?'

Silence followed. Lamont pressed his ear closer to the door.

'What are you trying to say?' Reagan's voice rose.

'Maybe you're not happy with the way things are,' Delroy paused. 'Maybe you think you deserve a bigger slice.'

'It's not about me. It's about Teflon. Gimme the word, and he won't last the night.'

'What, you wanna kill him in my office now? Is that smart?' Lamont heard the amusement in Delroy's tone.

'You're a gangster, not a businessman. Why do you need an office?'

'I'm both. That's why I'm rich. Teflon realises that. You never have.'

'Are you saying he's better than me?'

'I'm saying there's no profit in killing him. Learn to work with Teflon instead of against him. I want you on your best behaviour when he arrives.'

Lamont moved from the door and moved back down the draughty hall. The bribe he'd paid Delroy's people at the door had been worth it. He cut back around, knocked on the door twice and entered.

The office was old, particles of dust visible in the air. A large table dominated the room. The smell clung to Lamont's nostrils; stale cigarettes littering the overflowing ashtray, and the eye-watering scent of white rum.

There were two chairs in the room. One, an oversized throne-like leather chair. The other, a metal contraption more suited for a torture chamber, faced the desk.

Reagan leant against the wall, feral and wild-eyed. His afro-style hair was uncouth, his facial hair neater. He eyed Lamont, nodding. Lamont returned the gesture.

'Good to see you, Teflon. Take a seat,' said the dark-skinned, dreadlocked man in the big seat, Delroy Williams. Born on the Island of Grenada, he'd had fled to Britain after a murder in his home country. He ascended to power in the prosperous, bloody Eighties, resting at the top of the Chapeltown hierarchy. He eyed Lamont with a toothy smile not reflected in his eyes. Lamont sat on the hard-backed metal chair. Reagan bristled behind him. He ignored him, focusing his attention ahead.

'How's business?' Delroy continued, his chair creaking beneath him. From his own seat, Lamont noticed the buttons straining on the short-sleeved shirt the kingpin wore. Other than a shimmering gold watch on his right wrist and numerous rings on his thick fingers, he showed no signs of wealth.

'Business is business,' said Lamont. It was an ambiguous reply, but he wanted to learn why Delroy had summoned him. They were both high enough up on the food chain that they worked through people. He couldn't remember the last time he'd spoken face-to-face with Delroy.

'Business is important, don't you agree?' asked Delroy.

'I suppose I do.'

Delroy's mask vanished. 'Tell me why I've heard things about your team then?'

'What have you heard?'

'You don't know?'

'He probably told them to say it,' said Reagan, interjecting himself into the conversation.

'You don't need to talk about me like I'm not here, Rick.'

'Don't talk like we're friends,' Reagan grumbled.

'I'm talking to your boss, not you.' Lamont kept looking ahead. Reagan's mouth twisted.

'You fuc—'

'Stop.' Delroy didn't raise his voice, but it silenced the pair. Agitated, Lamont tapped a slender finger on the table as Reagan stewed, breathing hard.

'Don't take me for a fool. Do you know or not?' Delroy continued.

'Stop talking in riddles. Just be straight up,' replied Lamont. Delroy studied him. His dark eyes flickered towards Reagan for a moment, then back to him.

'Do you want a drink?'

Lamont didn't. He recognised the intent, however, and nodded. Delroy poured the remnants of the rum into a cloudy glass and handed it to Lamont. He wiped the glass and drank.

'Reagan, wait outside.'

'What for?' Reagan's voice rose.

'I'm trying to talk business with Teflon.'

Reagan didn't move.

'I should be in the room when you're dealing with him.'

'Why? Because you can handle me?' Snapped Lamont without thinking.

'What—'

'Ricky, go.'

Reagan stomped from the room, slamming the door behind him.

'Dunno why you're always aggravating him.' Delroy wiped his eyes. He looked exhausted and sounded less confident than he had earlier. Lamont wondered if it was an act.

'He's emotional. It's not my problem.'

'Until he makes it your problem. I dunno what it is with you two, but Ricky hates you. I don't think you're his best friend either.'

Lamont shrugged.

'Your people are talking shit. They're saying the supply is weak,' said Delroy, realising they were finished discussing Ricky Reagan.

'Do you have names?'

'Forget names. I don't want that crap out there, so get your people in line and sort it. Got that?'

Lamont continued to assess him. The kingpin scratched at his face with a paw-like hand, leaning backwards.

'I said, got that?'

'I suppose I do. Anything else you want to discuss?' Lamont asked. Delroy eyeballed him.

'We've got something coming in a few days. Save it for the drought. We'll tell your people when it's here.'

———

'SOMEONE'S BEEN TALKING.'

Lamont slumped in the passenger seat as Shorty drove away from Delroy's at speed, loud music pumping from the ride. It was a new mixtape by some brash kid Lamont wasn't familiar with. All of Shorty's music sounded the same, though.

Lamont rubbed his temples, his head pounding. The car was stuffy, the smell of weed overpowering. He turned off the music.

'Oi! What are you doing?' said Shorty.

'I'm talking. I don't want to shout over whatever rubbish this is.'

'Ask then. Don't just reach for my shit,' snapped Shorty. A small peanut shell coloured tank of a man, he would bring drama to anyone who wanted it. Brutal and animated, he kept himself in ferocious shape by spending far too many hours training and working the bars in the park.

'Listen then, please. The big man's upset that we said his product was weak.'

'It is, so what's he crying about?'

Lamont shook his head. 'That's not the point. I don't want people talking out of line.'

'People are feeling the pinch, L. We're not making the same off this weak shit. You need to run that to Delroy.'

'Leave the supply to me. While we're paying wages, I want no one talking out of turn. Sort it.'

Shorty cut his eyes to Lamont, not liking the bite in his friend's tone.

'Fine. It's handled.'

'If anyone complains, tell them we'll make it up on the next go around,' said Lamont.

'How? With more crap?'

He didn't bother responding.

―――

'Same old then?'

Shorty had dropped Lamont off at the Park Row apartment of Xiyu Manderson. Known as *Chink*, his nickname came from his light eyes and facial features, inherited from his Chinese mother.

He'd grown up poor in Meanwood. Bullied by the tough kids of his neighbourhood, he learned to stay out of sight, developing a skill with numbers and gaining recognition as a proficient mathematician.

Chink and Lamont had become friends in their teens, and he'd followed Lamont into the drugs game, using his talent for figures to help them gain a foothold. He was smart with his money, and his home represented this. It was spotless, bereft of even the slightest dirt. The furniture combined *The Baroque* with a few modernist pieces, such as Andy Warhol. The windows were wide, all-encompassing, the walls various shades of white and cream. A solid bookshelf displayed various self-help books and history tomes.

'The quality will be shit again.' Lamont rubbed his eyes, sinking into the plush, linen sofa. Chink watched.

'You need to sleep.'

'I will. I thought you needed an update,' Lamont stifled a yawn.

'And Shorty couldn't tell me? Where is he, anyway? Outside smoking ganja?'

Lamont grinned. Shorty and Chink worked alongside each other, but their differences were clear. Shorty was rough and tumble; direct, keeping immersed in the streets. Chink moved behind the scenes, weighing up the profits and flushing them through careful investments.

Chink thought Shorty was a thug, and Shorty believed Chink was a spineless pretty boy. Lamont did his best to keep them apart unless necessary.

'He dropped me here. Had something to do.'

'It was his people spreading those rumours. You know that, don't you?'

'I know.' Lamont was fully aware it was Shorty's guys talking loosely. Shorty didn't respect Delroy or his team, and it was filtering down to the lower ranks. The thought of the drama made his head hurt more. He hoped he had suitable painkillers at home.

'So, tell him. Make him run his crew better.'

'Shorty's fine. Be on hand to coordinate.'

'I know the drill. We're overpaying for crap gear, though. It barely stands up to a cut, and Shorty's people aren't the only ones with complaints. Clients aren't happy.'

'They're still buying.'

Chink's eyes narrowed. 'Yes, they're still buying. Is this how it's going to be? We let Delroy keep diluting the product and wait for our clients to go elsewhere?'

'I've got it covered,' Lamont muttered.

'Do you? Because we already had one venture fuck up. Or did you forget Party in the Park?'

Lamont hadn't forgotten. The plan had been to set up a team of dealers to distribute drugs in the park, and to supply after parties that sprung up after the annual event. He'd had everything in place, but the weak product meant that the buyers copping the drugs opted to work with different dealers.

'Chink, I said I have it covered,' Lamont repeated. He rubbed his head. The headache felt worse now.

'What is with you?' Chink asked.

'Nothing.'

'You look like shit. Something's happened.'

Lamont took a deep breath. 'I got into it with Ricky Reagan.'

Chink grimaced.

'Was that smart?'

Lamont shrugged.

'Did you tell Shorty?'

Lamont smiled. Chink had a habit of asking questions to which he already knew the answer.

'What happened?'

'He kept interrupting when I was talking to Delroy, so I put him in his place.'

'You and your vendettas.' Chink shook his head. Lamont didn't want to talk about Reagan. He didn't want to talk about Shorty or any of it, even though he needed to. He needed to stay on top of the situation, but he couldn't bring himself to care right now.

'I'm tired, Chink.'

'Sleep.'

Lamont looked at him. 'You know what I mean.'

Chink sighed. 'Why do it then?'

Lamont pondered Chink's question. It gnawed at him daily. He took a deep breath, marshalling his thoughts.

'People depend on us to get paid. We used to control everything. Now, it's like a fucking machine. And we're just going along.'

'You don't think you have power?' Chink raised an eyebrow.

Lamont shook his head. 'That's not what I'm trying to say, but, I can't keep making excuses for the life I'm living. Something has to change, and soon.'

'Like?'

'People used to listen,' said Lamont, needing to get the words out. 'Now they don't. Our world used to be about money. Now everyone has something to prove.'

'Didn't we too? Maybe that's the problem, L. You made it. Cars, money, that mini-mansion you've got. There's nothing left to prove.'

'How can I live like that, though? How can anyone live like that? With nothing to prove. No order.' Lamont paused, his voice filled with emotion.

'What happens if I stopped playing by the rules? Does this thing we built fall apart?'

'Is that why you do it? To stop it all tumbling down?' said Chink.

Lamont couldn't answer.

———

THAT NIGHT, Lamont struggled to relax, drifting into a fitful sleep just after four. When he woke, his head still pounded. He dragged himself to the shower, letting the scalding water beat down on his head and shoulders. He closed his eyes, willing the thump of his brain to cease. It was to no avail. He could have stayed in the shower all day, but readied himself instead.

Lamont had several missed calls from his sister, Marika. He stowed his phone and drove to his makeshift office, the backroom of a barber shop on Chapeltown Road. It was almost eleven now, and the barbers was in full flow.

The premises were reasonably sized, with four barber chairs and a tidy waiting area with weathered leather seats. The walls were adorned with flashy pictures of the different hairstyles available, along with a handwritten price list. There were magazines, and an entertainment system in the corner. Sky Sports News results flashed along the bottom of the muted TV. Loud reggae music played, and several of the older guys waiting were nodding their heads.

Lamont greeted them. Trinidad Tommy, the manager, approached, his lined face cracking into a smile.

'Trinidad, everything good?' asked Lamont. The man nodded.

'The crowd will be here soon. You sleep? You look tired.'

'I'm fine.' Lamont excused himself to his backroom office. It was much smaller than the main area, with only a heavy wooden desk, computer chair and several filing cabinets. He looked over the paperwork from his legal ventures and met people to talk business here. Cautious, he ensured it was swept for listening devices, just in case.

Sinking into his chair, Lamont opened the drawer, taking out an open packet of Pro Plus. He dry-swallowed two, glancing at the most valuable thing in the room as he wiped his mouth. It was a battered old chess set. The board was marked, the pieces chipped. He loved it, though. It reminded him of the good times. Fingering several pieces, he put them down and started to work. He pored over several statements, his mind drifting in no time.

'L?'

Rough hands shook Lamont. He woke. Trinidad stood over him, concern in his eyes.

'Are you okay? I was seeing if you wanted any food.'

Lamont stood, yawning.

'No thanks. I'll get something from Rika's.' He wiped his eyes.

Before leaving, he took another two caffeine tablets. As he started his car engine, his eyeballs throbbed. He blinked, pulled out and drove to Marika's. She lived in Harehills, but wanted to move after several incidents with her neighbours. He parked outside and strode in. Marika's place was small, but comfortable, the living room stuffed with toys and pictures of her children, Keyshawn and Bianca. The professional photographs were probably more expensive than the drab furniture. As always, the place was clean.

'Oh, now you wanna turn up?' She looked up from the TV show she was watching. 'I've been ringing you all day.'

'Have you got any paracetamol?'

She fetched him water and a few pills.

'Coffee?' she asked. Lamont nodded.

'Please. Black, no sugar.'

He plopped on the sofa, closing his eyes. Minutes later, he heard the cup being placed next to him.

'Do you want any food? I can warm something up.'

'Sounds good.'

Lamont closed his eyes again, relaxing to the sounds of his sister clattering around in the kitchen. When the food was ready, they ate, talking as they did so. They had their difficulties, as all siblings did, but the love was still strong.

'Why didn't you reply before? I rang you loads of times.'

'I had things to tie up. How much do you want this time?'

Marika pouted.

'How do you know I want money?'

'Don't you?'

'That's not the point.'

Lamont laughed, putting his plate on the coffee table.

'If you say so.'

'I know you've got it, anyway. You lot are killing it on the streets.'

'Says who?'

'Everyone. Keisha told me the other day that Ricky Reagan kept calling out your name.'

Lamont's stomach plummeted. During the day, he had fleetingly thought about the conversation he'd overheard. He'd always known Reagan didn't like him, but the fact he was so open about killing him was unsettling. It remained another reason to make sure he had all the angles covered.

'Is he trying to beef with you?'

'Don't worry about Reagan,' Lamont said, wondering if he could take his own advice.

Shorty sat in the dingy gambling house drinking straight glasses of Hennessy. He'd procured a table in the corner, enabling him to see all the comings and goings.

The gambling house was rife with the pungent smell of sweat, mingled with weed and beer. It was nearly midnight and loud, the music playing in the background drowned out by people talking. It comprised four playing tables, and a few smaller ones. Men crowded the tables, seated on wooden chairs with ripped, cheap leather seating.

There was a backroom with a pool table where the younger crowd congregated. In his corner spot, nobody troubled him. He wanted it that way.

Lamont took a few steps into the gambling house before greetings and requests from all around besieged him.

'Lamont!'

'Yes, L!'

'You good, man?'

Lamont had to buy the bar before being allowed to move. He trudged across the room and sat across from Shorty.

'Bloody vultures,' he muttered.

'You love it. How come you wanted to meet here? This ain't your scene.'

Lamont drank his beer and ordered another one.

'Not like you to drink and drive,' Shorty added. Lamont was a stickler for rules.

'I took a taxi. Dropped my car off.'

'What's going on then?'

Lamont sipped his drink, froth gathering around his mouth. He rested his elbow on the table, which creaked under the weight.

'Did you talk to your people?' he asked. Shorty expressed his disapproval by kissing his teeth.

'Why are you stressing? Forget Delroy.'

'Shorty, we talked about this.'

'We don't work for that fat motherfucker. We can say what we like.'

'While we work *with* Delroy, we stay quiet. Things are going on in the background. There's a plan in place.'

'What plan?'

A heavy hand clapped down on Lamont's shoulder before he could reply.

It was Reggie, one of the old crowd. Once a big deal in the streets, he was now an elderly man whose clothes hung on his frame. He had never planned for the future and had no money saved. It was a sad reality.

'Lamont! How are you?' Reggie's hearing was going, meaning he tended to shout.

'I'm doing well, Reg. How about yourself?' Lamont shook his hand.

'Life is hard. These young ones don't respect their elders. Not like you, Lamont.'

'Sit down with us. Have a drink.'

Reggie indulged, and Lamont slid to order him a white rum from the bar. Shorty glared at the old man. Reggie had clutched the same pint for hours. Shorty had seen it too many times. Reggie would stay all night for free drinks now.

They listened to his tales of the old days, his peeves about life and its disappointments. They started a game of dominoes, Reggie and one of his pals versus Lamont and Shorty. The wily pair decimated them. Shorty was decent, but Lamont was useless, and Shorty wasn't pleased about it.

'Stop messing about. You'd be trying harder if it was chess!' he kept saying.

They left, drunk and poorer. Reggie and his pal had taken them to the cleaners. Shorty wouldn't shut up about it.

'We didn't win a single round. That's ridiculous. You need to stop reading all the time and practise.'

'Piss off. You made me pay for it, anyway. Reggie and his white rums cleared my pockets too.'

'Dunno why you even bother with him. He's washed up. We can't use him anymore,' said Shorty.

'He's an example of how not to turn out. There's a lot to learn from Reggie and his era.'

'Sounds daft.'

Lamont didn't reply straight away, watching Shorty try to light a cigarette.

'Whatever. Where are you going now?'

'I've got a girl on Hamilton Avenue I'm gonna wake up.' Shorty touched fists with him. 'I'll get with you tomorrow.'

Lamont watched him stagger down the street. 'Catch you then.'

CHAPTER TWO
FRIDAY 2 AUGUST, 2013

LAMONT SAT in the back of the barbers, reading a newspaper and trying to ignore the raucous laughter coming from the shop floor. Shorty was supposed to be stopping by. An hour and a half later, he was nowhere in sight. Lamont yawned, stretching.

Trinidad poked his head around the door.

'That white boy's here to see you,' he said in his strong accent.

'Which one?'

'That loud one. Terry.' Trinidad kissed his teeth. Lamont sighed.

'Send him through.'

'Teflon, how's it going, my mate?' Terry strode into the office. Behind him, Lamont saw Trinidad shaking his head as the door closed.

'I'm living. What's new?'

'Mate, life is bloody good. I'm all over. Can't rest. Everything's happening. I'm trying to get my piece of the pie. Got these dudes in Halton Moor, right, they wanna buy—'

'I don't wanna hear that,' said Lamont. The office was swept for listening equipment, but he stayed vigilant.

Terry was a few years older and had been dealing drugs forever. Big money had passed through his hands over the years. Stupid decisions meant he still needed to hustle day in, day out to stay ahead. Lamont recalled him driving flash rides and throwing money around. Now he was struggling.

It was a lesson in how not to play the game.

Despite Terry's obvious flaws, he liked him. Terry could spin a story and draw in a whole room with his tales. He was the quintessential rich-for-a-day, broke-for-a-week type with a pound in his pocket and a dream in his eye.

'Tef, what do you take me for? I swear you act like I'm police or summat sometimes. You wanna check me for a wire?'

Lamont shot him an icy glare.

'You don't need to run your business by me. Got time for a game of chess?'

When he was concentrating, Terry gave a good game.

'Not today, mate, it's boiling. Let's go for a drive.'

'I'm meeting Shorty,' said Lamont.

'Let the little munchkin wait. I bet he was meant to be here about three hours ago. Go on, tell me I'm wrong.'

Lamont laughed.

'Where are you parked?' he asked.

'Behind you. C'mon, we'll drive up to Roundhay, and get a spot of lunch at the pub.'

Lamont nodded. He was hungry, and Shorty was AWOL.

'Lead the way.'

―――

TERRY DROVE, talking a thousand words a second, turning up the radio, trying to shout over it. Lamont stared out of the window, struggling not to laugh at the absurdity of the situation. Terry's gleaming blue Audi was a recent acquisition. He wasn't fooled. Terry was up to his eyes in overhead and trying to live beyond his means. The Audi had been purchased with profits, and now he was struggling to sell it. He had no idea Lamont knew.

Terry's BlackBerry pinged like crazy, but he ignored it, determined to tell as many tales as possible. He locked the car, and the two headed into The Deer Park in Roundhay, procuring a decent table.

Terry wanted to order a bottle of wine, but he vetoed, not wanting to get drunk.

'Anyway,' Terry was still talking twenty minutes later, pausing only to sip his drink and shovel forkfuls of fish pie into his mouth, 'I've got orders going all over the place. Mikey B's moving pills like a bloody pharmacy too! Reckon I could see twenty grand after everything's sold. Not bad for a week's work.'

'What's going on in Halton Moor?' Lamont ignored Terry's lies.

'Everyone wants a slice, don't they? I'm telling ya, I've got a good feeling about the future. Who knows, I might be in your league soon.'

Lamont cut into his steak. It wasn't the best, but it was decent for the price.

'This is good,' he said.

'Yeah, yeah. What's your plan, though?'

'For what?'

'Life. We never talk about you. What's your goal? Ten million?'

'One day at a time.' Lamont cut another piece of steak and chewed.

'Bet you've already got ten, haven't you?' pressed Terry. Lamont didn't understand why his situation was so vital to him. He shrugged.

'Well? What's the crack?' Terry was trying to hit Lamont up for a loan, and as usual, the wannabe kingpin was being evasive. He needed start-up capital to get his schemes moving. That was why he'd invited Lamont to lunch. He'd ruined it, though. Instead of asking straight up, he'd made up a story about Halton Moor.

The only element of his story with any truth was the part about Mikey B; he was moving a lot of ecstasy. He'd dropped Terry as a partner, though, and was making all the money without him. Terry needed to get back on his feet.

TARGET

'I'm okay,' said Lamont. He wanted to reach across and slap him. Lamont treated him like an alien entity, good enough to sit and play chess with for hours on end, but second-class, undeserving of knowing his secrets and thoughts. He believed Lamont was the most guarded person on the planet, and both despised and respected this mindset.

'Fine. How's your love life? Have you banged anyone good?'

Lamont laughed. Terry always brought the conversation back to women.

'Nothing serious,' he replied.

'Mate, you need to get out there. Tell you a story. Met this bird in town, right. Cracking lass, dead bubbly, tits you could set up a fucking home on. I take her home to my abode right, and . . .'

Lamont tuned out, finishing his meal as Terry rambled on about the filth he and the woman had got up to. He liked to talk, and Lamont liked to listen. It was another reason they got along. As Lamont wiped his mouth, his phone rang.

'Hello?'

'Where the fuck are you? I've been here for ages,' said Shorty.

'Just eating lunch. Won't be long.'

Shorty hung up.

'Let's hurry, Terry. Business awaits.' Lamont waited for him to pay the bill.

RICKY REAGAN DROVE through Chapel Allerton in a tinted Vr6. Rap music blared from the speakers, announcing his status. Even in the current heatwave, he rocked a gilet, t-shirt and converse sweatpants. He was armed and ready for any situation. In this game, he had no shortage of enemies.

A lit spliff hung from his mouth as he gripped the steering wheel one-handed. On the passenger seat was a bag of cocaine he was on his way to sell. Delroy had forbidden him from doing this, insisting he work through their network of distributors. Reagan wasn't paying unnecessary middleman fees. He could handle his own business.

Screeching to a halt, he exited the ride, eyes flitting in all directions, looking for anything out of the ordinary. Nothing sprang out, and he banged on the door.

'Ricky mate,' The man said when he saw Reagan standing there.

'Terry.' Reagan pushed past him into the living room, dropping the baggie on the table.

'Get my money,' he ordered. Terry hurried to do his bidding, his face pink. He returned with a stack of money, handing it to Reagan.

'There you go, mate.'

Terry reached into the baggie, scooping out a small amount of the powder with his little finger and snorting it, breaking into a coughing and sneezing fit as the coke hit his sinuses.

'Top stuff!'

Reagan didn't respond, focused on checking his money was correct. Terry watched, lip quivering from cocaine and paranoia.

'Do you know Carlos? That DJ in town? I'm cool with him. You ever need tickets for his shows, I'm your man.'

No reply. He took a deep breath, noticing his hands shaking.

'He's got this half-Brazilian girlfriend too, mate. I'd do all kinds of shit to her. She—'

'Shut up. I'm gone. Bell me when you need more,' snapped Reagan.

Terry nodded and waited for him to leave. He locked the door and hoovered two lines of cocaine, his heart hammering.

———

REAGAN SMILED as he jumped back in his ride. He had Terry right where he wanted him. Soon he would force him to take more drugs, extending him credit and dragging him further into the hole. Terry was a victim. People like Reagan bled victims. That was the game.

Pulling onto Francis Street, he spotted K-Bar, one of Shorty's lieutenants, holding court on the road with some of his people. He cruised by, winding down the window and grilling him. To his credit, K-Bar didn't turn away. He met his gaze with a steely one, not backing down as Reagan vanished around a corner.

SHORTY AND LAMONT hopped out of Shorty's Golf. They were parked on a nice street in Oakwood that screamed *family*. Lamont always felt a sense of peace when he looked at the large houses with their spacious gardens. He followed Shorty, who knocked hard on the door, kissing his teeth and knocking again when the owner didn't answer.

The door swung open, and a woman faced them, panting as her auburn hair fanned her face. She looked at the ground for a moment, taking a deep breath before addressing them.

'God, Shorty, why can't you wait? I've told you before about knocking like that.' She ran her fingers through her hair, pea-green eyes boring into him. Both men stared before coming to their senses.

'Answer quicker next time then.' Shorty pushed past her. 'Where is the most beautiful girl in the world?'

'Daddy!' A tawny bundle of joy charged from the living room and into Shorty's arms. He smothered her with kisses, carrying her back into the room.

'I'm trying to get her settled. Don't get her excited,' said Amy. When Shorty gave no sign he'd heard, she turned to Lamont, hugging him.

'How are you, L? It's been ages.'

'Too long. I'm good, Ames. You?'

Amy and Shorty had been high school sweethearts, their affair far from conventional. She had been the intelligent, studious type, Shorty, hot-headed and streetwise. Their dalliance shouldn't have worked but had. The relationship was torrid and rocky, mingled with affection and a lot of passion.

After school, they had lost track of one another. Shorty hit the streets, getting another woman pregnant when he was twenty-one. After reconnecting with Amy years later, Grace was born.

Nowadays, she worked for a large marketing company. She made a good living, but with the money Shorty threw at her, she didn't need to. It was yet another reason Lamont admired her. She had character.

'I'm good, L. Just working hard and looking after that little madam,' said Amy. They both smiled now, hearing Grace giggle as Shorty tickled her. It amazed Lamont to witness his transformation whenever he was around Grace. The street goon persona diminished, he became much happier, more carefree, dominated by the will of a curly-haired four-year-old with an infectious smile.

Lamont understood that Shorty was making up for not seeing his son, who had moved away with his mother, by being there for Grace. Along with giving Amy money, he spent as much time with Grace as he could.

After playing with Shorty, Grace held out her arms to Lamont, and he gave her a hug and kiss.

'Hello, Gracey-Wacey. Shall we go to the shop?'

Grace nodded. 'I want a Ribena, Uncle. L.'

'C'mon then. Back soon, you two.' Checking to see if they wanted anything, he swung Grace onto his shoulders. Amy and Shorty heard the pair singing as they pranced down the road.

'Lamont should have one,' Amy remarked.

'One what?' Shorty glanced at her.

'A kid. I think he's ready. He has that look when he's around Grace.'

Shorty snorted, dismissing her words. 'L's all about his money. He doesn't need a kid fucking up his flow.'

Amy's brow furrowed, her forehead crinkling. Her mouth opened and closed as she impaled him with a glare.

'Does Grace *fuck up your flow?*'

'Course not. Me and L are different.'

'Maybe. I think he needs it, though.' Amy paused. 'Don't you think he looks . . .' She hesitated again.

'Looks what?'

'He looks exhausted, don't you think?'

'What are you on about?' Shorty resisted the urge to yawn.

'He looks lonely and tired.'

'Lonely? L can get it whenever he wants. He's not lonely.'

Amy shrugged, exposing her neck. His laughter abated as he took in her beauty. As much as she irritated him, the attraction surged within, and he couldn't fight against it. Amy felt his eyes roving her body. Despite her instincts screaming not to, she met his gaze. He invaded her space, capturing her mouth in a vicious kiss, their bodies close enough to feel the others' thudding heartbeat.

'Shorty, they'll be back in a minute,' said Amy, moaning. He ignored her and kissed her pale neck, sending desire shooting down her spine. Before they could take it further, his phone rang.

'Fuck off,' he grumbled, reaching for it. 'Yeah?'

LAMONT AND GRACE returned to the house with enough treats to fill a confectionery. He opened the gate and arched an eyebrow at the sight of Shorty and Chink waiting in the garden, not looking at one another. Grace ran to her dad.

'What are you doing here?' Lamont slapped hands with Chink whilst Shorty led Grace inside.

'I couldn't get hold of you, so I rang Shorty. I have news.'

Lamont checked his pockets. 'Must've left my phone in the car. What's up?'

'I've got us a meeting. You remember Marrion?'

Lamont did. Marrion was an associate Chink had brought up from Manchester a while back to boost their ranks. He'd met him once or twice, but disliked the people Marrion hung with. For that reason, he'd resisted bringing him into the inner fold.

'The Manny guy. Yeah, I remember.'

'He said Akhan's guys were keeping tabs on him. I've taken the initiative and reached out,' said Chink.

'Have you heard anything?' Lamont leaned forward. Akhan was a powerful supplier with links everywhere. He had interests in Leeds, but remained selective about who he worked with. Chink had been working on an introduction, and if Marrion's intel was correct, this would help.

'Not yet. Sounds promising, though. Marrion's seen them around a few times now.'

Lamont mulled it over, not wanting to take the word of someone he didn't trust.

'Put more feelers out. See what you can learn and keep me posted.'

Chink nodded, walking to his car. He drove away as Shorty came outside.

'Amy's gonna kill you for getting Grace all those sweets.'

'She'll have to catch me first.' Lamont grinned.

'Whatever. Where did Chink scurry off to?'

'To get us a new connect.'

Shorty frowned. 'You what?'

'Unlock the car, and I'll explain. I think my phone's in there too.'

CHAPTER THREE

SUNDAY 4 AUGUST, 2013

LAMONT SLOUCHED BEHIND the wheel of a nondescript Nissan. The car wasn't his; he never went to meet people regarding business in his own ride.

Chink had asked him to come to a warehouse out of town they owned. It comprised a large, open space with a table and assorted spindly chairs. Shorty and Chink waited when he arrived, Chink staring at the floor while Shorty messed about on his phone.

'Give me something good,' said Lamont.

'Akhan's people have a spot. Near that old mosque in the Hood. Do you know where I mean?'

Lamont nodded.

'Hares Avenue. It's a good spot. Police stay away from there. They're scared of pissing off the Muslims.'

'Exactly. They've invited us to see Akhan there,' said Chink.

'When?' Shorty asked.

'Tomorrow evening. Eight pm. Me and L will go in. You drive and wait.'

'Are you daft? I'm not waiting in the car.' Shorty crossed his arms.

'It's a meet-and-greet. Why do you need to be there?'

'Why do *you* need to be there?' Shorty's voice rose.

'I want you both there. We'll meet beforehand to prepare. Shorty, make sure K-Bar's on alert, just in case,' said Lamont. Satisfied, Shorty nodded. Chink raked his hands through his dark hair, his mouth tightening. Lamont watched them climb into their cars. He needed to ensure their egos didn't ruin a potential goldmine.

THE NEXT NIGHT, they headed to the meeting in another borrowed ride. Shorty drove, eyes darting between mirrors as he kept a lookout for the law.

When they pulled up on Hares Avenue, two Asian men stood outside a house, smoking cigarettes on the otherwise deserted street. They walked past them, approaching the house. Out of nowhere, half a dozen men surrounded them. Lamont glanced at Shorty, silently warning him to keep composed. After being frisked, the men led the trio upstairs into an opulent study. The room was quiet, a hint of incense in the air. Behind a smooth wooden desk, Akhan waited, perched on his seat. His elbows rested on the desk, hands locked, forefingers pointed outward towards the trio. His midnight-dark eyes assessed them, unyielding, his dark suit unruffled, head tilted to the side.

Chink and Shorty positioned themselves at opposite ends of the room. Akhan motioned for Lamont to sit opposite him, and they shook hands.

'You are Teflon,' he spoke softly, traces of an accent in his voice.

'I am. You must be Akhan.' Lamont met Akhan's eyes.

'I'm pleased to make your acquaintance.' Akhan's expression softened, recognising his intent.

'Likewise. I believe we can be of some use to each other.'

'I concur. We've both done our research. You, Teflon, are exactly the person we want to deal with.'

Lamont hid a smile, pleased it was going so well. It was this easy sometimes, especially if each party knew what the other brought to the table.

'I'm glad to hear it. For any deal to work, though, it is imperative the product remains consistent.' He didn't want the same problems that plagued his relationship with Delroy. He held his breath, knowing Akhan's reply would make or break the deal.

Akhan inclined his head a fraction. 'Our product is solid, I guarantee this. Let's discuss a price.' He scribbled a figure on a piece of paper, passing it to Lamont. He studied the number, hiding his surprise. It was much lower than he had expected.

'This is very generous.'

'If you require credit, I can offer bail on up to ten boxes.'

'I can pay upfront.' Lamont appreciated the offer. Akhan was offering credit for up to ten kilos, which was a huge upfront commitment.

'When you wish to do business, call this number and quote the code, *Mr J*. My men will provide you with the details and a sample as you exit,' said Akhan. Lamont assumed they were finished, and stood to leave. Akhan raised his arm, halting him.

'I also wanted to give you something else; a small token of friendship.'

'You've done more than enough.'

'Please, allow me to present you with this gift.' Whilst Akhan spoke, one of his men placed a black box laced with gold trim in front of Lamont. He felt Akhan's eyes on him as he opened it, stunned by the box's content.

'I'm led to believe you are partial to this brand.' Akhan smiled at Lamont's shock.

It was a bottle of *Centaure de Diamant*. An expensive cognac. Lamont held it in wonder, transfixed by the mahogany colour and elegance of the diamond-shaped bottle.

'I don't know what to say, Akhan. Thank you for this. It's *too lavish*,' his tone was hushed. Akhan shook his head again, implying it was nothing. Lamont gave the bottle to an equally impressed Chink to hold.

'Thank you for agreeing to meet. I think we'll both see the benefits of this arrangement.'

'It's a win-win situation.' Akhan shook his hand, and they left.

'THAT WAS A RESULT!'

Shorty bopped his head to the car music like a madman. There were moments when he could be joyfully childlike. His infectious mood caused Lamont to laugh too.

'Let's not get ahead of ourselves,' said Chink.

'We're sorted now. Those Asians are large,' said Shorty, forgetting his dislike of Chink in his elation.

'Not in the car.' Lamont wouldn't discuss business while they were driving. Shorty scowled.

'Can I taste the sample?'

'No you can't. Take us to Tek's,' said Lamont.

Chink waited in the car. He and Tek had their issues. Lamont knew of them and didn't press it. Tek opened the door to Shorty and Lamont, grinning at the pair like they were long-lost family. He was a middle-aged, burnout former chemist with a knack for drugs. Rail-thin and tattooed, he always seemed to have a spliff resting between his lips.

To most, he was an unreliable cokehead, but to Lamont, he was a genius who'd never reached the heights he should have.

'Tef, thought you were dead, mate!'

'He may as well be.' Shorty brushed past the pair.

'Ignore him. Are you busy?' Lamont led Tek into the house.

'A few peeps are coming over. What's the crack?'

'I've got summat for you to sample.'

Tek lit his spliff and inhaled before offering the joint to Lamont, who declined. Shorty took it.

'Follow me.'

Tek led them to a back room. When he switched the light on,

they were in a room dominated by huge, scientific-looking machines.

'What do you have for me then?' He asked.

'Shorty. Give him the ting,' said Lamont. Preoccupied with the spliff, he flung the pack at Tek, who caught it, and opened it with a small pocket knife. He placed the crystal-white powder into a glass vial, mixed up a solution, and added this to the same vial, before placing it into a large machine at the far end of the room.

'What the fuck is that?' Shorty asked.

Tek didn't reply. He hunched over the machine, pressing buttons and staring at several lines and equations that had appeared on the screen.

Shorty glanced over at Lamont, who watched Tek, his curiosity piqued. He had brought Tek product to test before and never had it elicited this reaction. He strode over to see the screen, which displayed a complex-looking graph. Tek was gazing at this, mumbling gibberish that only meant something to him.

'Go on, what does it mean?' Lamont asked.

'This beauty is a mass-spectrometry machine.' Tek gazed at the graph. 'It separates the individual components and identifies the chemical signature of the substances within the sample you provided.'

'What does that mean?' Shorty spoke louder, annoyed at Tek for ignoring him.

'It means, you're looking at cocaine that is around seventy percent pure.'

'Don't lie!' Shorty's eyes widened.

'There are other tests, but it's fantastic. The last stuff you guys gave me, I could barely get a reading.'

Lamont beamed. If Tek was correct, the product he had was better than anything else in Leeds. He could cut the cocaine four, maybe five times and still have the best merchandise. His excitement bubbled. Life was about to change.

'L, may I?' Tek motioned to the rest of the sample. They were in the living room now, remnants of dinner on the coffee table, mingled with several cans of lager. Cigarettes and weed stench hung in the air, mingled with Lynx. Lamont nodded. He'd earned a taste.

'Me too,' said Shorty, crowding over the coke Tek had now placed on his coffee table.

'Be careful, this is strong shit,' Tek warned as he scooped a large amount on the end of his car key. Shorty snorted the powder, his head jerking back as he spluttered.

'It's not all that,' he said, his face twisting. Lamont stared. Shorty's nose was dripping, and he hadn't realised.

'L, you need to bang that at least four times.' Tek scooped a small amount up with his pinkie finger and ingested it. 'You'll kill someone otherwise.'

Shorty cottoned onto his nosebleed, stemming it with a piece of tissue as he paced the room. Lamont beckoned him over.

'Get the word out. We've got some new shit. Get it pinging.'

'Say no more.' Shorty left the room. Lamont knew the drill. He would relay to K-Bar, who would arrange delivery and figures. The operation was fluid, large in scope and well-structured. Akhan's drugs would launch it into another stratosphere.

'Tek, we're leaving.' Lamont motioned to the coke. 'Keep that.'

'Cheers. Stay and meet my mates before you go, though. They'll be here in a sec.'

Turning to the window again, Lamont looked out at Chink. A car pulled in behind him.

'Chink's waiting,' he said. Tek replied, but he didn't hear a single word he said. A man climbed out of the second car, but the woman stepping from the passenger seat distracted him.

The world behind her melted. Raven-haired and long-legged, her pronounced curves were untamed by the conservative khaki jumpsuit she wore. Lamont's eyes blurred, unable to blink, unwilling to tear his eyes away.

'Tef! Are you listening?' Tek's voice rose.

'Sorry. What did you say?' Lamont remained glued to the window.

'What's Chink's problem? I paid him back.'

She entered Tek's garden. Sensing Lamont's presence, she looked up. For a moment, chestnut eyes met his rosewood own, then she was in the house. He stepped back. Tek played host, the conversation forgotten.

'Tone, good to see you mate. Can I get you a drink? A line?' Tek rambled, his mannerisms more vivacious under the influence of the drugs. 'Jenny, how're you doing, lass? Haven't seen you since we got stranded down in Brum that weekend.'

'L.' Shorty walked into the room before Lamont could hear Jenny's reply. His nose had stopped bleeding.

'Is it sorted?'

'K-Bar's on top of it. Who is *that*?' Shorty leered at Jenny.

'Your guess is as good as mine,' said Lamont.

'She's tasty.'

Lamont frowned, but marshalled his irritation.

'Calm down, player. We need to leave.'

Before they could move, Tek led his friends over to them.

'Let me introduce you. Tone, Jen, these are my good friends, Lamont and Shorty. You two, these are my long-time compadres, Tony and Jenny.'

Lamont and Shorty shook hands with them, lingering a second longer with Jenny. Close-up, she stole Lamont's breath; she wore a touch of makeup, hair flowing past her shoulders with loose bangs either side. It suited her.

They spoke for a short while, learning Tony worked in a bank, whilst Jenny ran her own florists. Lamont couldn't tell if the pair were together. If they were, he decided it wouldn't stand in his way. Jenny was extraordinary.

Chink glared at the pair as they climbed in the car a while later.

'What took so long? It's freezing in here.'

'You should have come inside then. Tek was proper hospitable.' Shorty wiped his nose again.

'Whatever, cokey.' Chink's lip curled as he glared. Shorty

ignored him and tried to start the engine, still dazed from the cocaine.

'I'll drive.' Lamont saw Shorty was confused. Chink watched them switch seats.

'How are we looking then?' he asked.

'I think you'd better order more benzocaine.' Lamont flashed his friend a large grin.

ONCE HOME, Lamont headed to his drinks cabinet and added the bottle of cognac to his collection. He gazed, touched by both the gift and the gesture itself. Akhan had found out what he enjoyed, which appealed to his ego.

During the meeting, he'd noticed not just power, but also the casual elegance only the wealthy possessed. He thought of Delroy, who had money but didn't use it with the same panache Akhan did. The timing was perfect.

There was more money to be made, and Lamont resolved to delay his departure a while longer. He fixed another drink and smiled to himself as he fantasised about his future.

CHAPTER FOUR
TUESDAY 6 AUGUST, 2013

TERRY WORTHY DROVE along the quiet street, looking for a parking spot. His clammy hands gripped the steering wheel as he turned down the thumping hip-hop song he'd been listening to.

Two youngsters waited, clad in dark tracksuits. One towered over the other. Terry scoped the lining of his muscle through his Nike top. His companion had a ratty smile on his pointed face. Terry signalled for them to get in.

'Let's make this quick.' He reached under his seat, handing the boy the drugs. The kid looked at the packet, passing it to his ratty associate. He went to open the passenger door, but Terry grabbed his arm.

'What the hell are you doing? Where's my money?'

'Inside,' the boy pointed at the house, 'I'll be two minutes.'

'I said I wanted to be quick.'

'It will be, man. Chill. Like I said, two minutes.'

'Don't fuck me about,' Terry warned. The boy nodded, not meeting his eyes.

'Yo, I know who you are, Terry. I wouldn't mess about a top boy like you.'

Terry smirked, satisfied that the kid knew his rep. The youngsters climbed from the car and hurried into the house. Once they brought his money back, he would clear one thousand pounds in profit for little work. He checked his watch a few minutes later when the kids didn't return. Grumbling, he climbed from the car and hurried towards the house. He knocked twice on the door, but received no reply.

Panicking, he burst into the derelict house. A cool breeze coming from the kitchen led him to an open back door. He reached the gate in time to see a taxi speed away.

'OI!' Terry shouted, but it was too late. The youths had vanished, and so had his drugs.

───

'I CAN'T BELIEVE how easy that was,' Timmy Turner laughed from the taxi. His plan had gone off without a hitch. He had played to Terry Worthy's ego, counting on the old relic thinking he feared him. The ounces they robbed would pay for their night, and they would have money left to flip.

'Told you. Terry's not gonna do shit,' said Ben, his thick-lipped, ratty-looking accomplice. He worshipped Timmy and followed him, trying to make money and get laid in equal succession. He failed most of the time, but Timmy liked him. Ben was entertaining in his own way.

'Where are we going?' the driver asked. Timmy gave him the address and pulled out his phone with a smile. Business was on the up.

───

REAGAN STORMED DOWN THE STREET, mobile phone in hand and danger in his eyes. He'd built an impressive reputation over the years, yet people still seemed to try him. Terry hadn't repaid him yet for drugs he'd received on credit, and now he was ducking his calls. Reagan could almost hear Delroy's voice in his head, telling him *I told you so*, lording it over him as he stuffed his fat face with yet another meal. As always, he would leave one hell of a message and remind the streets why they feared him.

With two phone calls, he had Terry's new location. A group of teenagers chilled on the road, laughing and joking, listening to music on their mobiles. Reagan quickened his step, pushing through the crowd. None protested. Some knew him by face, the rest by reputation.

As Reagan approached his destination, a figure climbed from a parked car and fell in sync with him. Younger and almost as ruthless, TC had worked with him for years. Reagan kept him close, using him for missions and to send messages.

Terry was a buffoon, but he was cool with Teflon, and some of his sneakiness may have rubbed off. He wasn't taking any chances. TC was armed and had no qualms about using his weapon. The pair of them climbed up the steps. At a signal from Reagan, TC kicked the door in. They charged into the living room, startling Terry.

'Ricky, mate—'

Reagan didn't hesitate. A single blow cracked the bridge of Terry's nose. He toppled to the ground, the air driven from his lungs as Reagan stomped on his ribs. TC watched with a smile on his face, keeping an eye out for intruders as Reagan kicked Terry again.

'You think I'm a prick? Thought you could take my shit and not pay?' He kicked him a third time. Terry curled into a ball, retching and moaning, holding his ribs.

'Ricky, mate, I got robbed. Please—'

'I don't give a fuck. Get up.'

Terry froze with fear.

'I said get up,' said Reagan. He struggled to his feet.

'Now, tell me how you're gonna get what you owe me?'

'Mate. I'm fucked. I've got nothing.'

Reagan signalled to TC, who drew his gun and aimed it at Terry.

'Not good enough.'

'I've got a mate doing pills. I'll get the money from him, I promise,' pleaded Terry, mucous mingling with the blood and tears. Reagan glared, breathing hard, smarting fists still clenched.

'You've got until tomorrow night. Don't think about running. I tracked you once, and I'll do it again. TC,' he turned to his accomplice, 'teach him a lesson before we go.'

MIKEY B WAS a former doorman turned pill seller. He'd stumbled into the game after door work dried up, and had done well. On the scale of things, he seemed like an ordinary decent guy. He kept himself in shape and had shovel-like hands that resembled *The Hulks*. He'd taken his hits, grinding to get into a solid financial position.

Now, Terry sat, trying to hit him up for money.

They were at Mikey's home. He'd moved from a spot in Cottingley to a bigger place in Moortown, liking the quiet. As the pair spoke, classic *Britpop* played in the background. Mikey took a deep swig from a bottle of Coors, facing the mess in front of him.

'I need you, mate,' said Terry.

Mikey sighed, putting the bottle down. Terry was his friend, but the guy gave new meaning to the word *fuckup*. He owed Ricky Reagan money and had no hope of paying it back in the time allotted.

'Please, Mikey. Gimme the five grand. I'll pay him, and that'll be the end.'

'How would you pay me back?' Mikey asked.

Terry hesitated. 'I could work it off.'

'You got yourself into this position because you couldn't slang the drugs, but I'm supposed to believe you're gonna pay me back? Do you think you can rip me off because we're mates?'

'I'd never rip you off! The difference is you won't kill me if I'm late. Reagan is serious. He will murder me if I don't get his money. I need five bags. I know you've got it.'

'Yeah, I've got it. Worked hard for it too. Why can't you ask Lamont for the money?'

'Are you serious? He'll set me up on some payment scheme, then Shorty will rip my head off if I miss it. How is that any better?'

'Who ripped you off?' Mikey hated the part of him wondering if Terry was making the whole thing up.

'Some youngsters. Do you know little Timmy Turner? Black lad, well built.'

'You mean Shorty's little cousin?'

'Timmy's related to Shorty?' Terry froze, eyes widening from the information.

Mikey shook his head. 'You can't be serious.'

'The sneaky little shit. I can't believe he skanked me.'

'I can't believe you let him. Speak to Lamont. Get him to make Timmy give you the money back.'

Terry hesitated. Mikey resisted the urge to smack his friend. He had no problem asking Mikey to loan him money, but he baulked at asking someone else for help.

'Take your chances with Reagan then. Either way, I'm not giving you the money, so there you go.'

CARLOS LOUNGED AROUND AT HOME, trolling on the internet. He was a smooth-skinned man with traces of Asian and Irish blood in him. He was about his music and was popular and outgoing.

Zoë was making them dinner and dancing to music. They were both so engrossed that they didn't hear the door until the person knocked louder. Carlos grumbled and went to open it. When he did, two men pinned him to the floor. They laid into him with punches and kicks, subduing him. Zoë heard the commotion and ran towards them, screaming. One caught her with a vicious backhander. She hit the carpet with a tremendous thud and lay still.

'Zoë!' Carlos tried crawling to her.

'We'll deal with your bitch later. This is about you,' One of them snarled. Through woozy eyes, Carlos recognised the man as Ricky Reagan. He had seen him in town and knew he was a big deal.

'Ricky? What the fuck, man? What is this about?'

Reagan grinned. 'You know me then?'

'Course I know you. Everyone knows you. Why are you doing this?'

The grin hadn't left Reagan's face. 'Ask Terry Worthy when I'm finished.' He hit Carlos again, knocking him out. He and TC turned their attention to Zoë, still sprawled out in the middle of the living room.

'Lock the door,' Reagan ordered.

———

Lamont watched the crowds of people as the taxi approached a busy street, teeming with clubs and loud music. Still buzzing from the meeting with Akhan, Shorty wanted to celebrate. Lamont was reluctant, but was talked into it. He'd spent his day dealing with an issue that had cropped up.

Terry Worthy had stupidly done a deal with Shorty's younger cousin, Timmy. He'd ripped Terry off, which Lamont found amusing. He didn't want to be associated with skanking, however, so Shorty had forced Timmy to give Terry the drugs back, issuing his cousin a stern warning.

The pair made their way to Normans Bar on Call Lane. A popular nightspot, it had a pure white ceiling, thin, dark brown pillars, comfortable purple booths, and a well-stocked mahogany and glass partitioned bar. Loud R&B music was being spun by the resident DJ, and the crowds were feeling it.

Shorty and Lamont fought their way to the bar and ordered bottles of beer. They were well-dressed and turning heads, but none of the females were biting yet. Shorty had his phone out, making calls, trying to get anyone else to come out.

'Losers.' He kissed his teeth. 'Everyone's moving soggy. Wanna go somewhere else?'

'I'm following your lead,' said Lamont. Shorty glared and was about to retort when he spotted something. His eyes narrowed.

'Back in a minute.'

Lamont sipped his drink and watched him disappear. He spotted a petite blonde standing nearby, wearing a short black dress and heels. She was pretty but wore too much makeup. As she swayed to the music, she grinned at him. About to go in for the kill, a movement by the entrance held his attention.

Jenny had entered, flanked by two other ladies. She wore a sleeveless top and loose-fitting trousers and was striding across the bar with her people like she owned the place. He stared, transfixed. His new friend sensed his attention wavering. She shifted closer, but it was futile. Lamont took a deep breath and stepped forward.

———

'IT'S TOO PACKED IN HERE,' moaned Kate. Jenny's best friend since their younger days, she was a cocoa-skinned woman with sultry features and an hourglass figure. She stared around the bar with barely veiled contempt, her glossed lips smacking together.

'Don't worry. We'll have a drink and go somewhere else.' Jenny led the way when a hand touched hers, halting her. Startled, she turned to protest when she realised it was the dealer she'd met at Tek's place, *Lamont*. The corners of his eyes crinkled as he grinned.

'Jenny, right?'

'You're Lamont. Tek's friend.' Jenny felt her friends staring, so she kept her attention on Lamont.

'That's right. What are you drinking?' He motioned to the bar. A blonde girl stood there, shooting daggers at Lamont and also Jenny, who picked up on this.

'It's fine. We can buy our own.' She wanted to put distance between them. The last thing she needed was trouble.

'I insist.' Lamont looked past her at her friends. 'Apologies, I didn't catch your names.'

'I'm Kate.'

'Michelle,' The other added.

'Nice to meet you both. You look gorgeous,' Lamont said. They beamed, pleased with the compliment. 'What are you drinking?'

Neither hesitated in ordering. With reluctance, Jenny did the same, unable to see the jilted girl now.

'Here you go.' Lamont passed their drinks, then paid with a fifty-pound note. He held out his glass.

'To exquisite company.'

Their glasses clinked, and they all took a sip.

'Are you by yourself?' Kate asked. He shook his head.

'My mate's around somewhere.'

'What about that girl?' said Jenny.

'Which girl?' Lamont frowned.

'The blonde one by the bar giving me dirty looks.'

'She's nobody. Don't worry about her.' Lamont didn't bother looking for the girl. His dismissive arrogance irked Jenny. She let it slide, watching him charm her friends with ease. She sighed.

'Are you okay?' Lamont asked.

'I'm fine.'

'I'll get you another drink. Who's up for champagne?'

Before they could answer, there were loud voices and screams. Lamont moved into a better position, unsurprised by what he saw.

―――――

AMY WAS on a rare night out. Since having Grace, her social life had dwindled. Her friend had dragged her out, insisting she needed it. After picking out a dress and sinking several glasses of wine to calm her nerves, she complied. She'd missed it more than she thought. Guys were all over her, and she enjoyed the attention. In the middle of dancing with one of her admirers, a voice made her freeze.

'What are you doing here?'

Amy whirled around. Shorty stood there, his face twisted with fury, his nostrils flaring.

'Hey, Shorty,' she said.

'Where's Grace?'

'At the bar, where do you think?'

'Don't play with me.'

Amy saw the muscles straining against his dark t-shirt, his eyes red.

'She's with my mum. What's your problem?' Amy fiddled with her bracelet. Shorty's eyes flitted to her dance partner.

'Leave. I need to talk with my girl.'

'Shorty, I am not your girl. We were just dancing. It's no big deal.'

'Mate, I don't want any trouble.' The man was already backing away from Amy.

'Move then.'

'Shorty, please just go. We can talk about this tomorrow.' Amy sighed when a bouncer waded over, sticking his chest out.

'Is there a problem over here?' He asked her.

'Yo, this is between me and her,' Shorty barked at the bouncer.

'Calm down, pal.'

'Fuck you.'

'That's it. You're out. Let's go.' The bouncer tried grabbing him, but he shrugged him off. Two more bouncers stormed over. The music had turned down, and everyone watched the standoff. The trio surrounded Shorty, but he didn't seem fazed. They grabbed for him, and he tussled with them.

'Get off him!' screamed Amy. Shorty continued to struggle, but they were overpowering him.

'Stop. That's enough.' Lamont was in the mix now. One bouncer paused.

'That you, L?'

'I need you to cut him loose,' said Lamont. 'Are you okay?' he asked Amy, who nodded, taking a deep breath. The bouncers let

Shorty go. After a glare from Lamont, he walked out, not even looking back at Amy. Debbie appeared at her side carrying two Amaretto and Cranberry drinks.

'What happened?' she asked, sensing the tension.

Amy stared at her friend, feeling tears pooling in her eyes, suddenly wanting to go home.

———

The following day, Lamont woke early. Instead of getting up, he lay back and assessed the night before. He'd calmed Shorty down and stuck him in a taxi, thankful he hadn't ended up arrested or hospitalised. By the time Lamont re-entered the club, Jenny had disappeared. He found his thoughts drifting towards her. He visualised her big brown eyes, long legs, her penetrating glare, and imagined what it would be like to watch her com*e undone.*

With a flourish, he climbed out the bed and hurried to get ready. He had a plan.

———

Tek stumbled downstairs, half-naked and grumbling. The loud banging at the door had ruined an otherwise perfect lie-in.

'I'm coming. Chill,' he shouted, tripping over a pair of stray Converse trainers by the door. 'Shit.'

Locating the key, Tek unlocked the door and glared at Lamont.

'L, man. What gives? It's proper early.'

'I needed to see you. Make some coffee and wake up.'

'This is my place, not yours,' Tek grumbled as he headed to the kitchen. In the time since Lamont had last been, the house was no cleaner. The ashtray on the coffee table was cluttered with weed roaches and cigarette butts. He perched on a chair and opened an energy drink he'd bought on the way, gulping it.

'What's up? Got another sample for me to test?' Tek took a hopeful sip of coffee.

'I'm not here about business.'

'Go on then. What's on your mind?' Tek made himself comfortable.

'That girl from the other night. What's the story?'

Tek laughed, spilling his drink. He ignored the billowing liquid staining his sofa as he sniggered.

'Surprise, surprise. I saw you eyeing her.'

'I'm curious, that's all.'

'When aren't you? Bloody hell, L, you run through these birds like Usain Bolt.'

'Stop messing about.'

'I'm not. C'mon, you think you're the only one? Jenny's got a lot of guys chasing her.'

'What do I need to know?'

'How the hell would I know? If I knew, I'd take a run myself.'

'I saw her last night. Do you have a number for her?' Lamont pressed. Tek drained his cup and got up.

'One sec.' He stomped upstairs, returning with Kate. She had a duvet wrapped around her body and a tired smirk on her dishevelled face. 'This sexy queen might help. Usually finds her way here after a night out.'

'He means he *took advantage* while I was drunk,' Kate's tone was glib. 'Nice to see you again, L.'

'Likewise. Where'd you lot go last night?'

'Down to Greek Street. You didn't think you had Jenny after one drink, did you?' Kate raised an eyebrow. Tek giggled. Lamont glared.

'Jenny's a tough nut to crack. You want her, you need to surprise her,' Kate continued.

'How?'

'She needs a driver,' Kate said after thinking for a minute, 'to do deliveries. She's advertising for it. Take her work number. The rest is up to you.'

'That works.' Lamont smirked.

Mikey B sat in Terry's tatty flat, watching his friend knock back another beer.

'Mikey, I fucking love you, mate.'

The drugs Timmy had brought back rested on the table next to two empty bottles.

'You've saved my skin! I can give these to that psycho.'

Mikey B shook his head. 'That's not gonna work. Ricky doesn't want the drugs, he wants his money. Have you got anyone else you can move it through?'

'Yeah, course. I've got loads of connections,' said Terry, as if he hadn't been ripped off. Mikey had to hand it to him; he didn't stay down for long. Whatever disappointment life threw at Terry, he took it.

'Why did you sell to Timmy then?'

Terry struggled to answer.

'He's a wrong sort. Why deal with him over someone else? You know what these youngsters are like.'

'I had plans, and I was in a hurry.' Terry scratched his face. 'It's cool now, though. I'll flip this work, pay Ricky, and that's the end. When I'm done, maybe we can talk about —' His phone rang. He answered, listened for a minute, then stumbled to his feet.

'I'm on my way. C'mon, Mikey! We need to go.'

The scrap of paper with Jenny's number burned a hole in Lamont's pocket as he lounged in his home, eyes closed as the sounds of *John Legend's Get Lifted* album filled the room. He grabbed the number, gazing as if it held the answers to a test. Smirking, he laughed out loud at the absurdity of his situation.

Lamont had things in motion, yet here he sat, scheming to get a date like some horny teenager. Jenny had him, though. No stranger to the fairer sex, few had ever captivated him at first glance like she had. He had a sudden brainwave whilst he made a cup of coffee. Before he could stop himself, the phone was in his hand.

'Jenny Campbell speaking?'

Lamont froze.

'Hello? Is someone there?'

'I'm calling about the delivery job,' he said, altering his voice.

'Excellent. Let me jot down the details. I need your name and the best contact number, please.'

Straight to business. Lamont liked that. He gave her a fake name and arranged a meeting for the following day. Determined to make a better impression, he had a surefire way to accomplish his goal.

Terry stood near the door, watching Carlos sob.

'What happened?'

Carlos glared at Terry, his tears dissipating.

'I'll tell you what happened. That psycho Ricky Reagan came to my house, beat the shit out of me and raped my girl. Because of you.'

'Mate, I—'

'Did you tell him about Zoë? Because he said I needed to blame you. Is that what you did?'

'Mate, you've got it all wrong. I said I could get him some tickets to a show. I never told him to do this.'

'Don't you get it? He sent you a message because you mentioned me. Because you always have to be the fucking big dog, talking yourself up, making yourself seem like the main attraction. All because you're an insecure little prick.'

'Steady on pal, I know you're upset, but—'

'Upset?' Carlos pointed upstairs. 'They raped the woman I love. She hates me. As far as she's concerned, it's all my fault, because I've got friends like you.'

Terry hung his head. He stared at the floor, feeling Carlos's pain, knowing how much he loved Zoë. Terry couldn't explain why he had brought her into his conversation with Reagan. He hadn't even thought the thug was listening. Now, Reagan had retaliated in the worst way.

'Carlos, I'm sorry,' He said, his voice thick with emotion.

'Get out of my house. I hope I never see you again.'

Terry was quiet as they left Carlos' place. Mikey drove along, listening to the radio. After a few minutes, he turned it down.

'You need to shift this gear sharpish and get that crazy cunt off your back. Okay?'

Terry didn't reply.

'Oi,' Mikey raised his voice. Terry looked up. 'I know you're upset, but you need to sort this. I'll stay with you until it's done; we'll give him the money together, make sure this is all done with.'

Terry nodded, feeling a profound guilt over what had happened to Zoë. She was a nice girl, and he had shouted his mouth off about her for no reason.

Mikey was on his phone. With a single call, he had a buyer for the product, and they were on their way to meet him. The only downside was they were selling cheap, killing Terry's profit.

Never had Terry felt so far behind the pack. Mikey moved pills, yet with ease, had secured someone to take the cocaine. Resigned to whatever happened, he stared out of the window.

Reagan met Terry outside a barber shop in Harehills. He leant against a Mercedes Benz in a designer tracksuit, laughing to himself. TC watched the pair, his eyes lingering on Mikey, sizing him up.

'Terry! Good to see you. You got that then?' said Reagan. Terry handed him the money without meeting his eyes.

TARGET

'Summat wrong, Tezza? You're not your usual gossipy self. No stories for me?'

Terry didn't reply, watching him thumb through the money. They were standing in public, and he was a known criminal, but he didn't seem to care.

'Got any more links? The last one you recommended, she was everything you said she would be. Isn't that right, T?' Reagan turned to his soldier.

TC nodded, licking his lips. 'Dead right. She was delicious.'

Terry looked up, eyes blazing. Reagan noticed, and his attitude changed. The playful manner dissipated. He dropped the stack of money through the open passenger-side window.

'You got summat you wanna say? Go on, say it.'

Terry didn't speak. Mikey stepped forward.

'I've got summat *I* wanna say,' he started. 'You may think it's cool to rape a bird, but it's not. You've got your money. Stay away from Terry now. This is done.'

Reagan frowned. No one spoke to him like that. He stepped forward. Mikey had two inches and some size on him. Reagan met his glare, eyes narrowed.

'Who do you think you are?'

'I'm the one who tells you what others won't. Rape isn't summat to brag about.'

Reagan shook his head. 'You don't wanna get on my bad side. I can promise you that.'

'Like I said, you got your money. Your business with Terry is over. That's the end.' Mikey B stared into his eyes.

'Is it?' Reagan's voice was full of malice. TC watched the exchange, debating whether to get involved. He had seen Mikey in the company of some heavy faces. It wasn't worth the aggravation.

'Rick, we've got that meeting. Let's deal with this later,' he said. Reagan nodded. Not taking his eyes off Mikey, he climbed into the passenger seat. TC started the engine, and they motored off down the street.

CHAPTER FIVE
THURSDAY 8 AUGUST, 2013

JENNY'S DAY WAS NON-STOP. A spate of summer events meant that she'd worked hard to meet orders whilst interviewing for a new driver. They were more like meet-and-greets, but she felt burnt out. She didn't want to hire the wrong person. The right driver could take her business to the next level. She was getting more opportunities from other cities. Her arrangements were unique, and people loved them.

The interviewees so far were awful. The first didn't have a licence but expected Jenny to give him a job *driving*. Another had been a horny lorry driver, who spent the entire meet staring at her chest and not-so-subtly rubbing himself. It was revolting.

Now, she was in her office checking that she still looked professional. She had put an apron over her blouse and smoothed her hair. She noted the bags under her eyes. The door to the shop clanged. The next applicant was here.

'One moment,' she called. Composing herself, she walked out and stopped short.

'What the hell?'

Lamont Jones stood by the door. He nodded, watching her with appraising eyes.

'Nice to see you again.'

'Lamont, I'm working.'

'Correct.'

'I'm expecting someone.'

'Walter, right?' Lamont mimicked the voice from the night before. 'I'm here about the job.'

Jenny looked him up and down. He wore a plum-coloured, creaseless shirt, black trousers, and expensive-looking shoes. In his right hand, he clutched a ring binder. The cocksure expression on his face annoyed her so much that she called his bluff.

'Okay then, *Walter*. Follow me, and we can begin.' Jenny locked the shop door and led him to the office. She slid behind her desk and motioned for him to take a seat.

'Let's get started,' she picked up a pen, ready to take notes. Her face was composed, and her manner brisk. 'Can I see your CV?'

Lamont handed it to her. She scanned it, impressed by the layout.

'Full name?'

'It's right in front of you.' Jenny scowled. 'Sorry. Lamont Jones.'

'Age?'

'Thirty-two years and six months.'

'And what do you do? Are you in employment?'

'This and that.'

'Care to be more specific?'

'Okay. Supply and demand,' said Lamont with a wink. Undeterred, Jenny wrote his responses.

'Do you have a valid UK driver's licence?' She continued. He nodded.

'I will ask a few work-related questions, just to see what kind of worker you would be.'

'Fire away.'

'Why do you want the job?'

'It has great benefits.'

'Such as?'

'A *stunning* work environment.' He met her eyes. She held his gaze for a second, then continued.

'What skills do you bring to the workplace?' Her tone remained unchanged.

'I make a good cup of coffee, I entertain, I have flawless speaking skills, people skills, humour.' Lamont counted the traits on his fingers. 'Do I need to continue?'

Despite herself, his reply tickled Jenny. To her surprise, he rose to his feet.

'Wait, don't answer that. I'll do a practical demonstration.'

'W-What?'

'I'll make you a kick-ass cup of coffee.' Lamont took two mugs from the cupboard and added coffee to them. Jenny watched, feeling like she was losing control of the situation.

'Aren't you going to ask how I want it?'

'Nope. I'm gonna *tell* you how to take it,' He winked again. 'Assertiveness, right?'

She didn't respond. His dismissive arrogance in the club had irritated her. Now, he seemed wittier than she had given him credit for. Before she could ponder any further, he placed a cup in front of her.

'Drink it.'

'It needs milk.'

'No, no. Take it black.' Lamont smiled again and sipped his own coffee. *He was playing games.* Jenny sipped the drink. It was strong, but not bad.

'It's good, right?' He watched her face.

'Let's press on. What do you have in the folder?'

'Apart from the CV, I've got my birth certificate, NI number, CRB form, driver's licence, qualifications, references, blah blah.' He pushed the folder towards her.

Jenny looked through the paperwork, again impressed by the layout. Lamont had gone to a lot of trouble to impress.

'Who is Martin Fisher?' She glanced at his references, noting the contact number.

'My boss. He owns a small gym. I work there from time to time.'

'You said earlier that your business was supply and demand.'

'I work recreationally. I *demand* my clients work their hardest to achieve their goals, and I *supply* the workplace, motivation and overall fitness expertise.'

Jenny hid a smile at the speed of his responses. He talked a good game.

'What are your hobbies and interests?'

'I like to play chess, I read—thrillers mostly. Slight film buff. I follow sports. I—'

'Like to drink champagne in clubs,' Jenny interjected. Lamont laughed.

'I'm isolated, but sometimes I need to be social.'

'Are you good at chess?'

'I know my way around the board. Do you play?'

Jenny nodded.

'We must play together sometime.' Lamont's rosewood eyes burned into her. She looked away.

'Let's push on. If I was to call you in the middle of the night and ask you to deliver to Birmingham, would you be able to do it?'

'I have *no problem* working through the night.' He let the double entendre hang in the air. Against her better judgement, she grinned.

'Okay. Wait—what's the time?'

'Quarter to six.' Lamont checked his watch.

'Really?'

'Time flies when you're having the time of your life.'

Jenny studied him. 'You don't give up, do you?'

'There's no fun in giving up. When are you going to let me take you out?'

'I don't date employees, Mr Jones. I have a strict policy.'

'So I have the job then? Because I'll quit to uphold the sanctity of your policy. I swear I will.' Lamont placed his hand over his heart. She laughed. He watched, beaming.

'It makes sense, Jen. We get along. What's one little date going to do?'

'Fine,' Jenny sighed. 'If it gets you to leave, I'll do it.'

'Splendid. I'll need that personal number, and I'll be on my way.' Lamont eased to his feet. The corners of her mouth twitched as she wrote her number on the corner of his CV. Tidying his paperwork, she closed his ring binder and handed it to him.

'Don't be ringing me at two in the morning about a booty call.'

'I'll try. If you get the urge, I'd be chuffed if you acted on it.' Lamont held out his hand. 'Thank you for taking the time to meet with me. I'm sorry I wasn't suitable for the role,' he deadpanned. Jenny shook his hand, impressed by his firm grip. She held it longer than was necessary, letting go once she realised this.

'I'll see you soon, Lamont. You drive safely.'

'I will.' With a mock-bow, Lamont left. Jenny gazed after him. When she realised she was staring at the door, she walked back into the office. She still had work to do.

―――

Timmy Turner and Ben stood in a queue in town, waiting to get into a club.

'I hope there's fit girls in here,' said Ben. Timmy scowled, but didn't reply. He was still sulking about having to give Terry Worthy his drugs back. Shorty had been furious, and he had been lucky to avoid a beating.

The queue inched forward until they reached the front. They were ready to step in and party when two beefy bouncers crossed their path.

'Not tonight, lads,' One of them said. He forced them to the side, then let the people behind them straight in.

'We queued for ages,' said Ben. The bouncer scowled.

'We're only letting mixed groups in tonight. Get some lasses and try again.'

'C'mon, mate, there's only two of us. We're not here to cause trouble. We wanna spend money,' Timmy tried negotiating. For a second, the bouncer looked receptive.

'Oi,' Ben prodded him. 'Your boy just let them three white boys in. That's tight!'

'You're not dressed right. Try again another time.'

'Prick,' Ben mumbled. Quick as a flash, the bouncer grabbed him by his shirt and dragged him away from the crowds.

'Think you're a big man? I'll break your neck.' He raised his massive fist.

'C'mon man, he's sorry.' Timmy tried calming the bouncer down. Ben was annoying, but he couldn't stand back and watch him get hurt.

'Shut it, or you're next.' The bouncer wrapped his hands around Ben's neck. 'I'm sick of you little black bastards. Sell a few drugs, and suddenly you think you're hard men? Not around here.'

Ben's arms flailed as the bouncer choked him. Timmy looked around for something to strike the larger man. He would have to use his fists. A voice stopped him mid-lunge.

'Timmy?'

He turned, surprised to see Chink's friend, Marrion Bernette, stood there. Timmy was bigger than most of his peers, but Marrion towered over him. He didn't recognise the men with him.

The bouncer released Ben, who leant against the wall coughing.

'You know these lads?' The bouncer shook Marrion's hand.

'That's Shorty's cousin.' Marrion pointed at Timmy. The bouncer paled. He knew who Shorty was. If word got out that he had manhandled them, he was dead.

'Fuck. Didn't know that.'

Marrion smiled. 'Now you do. They're with us.'

The club was filled with scantily clad women of all races and sizes. As the quintet made their way to the bar, Timmy and Ben stared in all directions.

'Put your tongues away,' Marrion said, laughing. His people ordered two bottles of Dom Pérignon. 'Where's Shorty?'

Timmy shrugged. Marrion nodded.

'Drink up anyway. Everything's on us tonight.' He motioned towards his crew, pointing at a tall, light-skinned man, and a shorter man. 'That's Antonio, and Brownie. You two, this is Shorty's cuz Timmy and,' Marrion nodded at Ben, 'what's ya name boss?'

Ben replied with his mouth full of vintage champagne. He had drunk two glasses already.

'Chill,' said Brownie, watching him pour a third. 'It's early yet.'

It was a lively night after that. They hit several clubs, spending big money in each. Timmy had two hundred pounds in his pocket. Marrion and his people had spent double that in the first club. He couldn't remember having a better night.

Dawn loomed when Marrion draped his arm around him.

'You're all right, kid; didn't think you'd keep up. How old are you again?'

'Eighteen,' Timmy slurred, drunk from all the high-class alcohol.

'You've got potential. Tell your cousin it's time you got a bump up. And a pay rise.'

'I'm trying,' said Timmy thinking of all the times he had pleaded with Shorty to elevate him.

'Give it time. Take my number. I wanna talk to you when we're not so drunk. I'll put money in your pocket.'

'You've done enough.' Timmy's words tumbled out. 'You lot paid for everything and—'

Marrion silenced him with a hard stare. 'If a man wants to give you money, take it, but make sure you find out what he wants in return.'

'Well, what do you want?'

Marrion watched him for a long moment.

'Friendship.' He looked past Timmy to a group of attractive girls who were studying the pair with interest. 'Let's go make summat happen with these slags.' He dragged him towards the girls.

TARGET

LAMONT LOUNGED in a café the following day as Jenny entered, owning the room as always. She slid opposite him and greeted him with a wide smile.

'I'm surprised you wanted to meet here,' admitted Jenny, noticing the puffiness under his clouded eyes.

'When the company's right, where you are doesn't matter. What are you drinking?'

Jenny called the waitress over and ordered a bottle of elderflower water, requesting a glass and some ice. Lamont couldn't take his eyes off her. She wore her work attire, just like last time they had been together. Even when she wasn't trying, she still looked spectacular. She wore a touch more makeup and a dash of red lipstick this time.

'You look beautiful.'

Jenny beamed again.

'Thank you.'

'Tell me about your work; why flowers?' Lamont asked as the waitress brought her drink.

'Not much to tell. I always had a fascination with flowers and art. As I got older, I put more into it.' Jenny twirled a stray lock of her dark hair as she sipped her beverage.

'How did you get started?'

'Worked hard. Borrowed money from my parents and rented a dingy shop. The rest is history.'

Lamont gazed as she spoke, taking in the slight curve of her eyebrows, the hint of pearly white teeth beneath those sensuous lips.

'And you? How did you get into *personal training,* was it?' Jenny made air quotes with her fingers. They laughed.

'I was in the right place. I'm personable, and I have a knowledge of how the human body works.'

'One of these days, we will talk about your real job.' She met his eyes.

'I look forward to it.' He drained his coffee. 'Can I get you another drink?'

Jenny shook her head. 'You shouldn't drink so much coffee.'

Lamont wiped his eyes, acknowledging her words with a nod.

'Are you okay? I wasn't going to bring it up, but you seem tired,' she continued.

'Too many late nights.'

'Lay off the coffee then. Drink water.'

'I will. I do.' Lamont tripped over his words.

'Good. Make sure you do. Filtered if possible.'

'You seem to have quite an interest in my well-being.'

'Just making conversation,' said Jenny. Shrugging, she glanced out of the window, the atmosphere chilled.

'I'm gonna get a bottle of water,' Lamont scratched his ear as he headed to the counter. He again tried to make small-talk after he returned with his drink. She reciprocated, but it seemed stilted. Soon, she looked at her watch and reached for her handbag.

'I need to go. I left my assistant in charge.' She stood. 'This was nice.'

'Agreed. You're good company.' Lamont slid to his feet. Jenny surveyed him.

'Would you like to go for a proper drink tomorrow?'

'Pardon?' Lamont hadn't heard her.

'Kate and I are going for drinks. Would you like to come?'

'What time?' He didn't even try playing it cool.

'We should be there for nine.' Jenny's features seemed to glow, and they both smiled. Lamont left a tip and followed her outside.

The sun rested in the sky, and there were no clouds in sight, a testament to a surge of good weather. It was too warm now for the jacket he'd brought, so he held it in his hand as they stood on the pavement.

'Can I give you a lift to your office?' he asked.

'I'm parked nearby. Thanks for the offer.'

'I guess I'll see you on Saturday then.'

'Friday,' Jenny corrected.

'Just checking,' leaning over, Lamont kissed her on the cheek. 'Take care.'

TARGET

'You too, Lamont,' said Jenny. With that, she crossed the road. Still grinning, he watched until she was out of sight.

'Fam, it's the best thing to do. We need to step up.'

Timmy sighed. It felt like he'd only slept for two minutes before his mum woke him, saying Jerome and Ben were waiting. He'd dressed and staggered out to meet them. They sat in Potternewton Park, passing a spliff around.

Jerome was older than Ben and Timmy. He was unruly, the type of person you wouldn't let in your house even if you knew them. Known for being shady, the streets shunned him, and he'd taken to running with Timmy because of this.

'Jerome's right, T. We need to make something happen,' added Ben. He kicked a stray can around, making more noise than was necessary. Timmy and Jerome both scowled.

'Leave that damn can alone,' Jerome told him.

'Fine. Chill.'

'We can make it happen. Let's make our case,' Jerome continued.

'Teflon's funny. He doesn't like people just creeping up on him.' Timmy had heard Shorty talking occasionally, and he had been clear on one thing; Teflon didn't like surprises.

'Trust me, this'll work. You're Shorty's cousin. He's waiting for you to step up to the plate. At your age, Shorty was moving kilos.'

Jerome's words hit home. Timmy remembered the times Shorty would stop by his house when he was younger. He always had fresh gear and always looked the part. Even at a young age, it had triggered something. He wanted to walk Shorty's path; wanting people to clamour towards him when he entered a spot. He wanted to be the main man.

Maybe Shorty had mentioned him to Teflon? Maybe they wanted him to take the initiative?

'Okay. Let's stop by and see him. He'll be down the barbers.'

'Checkmate.'

Ken kissed his teeth, staring at the board in frustration.

'How did that happen?'

'Easy. I sacrificed the Castle and forced you to commit the Queen. It was simple after that.'

'You think like an old man, I swear,' Ken laughed. He was a balding black man in his early sixties, full of stories about the old days. He spent most of his time sitting in the barbers, soaking up the atmosphere. Lamont liked him. He lived life and had taken full advantage of England after coming over from the West Indies in the sixties.

'I play to win,' said Lamont, hoping he would take the bait and challenge him to another game. He was about to reply when three kids walked in. Lamont recognised the one in the middle, but his phone rang before they could speak.

———

'You want a cut?' A barber motioned to the empty chair when he saw the youths.

'Nah, he does, though.' Timmy pushed Ben forward. He tried protesting but sat in the chair after a look from Timmy.

While the barber asked Ben what style he wanted, Timmy and Jerome stared at Lamont. He had looked at them for a second when they entered. Timmy thought he was about to speak, but his phone had rung. He remained on the call, doing more listening than talking.

Timmy gawped. Like Marrion Bernette, Lamont exuded power. He sat in the chair, well-dressed, aware of his surroundings. Timmy felt his mouth drying.

'Go on, go and speak to him.' Jerome elbowed him. Timmy stumbled, but maintained his composure and glowered at Jerome. Lamont had finished on the phone, now gazing at the chessboard.

'Erm, Teflon?'

Lamont's head rose. He regarded him with mingled curiosity and irritation. Timmy's hands were clammy now. He was out of his depth.

'My name is Lamont. You're Shorty's cousin. *Timmy*.' His words were clipped. Timmy hung onto every word.

'I was wondering if I could chat to you for a minute?'

'Do you play chess?'

'Nah, I don't.' He made a face.

'I see. What do we have to talk about?' Lamont's question wasn't meant as a slight, but he wished the ground would swallow him up. *This was a crap idea.*

'I . . .' His mind had gone blank. Lamont's expression was mild, but his eyes were a different story. They were boring into his. He looked at the floor, unwilling to meet the gaze.

'Spit it out,' said Ken, annoyed at Timmy's stammering. The whole shop erupted into laughter. Everyone but Lamont chuckled.

'I wanted to say sorry for what happened with Terry.' He got his words together. Lamont said nothing. His eyes implored for him to continue.

'Me and my people just want an opportunity to grow.'

Lamont stared at him for a few more seconds.

'Okay,' he said.

'You what?' Timmy was sure he hadn't heard.

'I'll give you an opportunity.'

Timmy's face broke into a wide smile.

'Really?'

'Have you ever cut hair before?'

'Cut hair? What are you on about?'

'I thought you wanted a job?'

'Yeah, but not working in here, I wanna . . .' Timmy realised his mistake. Lamont was toying with him.

'Sorry,' he mumbled, hurrying from the shop. Jerome followed.

'Yo, wait for me!' Ben called from the barber's chair to no avail.

'Kids nowadays,' said Lamont. Everyone laughed again.

'I can't believe we did that.'

Timmy punched the wall in frustration. He had been humiliated in front of Teflon and the locals in the barbershop. With his failure, the plan seemed ridiculous.

'It's cool,' said Jerome. They sat outside an old shop on Louis Street in the Hood. 'You're on his radar now. He'll be watching you.'

'Don't be thick. I shouldn't have done it.'

'Trust me, it's cool. Can't believe we ducked Ben like that, though.'

Before Timmy could reply, they heard the screeching of tyres. Shorty's car pulled up, and he leapt out, eyes bulging with rage. Timmy opened his mouth, but he raised his arm, silencing him.

'Don't say a word.' He turned to Jerome. 'Get out of here. I'll deal with you later.'

Jerome didn't need telling twice. Shorty glared down at his cousin as Jerome ran.

'Stand up.'

Timmy did as he demanded, aware of the throbbing pain in his hand. With no warning, Shorty slapped him hard in the face, sending him staggering. Anger flared up in Timmy and dissipated. Shorty would kill him if he tried to flex.

'Are you stupid?'

Timmy stared at the floor, his face and hand smarting.

'Yo, it was dumb, I—'

'Damn right, it was dumb. This isn't *The Sopranos*, you little prick. Did you think you were gonna walk up to Teflon, talk your talk, and he would give you a box of coke to move? You don't know how close I am to cracking your head open. First, you rip off Terry, and now this. How daft are you?'

Shorty had stopped by the barbers. When Lamont told him about the stunt, he'd gone ballistic. Timmy wanted to run with the wolves, but he wasn't ready yet. This proved it.

'I'm gonna tell you this one time; stop letting that fool Jerome put ideas in your head. He's where he is because he's a snake and a fuckup. No one trusts him with work. Why d'you think he's hanging around you? Cut him and that little prick Ben loose and get better friends before you try to make power moves.'

Timmy still didn't speak. The slap had mollified him.

'Get in the car. You're not working tonight. Don't fucking go anywhere either. Stay in and think about your next step because I'm tempted to slap you again. Get in. Quick.'

Timmy climbed in, his face burning with humiliation. He was glad that his people hadn't seen Shorty telling him off. As soon as his door closed, Shorty sped away.

CHAPTER SIX
FRIDAY 9 AUGUST, 2013

LAMONT ROLLED OVER, wiping his eyes and yawning. He reached for his phone. When he saw the time, he vaulted out of bed, cursing. He was supposed to meet Jenny at nine pm. It was already half nine. His body yearned for more sleep, but he needed to do this. As he stepped into the scalding shower, he soaped himself, thinking about the things that needed to change. Number one was the sleep pattern. He couldn't do this anymore. People respected him for being reliable. Falling asleep in the middle of the day wasn't reliable, and it wasn't productive.

After a quick shower, he hurried to the closet and picked a pair of jeans and a long-sleeved top. He fastened his watch and slipped on a pair of shoes. His hair was a mess, as always. He'd run a comb through it, but it resisted the bristles. He looked at his face. His eyes were bloodshot, and he could do with a shave. It would suffice, though. As he dialled a taxi, he hoped it wasn't too late.

The taxi driver was stoic, which he appreciated. Already sweating from the muggy heat, he climbed from the taxi and almost collided with an overweight drunken man bellowing at the top of his voice and staggering.

There was a queue to get into the bar, lengthened when a couple kicked off near the front when the bouncers said they weren't dressed right. After the wide-boy threatened to come back for them and the bouncers laughed it off, Lamont entered the bar, navigating through a mass of bodies. He felt the old-school vibe, the crowd dancing to *Mary J Blige*. The bar was a modern monstrosity, with lots of chrome and glass. Everyone was out in their finery.

Lamont made his way through the crowd, looking for Jenny, hoping she hadn't left. He was halfway to the bar when he saw her sitting in the corner, smiling as a guy talked to her at length. Kate was there, but didn't look as happy as Jenny. He ordered a gin and tonic from the bar and walked over.

'Sorry I took so long.'

'Lamont. I thought you'd stood me up.' Jenny's face was unsmiling.

'Something came up. Let me make up for it by getting drinks.'

'No need. Tristan took care of us,' said Jenny. Lamont gave the man his attention. He had a square head and a similar build to Shorty, looking like he spent a lot of hours in the gym. They sized each other up.

'Nice to meet you, Tristan.'

They shook hands. Lamont turned his attention to Jenny. She wore a blue Peplum dress and black heels, her hair coiffed and teased, skin shimmering in the low lights of the bar. It was the first time he'd seen her so dressed up, and he struggled to avoid staring.

'Sensational,' he murmured. Jenny smiled tightly.

'What about me?' Kate piped up.

'I was getting to you,' said Lamont, laughing. Jenny's face remained impassive. She spoke to Tristan again, and the man shot him a smug smile.

'Why were you so late then? Tell the truth?' Kate kept up the conversation. He appreciated the distraction.

'I haven't been sleeping well. Dozed off and overslept.'

'Don't let Jen hear you say that. She'll have you doing yoga and meditating before the night ends.'

'I'll bear that in mind.' Lamont glanced around the room,

unable to understand the exclusivity of the bar. Apart from the music, there was no theme. The floor was sticky under his feet, and the bar staff were rushed off theirs.

'What do you think of this place?'

'Chrome isn't my thing,' admitted Lamont. He kept his eyes on Kate, trying not to think about Jenny growing closer to Tristan. He glanced in Lamont's direction as he swaggered to the bar.

'My friend wanted to open a bar. Couldn't get the funding, though.'

'You should have sent him to Tek for a loan.' Lamont winked. Kate laughed.

'What are we talking about?' Jenny stood between them, brushing her arm against his. The fleeting movement warmed his stomach.

'Lamont was giving his opinion on this bar. He thinks it's tacky.'

'It is. I was telling you this last time,' Jenny said. 'Why did we pick such a pretentious place?'

'Because we wanted to show Lamont how upscale we were.'

'Lamont's a man of mystery. We went on a date, and he took me to a greasy spoon,' said Jenny. She clicked her fingers to the beat as she spoke.

Lamont's ears pricked. 'That was a date?'

She gave him an appraising glance as Tristan came back with three drinks.

'Sorry, mate. Didn't know what you were drinking.'

'No problem.' Lamont took another sip of his gin and tonic, his eyes surveying the bar. He spotted a stunning honey-shaded woman near the bar with her friends. She kept looking in his direction and smiled when she caught his eye. He grinned back, then continued drinking his drink.

'You seem to find them every place you go, don't you?' Jenny watched.

'What do you mean?'

'I think you know.'

'I'm just here to drink with you, Jen. Don't worry about any other ladies.'

'I didn't say I was.'

Kate, Lamont and Jenny talked for a while. Tristan felt squeezed out and skulked away.

'So, L, what do you like about my girl Jen?' Kate asked. He looked at Jenny to see her reaction. Her face remained unreadable.

'She opened my eyes,' admitted Lamont. He saw from their reaction that his answer had surprised them.

'How do we know you're not just trying to bang and tell your friends?' said Kate. He wondered if they had planned these questions before he turned up.

'Because I'm a grown man who doesn't need to run and tell the world my business.'

'Can you get girls? Or is it only when you buy champagne for them?' Kate wasn't pulling any punches.

'I do okay. If I need to,' said Lamont.

Kate glanced around. 'So, if I said to talk to any girl here, you could?'

'If I needed to.'

'Do it then.'

'No.'

'Why not?'

'Jenny's opinion means more.'

They locked eyes, neither backing down. A third voice piped up.

'Do it.'

They both looked at Jenny. She stared back.

'What?' Lamont gaped. Jenny's eyes sparkled.

'I want to see if you walk the walk. If you do it, I'll give you a kiss.' She met his eyes for a moment. He felt the desire for this woman surging throughout his veins. He didn't care who saw. Her eyes continued to twinkle as she waited.

'A kiss?'

'That isn't enough?'

'It'll do. For now. Pick a girl.'

They did. A round-faced, smooth-skinned black girl twirling a straw in her drink sitting in an adjacent booth. Lamont sauntered over. The girl didn't sense his presence, engrossed with dipping her straw in her glass.

'You seem sad,' he noted.

'I'm not interested.' She didn't move.

'In what? *Happiness*?'

Now she looked up.

'You're going to make me happy?' She asked.

'I'm going to buy you a drink, stop you from drowning that straw. Any drink you like apart from champagne,' said Lamont.

'Why not champagne?' She looked intrigued now.

'I realise it sends the wrong message. Makes me seem like a prick who throws money around.'

'Maybe you can't afford it.'

He laughed. 'There's always that.' He held out his hand. 'Lamont.'

'Robin,' she responded.

'Well, Ms Robin, what can I get you?'

'Who's this?' A man stormed over, his face shiny, eyes narrowed. He towered over Lamont, broader and almost bristling.

'Hey, babe. This is Lamont.'

'What's he doing here?' The man's eyes hadn't left Lamont's. He stood.

'I was talking to a new friend. Don't worry about it.' He walked away, defusing the situation. Jenny and Kate laughed as he took his seat.

'Nice try. I guess your skills weren't good enough,' teased Jenny.

'That's not fair. She had a man.'

'Doesn't matter. You failed.'

'Guess I better get another round in.'

Later, they left the bar. Lamont's head spun from the buzz of the liquor. He hung close to Jenny, his hand skimming her waist as he guided her outside.

'Where are we going now?'

'We're meeting friends. I'm not sure where you're going,' said Jenny, laughing. He gazed, thinking about what he wanted to do to her, watching her in her sexy dress. He gathered her into his arms, pressing her body close to his.

'Don't keep me waiting,' he whispered.

'I'll try not to.' With a nibble of his ear, she broke the embrace and sashayed away with Kate. Lamont watched them with a grin. He hadn't worked so hard in years. Jenny had him hooked, and worst of all, she knew it. Turning, he went to hail a taxi.

'You're just teasing him now.'

Kate and Jenny walked towards Brooklyn Bar. The cool air sobered them as they navigated past groups of drunken guys whilst avoiding being groped.

'I'm just making him work for it,' said Jenny. Kate rolled her eyes.

'Are you serious? Didn't you see the way he looked at you? Lamont wants you, Jen. You can see it in his eyes. He's jumped through hoops to get close to you.'

'We both know what he does, though,' Jenny lowered her voice, eyebrows drawing together. Kate was quiet as they crossed the road.

'Lamont seems decent, and you're a good judge of character. Don't make him wait forever, though. Either you take it further, or you don't.'

Jenny didn't reply. She knew Kate had her best interests at heart. They were always honest with each other. Lamont was in a dangerous business, and she didn't understand why. He seemed to have everything going for him, yet she sensed a vulnerability emitting from him. The more she was around him, the more drawn she became towards finding out what he was all about.

'Let's see how it goes.' Deep down, she knew she had to decide.

———

THE NEXT NIGHT, Lamont went to see Marika. He noticed a Mercedes parked across the road as he approached the house. He had seen it before but couldn't think where. Shrugging it off, he opened the front door, startling Marika in the hallway.

'You scared me, bro.'

'Let's go for dinner. My treat. Are the kids in?'

She shook her head. 'They're at Clara's.'

Lamont almost asked if she ever looked after them. He held his tongue.

'Me and you then. Anywhere you want to go.'

'We've already cooked. Auntie's here.'

Lamont took a deep breath, resisting the urge to leave. His stomach lurched as he followed her to the living room. Auntie Carmen sat there like she owned the place. She was their father's older sister. He hadn't seen her in years, but she remained the same; beady-eyed with a shit-eating smirk.

'Lamont. How are you?' She tapped her cheek. He held his breath as he kissed it. She'd only done this because Marika was around. To say they didn't get along was a colossal understatement.

'I'm fine, Auntie. How are you keeping?'

'Are you still in that barbers pretending to work?' Auntie ignored his question. He took another deep breath, controlling himself. Just then, Marrion Bernette walked out of the kitchen, stopping when he saw Lamont. An awkward silence ensued.

'Nice to see you again, Marrion.'

Marrion nodded, seeing the game.

'You too, Lamont. Hope everything's cool.'

'I assume you're staying for dinner?'

'He cooked, and we invited him. Unlike some people,' said Auntie.

'L, you don't mind chicken do you?' asked Marika before he could respond.

'Chicken is fine.' Lamont took the seat furthest from Auntie. She watched him with her piggy eyes, desperate for him to say something else she could rip apart. He wouldn't give her the satisfaction. He stared at the TV, pretending to be interested in the mundane reality show on the screen. The tension thickened.

Later, the four ate the tasteless food in silence. Lamont twirled his fork around on the plate, not wanting to chew the rubbery chicken, wondering about the pair. He hadn't introduced them. He didn't like having his worlds so close together. Marika obviously wanted him to ask about the situation, and for once, he played right into her hands.

'What's going on here?' He laid his fork down. Marika and Marrion looked at one another.

'With what?'

'You two. Am I missing something?'

'What do you want me to say? We like each other,' said Marika.

'How do you even *know* each other?'

'We met in town.'

'Is that a problem?' Marrion wanted his answer.

'It's nothing to do with him. It doesn't matter if he has a problem.'

Lamont shot Auntie a venomous glare.

'Eat your food. No one's talking to you.'

'Don't talk to her like that,' said Marika. Auntie waved her off.

'It's fine, baby. He doesn't scare me. He's a miserable little boy still trying to control his sister after all this time. It's pathetic,' she spoke to Marika, but looked straight at him. His ears pounded, rage searing. He shot to his feet, needing to leave before he exploded.

'That's it, run off. You're nothing but a poor excuse for a man. Your parents would be ashamed of the person you've become.'

The room went silent then as Lamont froze, glaring into Auntie's smug, satisfied face, his hands shaking.

'Don't talk about my parents,' he said, trying to get himself under control.

'Touched a nerve, have I?'

'L, don—' Marika started.

'Stay out of this.' Lamont's eyes hadn't left Auntie's. 'You wanna talk about touching nerves? How about the stories about you in the gambling houses? The things you did? You're nothing but a gold-digging con woman.'

'L!' Marika said as Auntie's face paled.

'I said, stay out. She started it. I'm finishing it.' Lamont turned to Marika, then focused on Auntie. 'What have you ever done? You're a sad, twisted harpy of a woman who can't face it that life left her behind.'

Auntie's mouth opened, but she couldn't speak. Tears pooled in her eyes. Marika jumped to her feet.

'Get out, L.'

He didn't argue. He heard Marika comforting Auntie as he stormed away. Lamont had started the engine when Marrion hurried outside.

'Lamont, listen, I'm sorry about the ambush.'

'I don't have time for this.' Lamont sped off, driving through the streets like a madman. He regretted losing his temper. He'd allowed Auntie to get into his head. The crocodile tears she put on had worked like a charm. Despite her roughness, Marika had a vulnerable interior. Auntie was an expert at exploiting this.

Once home, Lamont grabbed a bottle of vodka and a glass, ready to drink his anger away. After the successful meeting with Akhan and the time he'd spent with Jenny, he wondered if tonight was a sign that his luck would change. His instincts shot tonight. He'd played right into Auntie's hands by not leaving the second he saw her.

The first glass went down smoothly. Lamont poured another and downed that one too. There were too many bad memories where Auntie was concerned. He loathed her; her nature, her attitude, her appearance and, above all, her ability to make him feel like a helpless child whenever he was in her presence for more than a few minutes.

The bad times in his life began when he was forced to live with Auntie after his parents' deaths. There was no preparation, and life after that was shaped for him. He closed his eyes, taking a deep breath.

Another glass, then another, and another. By the time he passed out on his sofa, only a trickle of liquor remained in the bottle.

CHAPTER SEVEN
SUNDAY 11 AUGUST, 2013

LAMONT STOOD in front of his parents' gravesite, staring at their names etched on the front of the marble headstone. His shoulders shook as he laid down some flowers.

The argument with Auntie had brought him today, but he visited at least twice a month, sometimes with Marika and the kids, most times without. He switched his phone off on these occasions. Business didn't exist.

He'd loved his parents; a redundant but necessary statement. They had grown up in poverty, working hard to rise above it. They were well-liked and bound by their words and values. Without realising, they had instilled similar morals in their eldest child, morals he had adapted to make the drugs game work for him.

Lamont wondered if they would be proud of him, and the way he too had battled through poverty.

A slight chill spread through the cemetery, and he pulled his jacket a little tighter. How long he stood there, he didn't know. He reached down and touched the marble, feeling a single tear run down his face.

'I love you both,' he whispered, turning to walk away. As he started the car and switched his phone on, it rang.

TARGET

'Hello?'

'Mr Jones. Are you free later?'

Lamont gripped the phone closer to his ear, startled. Saj was Akhan's point-man. He'd spoken with him after the initial meeting with Akhan, finding him to be funny and personable.

'What time?'

'Nine pm.'

'Where?'

Saj gave him the details and hung up. Lamont drove away from the cemetery, wondering what Akhan wanted. Saj hadn't mentioned him by name, but it was obvious he had called on Akhan's behalf. He would call Shorty and give him the location, just in case.

TIMMY ROSE EARLY. He wasn't working, so he took his time. After getting ready, he threw on a t-shirt and tracksuit bottoms and hit the block. He nodded to a few familiar faces and strolled around the streets. Chapeltown had been his home as long as he'd been alive. He couldn't imagine living anywhere else. Timmy knew everyone. They knew him and his family. Nowhere exuded the same energy as Chapeltown. Even with the violent reputation it had cultivated in the eighties and nineties, it was a community, and he pounded the concrete pavement with a personal sense of pride. He saw Jerome and Ben when he turned onto Frankland Avenue. Ben watched for police while Jerome dealt with a sale.

Timmy waited until they finished before walking over.

'Yes, Tim.' Jerome pocketed the money and slapped hands with him.

'What are you two doing apart from looking suspect?'

'We're on our grind, fam. You know how I do it. I don't rest; I need to follow that money.' Jerome wore a black tracksuit with the hood up. Any police cruising would know what he was doing.

'Whatever. What's the plan then?'

Jerome shrugged. 'I'm looking to go out tonight, but my funds are low. Why do you think I'm here?'

Timmy laughed. Jerome was always broke. He had to buy product from whoever was around. Usually, he got ripped off, but had to take it. Timmy felt sorry for him. Without Shorty, he would be in the same position. It gave him food for thought.

'Ben, is your mum around? We can go smoke at your house later,' said Timmy.

Ben shrugged. 'Doesn't matter if she's round or not. She'll fuck off to her room if we're there.'

'That's a bet, then. We'll buy a bottle and a draw.'

'By the way,' Jerome interrupted, 'did you know about Reagan? He smacked up Terry. You know Terry Worthy, the one who's always talking shit.'

Timmy and Ben shared a glance. They had ripped him off, but hadn't known someone had beaten him up over it.

'Is he okay?'

'Yeah. Must have paid his debt, too, because he's still alive. Heard Reagan went on extra, though. You know Carlos, that DJ in town? Word is that Reagan ran up in his yard and raped Carlos's girl in front of him,' said Jerome, cackling with laughter.

'That's not funny.' Timmy glared.

'What's not funny?'

'You can't be laughing about raping someone. That's disgusting. What if it was your sister he raped?'

'I'd put a hole in his head. Terry's a pussy. So is Carlos. He's always playing that dead Funky House shit. No wonder he laid there and let it happen.'

'Even if he did, you're a piece of shit for laughing.'

'Miss me with all that sensitive talk. You're a nobody. You only get status because of your cousin. Where would you even be without him?'

'This isn't about Shorty.'

'It's about you. This game is cold. You wanna run around feeling sorry for all the pussies, go work for Oxfam.'

TARGET

'C'mon, you two, let's chill. We don't need to be arguing,' said Ben.

'Shut up. Everyone knows you're Timmy's bitch. Just stay out of the way.' Jerome's remark stung Ben, and it showed. Timmy was about to support him when his phone rang.

'Yeah?'

'Damn, someone's in a bad mood,' A voice laughed on the other end.

'Marrion?' Timmy moved away from Ben and Jerome, both of whom continued to bicker.

'No names, kid. Where are you?'

'I'm in the Hood. Something wrong?'

'I'm gonna send someone to scoop you up. Meet them at the Petty Station at the bottom of Roundhay Road. Just you.'

'Okay.' Timmy hung up. Ben and Jerome were nose to nose, shouting at each other but not doing anything.

'I'll get with you lot later,' he said. Both boys looked at him.

'Where are you going?'

'Yeah. We're meant to be chilling.'

'Summat's come up.' Timmy hurried to the petrol station, mooching around near the pumps. A few minutes later, a midnight blue BMW pulled up. Brownie motioned for him to get in, and they drove off.

'What's happening, kid?' Brownie pulled into traffic, turning up the volume on his CD.

'Nowt, B. What does Marrion want?'

'Relax. It's all good.'

Timmy wasn't convinced. Brownie seemed cool, but he didn't trust him. His eyes were like flint. Even when he was trying to be reassuring, it made him more anxious. He stared out of the window until they reached the destination, a house on Bayswater Terrace.

Two youths sat in the living room, playing Fifa on the PlayStation 3. They nodded at Brownie, paying Timmy no attention. Marrion waited in the kitchen. He grinned when he saw Timmy and touched fists with him.

'Yes, youngster. Good to see you again! What's new?'

'Same old; just doing my thing,' said Timmy. Something about Marrion made him tongue-tied. He didn't want him thinking he was an idiot.

'You're probably wondering why I called you up. I wanna put some money in your pocket, like I told you. I want you to do a few drop-offs for me. Easy money.'

'That's cool, but I work for—'

'Teflon. I know you do. I'm not stepping on toes. When you're not working, you can always get money with me. No law against that.'

Timmy thought it over. He could learn a lot from Marrion and accepted because of that. The money was a bonus.

'Okay, I'm down.'

Marrion grinned again.

'Good man. Antonio'll get you straightened out. I've gotta jet. I'll be back later.'

―――

LAMONT ENTERED the restaurant where he had arranged to meet Saj. He had been before, always enjoying the layout. On entry, there was a large stocked bar area with a smooth black wood finish. Solid beams of light resonated from the middle of towering marble pillars. As he was shown to the table, he noted the soft jazz music being played on the stage, patrons nodding their heads along with the instruments.

In the main area, there were dozens of round gold-topped tables. As he approached, Akhan and Saj held glasses of water, talking in genial tones. Lamont shook hands and took a seat.

'Nice to see you again, Teflon,' Akhan spoke first.

'You too, Akhan. Thanks again for the gift.'

'It's nothing. As I may have mentioned, I don't drink, but I'm told that brand is exquisite. Have you tried it yet?'

'I'm saving it for a special occasion.'

Akhan smiled. 'Don't save it for too long. Would you like to order a bottle for the table?'

Lamont shook his head. 'Water will be fine.'

While Lamont looked at the menu, Akhan again studied him, reminded of the feedback he had received from his sources. Trinidad Tommy and Ken were respected men he had known back in the day when they were all young Turks. Both agreed that Lamont was a force. His people worked hard for him and lived well.

Once they had ordered, and the waiter had gone, his manner changed. He no longer smiled, now businesslike. Lamont straightened in his seat.

'Where do you see yourself in five years, Teflon?'

Lamont hesitated. Akhan sensed his uneasiness, impressed by how guarded he was.

'I promise you, I have no ulterior motive. This is for my interest.'

Lamont nodded. 'I see myself in a position of power.'

'Are you not in one now?'

'You tell me. You're the one asking the questions,' said Lamont. Akhan acknowledged this with a small smile.

'Do you have any close family?'

Lamont was sure he already knew the answers to these questions, but humoured him.

'I have a younger sister.'

'What does your sister do?' Akhan's eyes hadn't left his face.

'She's trying to find herself.'

'And you're helping her?'

'In a manner of speaking.'

'What about friends? Do you have friends?' Akhan switched gears.

'I have friends, and I have acquaintances.'

'How do you differentiate the two?'

'Sometimes I don't. Some I work with. Others I socialise with.'

'You're most likely wondering why I am asking all these questions,' said Akhan with an almost self-deprecating smile.

'I presume you're trying to get to know me, to understand what makes me tick.'

Akhan smiled again, wider this time.

'Why do you do it?' Akhan didn't have to explain what he meant. Lamont understood the question. He had expected it earlier.

'It's easy money if you know what you're doing,' he said.

'And do you?'

'I'd like to think I do. I'm sure I could do more, but there are ways I could do worse.'

Akhan smiled, impressed with his answers.

'I hear good things about you, Teflon. It's why I wanted to work with you. You could go far in this business.'

'I don't know about that.'

'I have been in this game far longer than you, and I've seen many people and a lot of things. You have all the traits.'

'I won't be doing this forever. As soon as I'm able, I'll walk away.' This was the first time Lamont had shared this with anyone outside his circle. Saj glanced at him, but Akhan seemed unmoved by the statement.

'What would you want to do instead?'

'Live off the money. I don't want the risk forever.'

'No one does. That's why you buffer yourself from the operation. With the right backing, a man like yourself could earn tens of millions.'

When Akhan said the words *tens of millions*, Lamont felt a tingle. He loved the idea of having that much money, but he was sceptical. The game was played for keeps. He had done well to navigate it, but he knew he couldn't last forever. No one could.

'I'm not greedy,' he said.

'It's not about greed. It's about worth. Why be rich when you can be wealthy? I'll get you where you want to be. Scratch that: where you *need* to be.'

Before Lamont could reply, he noted a familiar party. Delroy

TARGET

Williams sauntered into the restaurant, followed by his son Winston, Reagan, and another man he knew was called *Mack*. Delroy faltered when he saw them. He and his entourage were shown to a table near theirs.

'Are you okay?' Akhan noticed Lamont's distraction.

'I'm fine.' He felt the table shooting him looks. Delroy stood, scraping his chair. Winston whispered something, but his father ignored him and approached the table. Lamont waited for the explosion, the inevitable scene that Delroy would cause. He hadn't reloaded with him and now sat in a restaurant breaking bread with a new supplier. To his surprise, Delroy ignored him and approached Saj with his hand held out. Saj studied Delroy, then shook his hand.

'Good evening, Delroy. How is everything?'

'Everything is well. Just treating the troops to some food.' Delroy waved his hands toward his table of goons, all of whom were glaring at Lamont. Lamont sipped his water, gazing at each man.

'That's good. Keeps the morale high,' said Saj. Akhan hadn't paid Delroy any attention. Delroy looked over at Lamont for a second, then turned his attention to Akhan. He met Delroy's eyes for a moment, nodded, then picked up his drink and spoke to Lamont as if Delroy wasn't there anymore. Delroy's mouth tightened, but he maintained his composure.

'Enjoy your meal, anyway,' he said, sitting back down at his table.

Lamont continued to make conversation with Akhan, but in his head, he analysed the exchange he had just witnessed. He had known Delroy for years, and he'd never seen another man humble him. Lamont allowed the events to process in his mind as he sipped his water.

———

'He's taking the piss.'

Delroy and his men camped in his office. After running into Lamont, he insisted they eat and leave.

'You can't deny it now, Del. I should have stabbed the cocky prick with my fork. He disses our people then steps out with a new supplier. It's bullshit.'

'Reagan's right. You've supported that little shit, now he's violating? Del, gimme the okay, and I'll take care of him,' added Mack, another of his lieutenants.

Winston watched his father smoking a cigarette. His fingers twitched. He wasn't used to him looking nervous, and it made him uneasy.

'I don't care who he's working with now. These are our streets. We can't let him get away with disrespecting us. Every day that little prick seems to grow bolder. Let us off the leash,' demanded Reagan.

Delroy shifted in his seat.

'No.'

'What do you mean?'

'Do nothing to Lamont. I mean that. He is now off limits.'

'Why?' Reagan's eyes popped, his nostrils flaring. Mack looked just as furious. Delroy couldn't believe he had to explain it.

'Do you know who Lamont was with?'

'Yeah. Two flash Pakis. So what?'

Delroy shook his head at Reagan's stupidity.

'That was Akhan.'

Winston sat up now. He had heard his father talk about Akhan, but had never met him. He hadn't looked like much, but looks were often deceptive in their world.

'So what?' Reagan shrugged.

'Do you know who Akhan is? Don't you think it was strange that he was meeting with Lamont?'

'Nah, I don't. He looked sneaky. I know for a fact how sneaky Teflon is. We should chop the pair of them.'

'Shut up and listen. Akhan is an entity. He doesn't meet with just anyone. This could be terrible for us. If he's working with Lamont, then it could be catastrophic.'

An awkward silence and blank stares greeted his statement. Lamont had leapfrogged him. He had been outmanoeuvred, and it didn't sit well. On some level, he agreed with Reagan. He was the boss, though, and had to move accordingly. This went beyond drugs. Akhan had his fingers in many pies. If he was cutting Lamont in on his action, then this would make him a bonafide rival.

'Catastrophic, how?' Winston spoke first.

'It would give him access to tremendous power. Akhan is more than a drug dealer. He's a warlord with dealings in every city. We have to be careful. The other gangs would never sit back if they believed we were doing anything to disrupt the rhythm of things. They would come down on us hard.' Delroy paused, as if confirming his decision. 'We need to wait on this. The blow must flow.'

CHAPTER EIGHT
MONDAY 12 AUGUST, 2013

LAMONT SAT IN THE BARBERS, listening to the chatter of locals while reading a newspaper. There was a buoyant atmosphere in the air, the warm weather bringing out the joy in everyone. He was so engrossed that when the door banged open, he didn't pay attention until the room fell quiet. Glancing up, he folded his paper and slid to his feet.

Mack stood in the middle of the room, his bodyguard bringing up the rear. Everyone in the room knew Mack and the overall trouble he brought to the table. He was an incorrigible criminal who had never learned to be subtle. Because of this, he made money, but never achieved success. When Mack glared at him, he knew his lazy day had ended.

'Teflon, me and you need to talk.'

'Nice to see you, Mack. Are you hungry? We were about to get food.'

Mack's mouth twisted. 'No, I'm not hungry. Don't try showing off for these idiots, because I'll finish you.'

All eyes were on Lamont. He remained placid as if talking sports rather than being threatened by a goon.

'How can I help? Does Delroy need something?'

'I'm here for me, not him. He likes you. Me, I think you're a fake, up-his-own-arse, pretty boy. You think you could test me back in the day?'

The tension kicked up a notch. Lamont noted Mack's insecurity; his desperate need to prove himself a tough guy. It was pathetic.

'Mack, I don't know what your problem is, but that was then,' he replied. Mack glanced at Spinks, who stifled a yawn, then turned back to him.

'I'm putting you on notice, Teflon. You've had a good run, now you need to pack it up. If you don't, it's over. You won't make it to your next birthday.'

A smile flitted across Lamont's face, taking everyone by surprise. Mack needed a reason to make a move. It was obvious. Now more than ever, Lamont wondered what he had told his team. He hadn't heard from him since the scene in the restaurant. The product Akhan had given them was off the scale, though, and they had almost sold out in two days.

'Why the fuck are you smiling? You think I'm taking the piss?'

Lamont shook his head.

'No, I know you're serious. Why don't you give me time to consider my options?'

'You think this is a joke? You know what? Get this idiot, nephew,' Mack ordered. Spinks stepped forward, only to find his path blocked by two tough-looking local goons. Lamont recognised them as some of Shorty's associates. Spinks stared them both down. Behind him, Trinidad Tommy picked up a nearby razor.

'It's time for you to go,' said Lamont. Mack's eyes blazed.

'Big mistake, Teflon. I'll be seeing you.'

They left. Lamont watched through the window as they tore through traffic in a Land Cruiser.

'L, are you all right?' Trinidad asked after a minute. Lamont grinned, expertly hiding his annoyance.

'Why wouldn't I be?'

In the heart of the Hood, Shorty chilled in a garden, a spliff to his lips. The heat had sapped his energy, so he was content to smoke and move only when needed. K-Bar was out handling business, but a few of his crew were alongside Shorty, cracking jokes and talking nonsense.

'Shorty.'

Everyone looked up when Blakey, his affable errand boy, jumped from his car after it screeched to a halt.

'Sup, B?'

'Have you heard about L?'

'What about him?'

'He had a run-in with Mack.'

'What? When?' Shorty sat up.

'Mack was talking reckless about an hour ago, going on about how Lamont's not gonna make it to his next birthday. Spinks tried amping, but our people backed it.'

Shorty kissed his teeth, flinging the joint to the floor. He found his phone and called Lamont.

'Why didn't you tell me?' He barked as soon as he picked up.

'Hello to you too,' replied Lamont.

'Don't joke. Why didn't you tell me?'

'It's not a big deal.'

'Course it is. It's a violation.'

'Don't overreact. It's the desperate move of a desperate man. We'll speak later.'

'Fuck,' snapped Shorty when he'd hung up.

'What did he say?' asked Blakey.

'He's a prick. I swear, he doesn't get it. He thinks life's like them fucking books he's always reading. Mack punking him isn't good for anyone.'

Most of the crew shared looks. They had never heard Shorty talk so viciously about Lamont before.

'What are you gonna do?' Blakey spoke up again. Shorty's veins protruded in his thick neck as he clenched his fists. Sometimes Lamont overlooked the power of reputation. Shorty didn't.

TARGET

'I'm gonna get with the Tall-Man, and we'll handle this shit. B, you can drive me.'

'Want me to come in?'

Blakey pulled up outside a house on Hillcrest Avenue. It was nondescript and looked no different to the surrounding houses. The small, boxy garden was home to a few plants, but mostly it remained barren.

'I won't be long.' Shorty knocked once on the door before entering. He paused in the living room. Two youngsters sat, both aiming guns at him. When they recognised him, they lowered the weapons.

'Tall-Man about?' Shorty asked.

'Course I am,' A voice said from behind him. He flinched, turning.

'Fuck man, you scared the shit outta me.'

Marcus smiled, his obsidian eyes darker than coal as he greeted Shorty.

'Nothing scares you. What's the deal, though? You don't just stop by.'

'We've got a situation. Someone's messing with *The President*.'

Marcus's attitude instantly switched from pleasant to cold.

'Wait outside,' he told the youths. He motioned for Shorty to sit, remaining on his feet. 'What happened?'

'Mack threatened L. Said our boy wasn't making it to his next birthday.' Shorty watched his face as he explained.

To people in the Hood, Marcus Daniels, aka *Tall-Man*, was a certified legend. A musclebound maniac who cared for little in the world and terrorised those who crossed him. Not only was he vicious, but he also kept a stable of like-minded goons who would carry out whatever degrading task he gave them. Most of all, Marcus allowed no one to trouble Lamont and Shorty. Mack was in for a rude awakening.

'Mack said that? Delroy's Mack?'

'His people have been out of pocket for a while. It's like they wanna start something.'

'Okay. We'll sort it,' said Marcus, his tone neutral. Shorty wasn't fooled. Marcus was more dangerous when he was quiet.

'Cool. I'll put L up on what we're doing.'

'Leave him. Meet me here tonight. We're gonna go hunting.'

Shorty smiled. They worked well together and had handled business in the past.

'You got it, fam.'

———

AFTER SPEAKING WITH SHORTY, Lamont drove to Marika's, happy to see Marrion's car wasn't there. She lounged in the garden, drink in hand, watching the children playing.

As soon as the kids saw Lamont, they shouted his name. Bianca dragged him to the paper shop. They returned laden with sweets and drinks. As Bianca showed her mother the spoils, Marika smiled at her brother, but said nothing.

'Can we talk, sis?'

She nodded. While the children argued over sweets, they moved to one side.

'I'm sorry about the other night.'

'I hate that you can't get along with Auntie. We're family. We have to stand by each other.'

Lamont's jaw tightened. His experiences with their aunt differed from hers.

'I know,' he said.

'Can't you try? Do you hate her that much?'

'Yes.'

'Apart from my kids, you two are the only family I care about. How do you think it makes me feel that you can't get along?'

'It's not about you. You know that.'

'It's shit, L.'

'Just leave it.'

'I can't,' said Marika. The kids glanced their way for a second. 'Anytime I try to talk about it, you won't. Auntie's the same. What happened?'

Lamont hugged her. 'Rika, you're better off not knowing.'

Marika made a noise of disgust.

'Forget it. C'mon, let me make you a cuppa. I'll tell you all about Marrion.' She got one last shot in, leading him inside.

MACK SAT IN JUKIE'S, a gambling spot in the Hood. He had been there all evening, making loud remarks about Lamont as he grew drunker.

'Tell you one thing, Juke,' he said to the barman and mild-mannered proprietor of the spot, Jukie, 'we've been too easy on this new breed; let them get away with too much.' Mack paused, taking another hearty swig. 'It's all good; I'm gonna sort the lot, starting with that flash cunt, Teflon; the weak little prick who's never done an ounce of time in the nick.'

Jukie nodded and smiled, the whole time thinking how foolish Mack was. He heard about things in Chapeltown as they happened, and knew about Mack threatening Lamont. He'd also heard Lamont had got the better of Mack, and wasn't surprised. Though some of his regulars spoke enviously of the youngster, Jukie recalled the fire in Lamont's eyes when he first sold drugs. He'd risen to a higher level than many had imagined. Mack was allowing jealousy to cloud his judgement.

Jukie kept his opinion to himself, though. Mack was a friend and a paying customer.

'Can I get you another?'

'Nah. Think I've had enough. Spinks,' said Mack, interrupting his nephew's game of pool he was having in the corner. 'Get the car.'

'Can't I—'

'Now.'

Spinks glared, but heeded the command.

'Kids nowadays,' Mack called after him.

Spinks fumed as he stomped down the quiet road. When his uncle had first suggested he work for him, he'd figured it was an easy way to get rich. Now, he realised he was wasting his time. Mack was cheap and too focused on petty vendettas to teach him anything worthwhile. He took liberties, and one day, he would push too hard, and Spinks would end him.

Spinks stomped toward the Land Cruiser. He'd paid a crackhead a fiver to watch it, but she had absconded and not done the job. He would slap her when he saw her.

Spinks was about to climb in when he heard footsteps and sprang into action. Pivoting, he blocked his assailant's hit, then tried to hit his opponent in the face. They tussled, seeking to overpower the other. Spinks hit his attacker with two body shots, then cocked his fist back to deliver another blow. A hand of iron snatched his. Surprised, he turned and was caught with a vicious uppercut. His eyes rolled back in his head, and he crumpled to the floor.

Marcus surveyed the young man. He had held his own with Shorty, and for that, he had earned his respect.

'Prick.' Shorty kicked the unconscious Spinks in the head. 'Tosser got me in the stomach. I should blast him.'

'Forget it. He's not gonna be helping anyone. Stick him in the boot, and we'll handle his Uncle.'

———

After leaving Marika's, Lamont headed home to unwind. His eyes burned, but he had gone through this pattern a lot. If he tried to sleep, he would only lay in bed. It was pointless.

He fixed himself a glass of gin. Mack's threats had unnerved him. Like Reagan, Mack could cause trouble without thinking. He needed to watch out for him and keep Shorty calm at the same time.

Before he could even consider walking away from this life, Lamont needed to ensure his pathway was clear. It was vital if he ever wanted to live. That meant doing something about Mack.

He picked up the book he had started re-reading, *The 48 Laws of Power*. He'd absorbed the lessons years ago, but liked to refresh his memory.

A sudden knock at the front door caused him to slide to his feet, frowning. Few had his address, and the ones that did wouldn't turn up without phoning. His brain was in overdrive as he hurried to the door. He opened it and paused at the sight of Jenny.

'Surprised?'

'Very,' admitted Lamont. 'Come in.'

Jenny followed him. She'd had an image of what she'd expected his place to look like, and it exceeded expectations. The walls were a light brown colour, the furniture dotted around a similar shade. Soft music played from a tasteful dock resting above a marble mantelpiece. There were several paintings on the walls, an old chessboard and various paperbacks and pieces of paper scattered around the coffee table. Based on the mahogany drinks cabinet in the corner, he seemed to enjoy the best of everything.

'I'll be back in a minute. Have a seat.' Lamont left the room and hurried upstairs. A door slammed. Jenny continued her assessment of the room until he returned, looking a little more relaxed and refreshed.

'Sorry about that. What are you drinking?'

Jenny picked out a bottle of red wine. He poured them each a glass. They toasted and sipped. She took another sip, enjoying the thick, fruity texture. Lamont observed her. She met his gaze.

'You want to ask me something.' It wasn't a question.

'A few things. How did you get my address?'

Jenny smiled, not in any hurry to answer.

'Does the name *Frankee* mean anything to you?'

It did. Frankee was a girl he'd known years back.

'Frankee told you where I lived?'

Jenny shook her head. 'I asked around.'

'Why?' He wondered why she had mentioned Frankee's name.

'You said not to keep you waiting. You learn more about a person when you turn up.'

'True,' Lamont admitted.

'Every time, you always seem so together. I wanted to catch you off guard.'

'You succeeded. Is that the only reason you came?'

'No. I was horny too,' said Jenny. They laughed.

'It happens. You might want that booty call.' Lamont played along. She bit her lip, but didn't respond. He sipped his drink, feeling more awake and enjoying the company. As attractive as she was, he appreciated her humour more than her looks at the moment.

'Did you find a driver?'

'Yes.'

'Bet he didn't make half the impression I did,' said Lamont with a wink. Jenny giggled.

'You think a lot of yourself, don't you?'

'Is that a bad thing?'

'There's a fine line between cockiness and confidence.'

'I'm aware of where that line is.'

'I'll bet. You're too smart for your own good. That's why you've got such a rep.'

Lamont shifted in his seat.

'What's my rep?'

'You're a player. You're not interested in settling down and having a relationship.'

'That's not entirely true. It's just not my main priority right now.'

'What is? Selling drugs?' Jenny blurted before she could stop herself.

'Amassing wealth.'

'And you don't care how you make that wealth?'

'I didn't say that.'

The awkward tension hung in the air. Jenny wondered again what was going on in his head, what drove him. He was keeping something hidden from her, and the more she was around him, the more determined she became to uncover it.

'I didn't expect you to live here,' she admitted.

'Why not? Too out of my league?'

'Yes.'

That got a laugh out of him.

'It's quiet out here. I can relax.'

'Must impress the ladies too.'

'Are you trying to imply something?'

'Why would I do that?'

'If I didn't know better, I'd say you were jealous.'

'Good thing you know better.' Jenny picked up the book.

'You were slamming doors upstairs before. Hiding something?' she asked as she put it back.

'A state-of-the-art, all-purpose drug lab.'

'Unsurprising.'

'Did you come here to assassinate my character?' He rolled his shoulders, his face playful. She stuck out her tongue.

'Sorry. Sometimes the comebacks have their own mind.'

'You're forgiven. For now. Can I top you up?' He gestured to the bottle.

'Trying to get me drunk?'

'I don't need you drunk to get what I want.'

'Oh?' Jenny raised an eyebrow. The whole vibe had changed now. Her voice was amused, tinged with a sexy huskiness.

'Trust me.' Lamont rose to his full height. Jenny stared up at him, daring him to make the first move. She didn't resist as he kissed her, slowly at first, then gathering momentum. His arms enclosed her, crushing her breasts against his hard chest as he brought her towards him. She felt his arousal pressing into her, and she ground against it, eliciting a moan. Lamont couldn't take anymore.

Before he could act further, Jenny slipped from his embrace, adjusting her clothing.

'I'll be leaving now,' she said, her breathing ragged.

'Are you for real?'

'Yes, I am.'

'You can't leave me like this.' Lamont pointed to his crotch.

'Watch me.' Jenny blew a kiss and left. He stood still, breathing hard, horny beyond all normal reason. After a moment, the corners of his face stretched into a smile.

Game on.

———

MACK STAGGERED out of the gambling spot, trying to light another cigarette with shaky hands. The night air jolted his senses, sobering him as he tottered down the street and turned the corner. The Land Cruiser was there, but Spinks was gone.

Mack muttered under his breath, then reached for his phone. He relaxed at the sound of footsteps and prepared to tear his Nephew's head off.

'Where the fu—'

His words stuck in his throat. Shorty stood in front of him, staring at him through cold eyes. He backed away, looking for a weapon or distraction. He knew what time it was. He knew what Shorty was capable of.

'We don't need to do this,' he blurted. 'Teflon's making a mistake.'

A twisted smirk appeared on Shorty's face, illuminated by the streetlight and making his features appear grotesque. His dark eyes looked beyond Mack at something behind him. He turned, his stomach dropping at the terrifying sight waiting.

'Fuck.'

Marcus Daniels loomed, blending with the night. The doleful look on his face worried Mack far more. He knew of the devastation that Marcus was famous for and never imagined they would catch him slipping.

'Listen, you know what Delroy will do if you touch me,' Mack babbled as the fearsome enforcers approached from either side. He backed away until he was against the door of his car. 'This is bad business. That thing in the barber shop, it—'

Shorty caught him with a wicked hook. His face shot to the side, but he stayed upright. Marcus blocked his escape, and Shorty hit him with vicious flurries. He tried to rise and fight him off, but Shorty was an animal. A knee to his stomach caused him to throw up, the vomit barely missing Shorty's trainers.

This seemed to anger him, and the last thing he saw before things went black was Shorty's trainer heading towards his face.

CHAPTER NINE
TUESDAY 13 AUGUST, 2013

A FIERCE KNOCKING at the door ruined Lamont's sleep. He climbed from bed, checking he hadn't dribbled in his sleep. Chink waited, sunken-eyed, gripping his phone, jaw clenched.

'Thanks for waking me up. Do you want a coffee?'

Chink followed him into the house.

'We've got a situation.'

'I gathered that. Coffee?'

'L, this is serious.'

'I need a coffee. I'm knackered. Gimme five minutes and tell me all about it.'

Chink held his tongue, nodded and sat down, flicking through the channels to the news. Lamont fixed himself a cup of black coffee and joined him.

'Okay, I'm listening.'

'Mack's in hospital.'

Lamont put his coffee down.

'What happened?'

'He and his bodyguard got jumped near Jukie's place. Marcus and Shorty did it.'

Lamont closed his eyes, trying to control his emotions. This wasn't good.

'Did Mack threaten you yesterday?' Chink watched him.

'Yeah,' he admitted. Chink's mouth twisted, scarlet blotches tinging his porcelain features.

'Did you order them to attack him?'

'Course not. Have you spoken to Delroy's people?'

'Not yet. They'll be in touch, though. That's a given.'

'You're right. I'm gonna go get ready. Track Shorty down.' Lamont hurried from the room.

SHORTY LOUNGED in his living room, smoking weed and drinking Hennessy from the bottle as an old *Jeru the Damaja* track played in the background. Mack's assault had been the highlight of his week. Delroy's crew had always thought they were untouchable, and now they had been humbled. He grinned at the memory of kicking Mack in the head and raised the bottle again.

A hard knock at the door startled him. He reached under the sofa cushion, came up with a gun, and cut the music off.

'Who is it?'

'Me.' Lamont's tone was clipped.

'What's up?' Shorty opened the door and touched fists with him. Chink brought up the rear. He didn't acknowledge Shorty.

'Shorty, you know what's up. What happened?' Lamont got to the point.

He sat back down and relit his spliff. The pungent aroma wafted through the air, upsetting the eyes of both Lamont and Chink.

'What do you want me to say?'

'I want to know why you thought it was feasible to put one of Delroy's top guys in the hospital,' said Lamont. Shorty shrugged.

'You know why I did it. That's what I do; I hurt people who step out of line.'

'Do you think Delroy's just gonna sit back and take this? What do you think's gonna happen next?'

'I'm ready for whatever. You already know that. We weren't gonna let Mack think he could talk to you like a prick in public.'

'Who's *we*? You and Marcus?'

Shorty just looked at him.

'This is gonna be bad. Don't you realise that? Delroy can't let this slide.'

'It'll be big,' Chink piped up for the first time. 'Delroy's people will retaliate.'

'So what? I'm not scared of him or his people. That's a fact,' replied Shorty.

'The fact is that you did something stupid, and now we'll all suffer. It's not about fear; it's about recognising that beef doesn't make us money. How can we get paid through the streets if we're at war?'

'Listen, you've never gotten your fucking hands dirty, so miss me with the *we* shit. It's my ass on the line, not yours,' said Shorty.

'Is that what you think? Delroy's gonna come for the lot of us. It won't matter who has shot people and who hasn't. You made the wrong call.'

'Whatever. You'd have let Mack get away with it, and he'd be debting you an hour later. You're good with numbers, Chink, but you know fuck all about the streets.'

Lamont sensed the situation escalating.

'It's pointless to argue. Shorty, sober up. Chink, get Winston on the phone. Tell him I want to see him.'

Both nodded. Lamont yawned, debating where he could get an energy drink or some Pro Plus. Carnival was close. He had the potential to make an explosive amount of money in a short period. It was essential he and his team did whatever was necessary to toe the line.

TARGET

'What are we gonna do then?'

Reagan stood in front of Delroy, watching the old prick dither over something that needed no thought. Teflon and his crew had violated again, and he was ready to lay waste to the lot.

Delroy sat at his desk, chain-smoking, stubbing each cigarette into an oversized marble ashtray.

'Wars cost money,' he said.

'So does losing respect. What will people say if you let Teflon get away with slapping around one of your guys? You think crews are gonna wanna reload with us? They're gonna jump on his dick and deal with his people. We need to retaliate. Now.'

Delroy sighed. Reagan was right whether or not he wanted to admit it.

'Get Chink.'

'*Chink?* We need to get Teflon; Shorty, at least.'

'Eye for an eye. We do to Chink what they did to Mack, and then we let them make a move.'

Reagan scowled. It was better than doing nothing. With a defiant nod, he went to put the word out to his team. Chink was finished.

That night, Shorty chilled with a few of his guys, enjoying the dark atmosphere of a club on Briggate, in the city centre. He needed it after a long day. Shorty hadn't liked the way Lamont and Chink had approached him. They didn't understand the streets like he did. You had to go above and beyond to protect your rep sometimes. Lamont was skilled, but he'd had it easy because of the things Shorty and Marcus did to people who violated.

He poured himself another glass, making a mental note to send someone for energy drinks from the bar. He was lagging after being up for two days. Scanning the room for talent, he jolted when Blakey leaned in close and got his attention.

'Check out who just walked in.'

Shorty glanced up, surprised to see Ricky Reagan heading towards him. TC flanked him and another big-headed dude he didn't recognise. Several nearby locals aware of the situation watched, awaiting drama. Shorty noted the wide grin on Reagan's face. A prickle of unease ran through his body.

'Shorty, what's happening?' Reagan held out his hand. He shook it, playing along.

'What can I do for you, Rick?'

'Just thought I would stop by, show love to you and your team. This whole beef thing, it could get outta hand. It's nice that we can step out like this with our teams and relax.'

Reagan's words were soft, but he detected the obvious malice beneath them. He was letting him know he was coming for him. Shorty appreciated his guts, but he didn't like the disrespect. He promised himself right then that he would fall, no matter what Lamont said.

'Glad to hear it. B, get bottles for Rick and all his crew. Make sure it's the good stuff too.' Blakey hurried off to carry out the order. Reagan's smirk remained in place.

'Teflon about? I wanted a chat with him,' he started. Shorty shrugged. 'No bother. Maybe he's with that little thing we've seen him with. I'll catch up with him another time.'

'I'm sure you will. Some advice, though.'

'Go on.'

'Take the bottles and go, before you and your whole team get dropped.'

Reagan burst into mocking laughter, 'Is that a threat?'

'Yeah, it is. Come for Teflon or any of us, and it's gonna get bad for the lot of you.'

'Oh yeah?' Reagan's mask of civility slipped.

'Yeah. Tell that fat prick you work for that the clock is ticking on his ass too. It's open season on all of you.'

'Let's go now.' TC stepped forward. Reagan put his hand out to calm his friend. He'd noticed what TC hadn't. Shorty's people slowly surrounded them. There were at least half a dozen; too many to take on.

'I'll pass it on. I guarantee I'll see *you* before you see *me*, though. Keep your flat-ass drinks.' Reagan nodded, leading his team away. Shorty's people watched Shorty, expecting a reaction.

'Fam, they were out of line,' snarled K-Bar. He'd wanted to wipe the smug look off Reagan's face while he was talking.

'Yeah, they were. We came to have a good time, and that's what we're gonna do. Business can wait until tomorrow.'

IN ANOTHER PART OF TOWN, Chink stood outside a bar, smoking a cigarette. His new minder, a Birmingham goon named Polo, was watching out for him. Chink couldn't see him, which was the way he wanted it. He didn't think Delroy's goons would try anything in such a public place, but it was best to safeguard against it.

He finished his cigarette and lit another. A drunken girl tottered over, asking to use his lighter. He obliged, and she thanked him, trying to make small talk, but he blanked her. She was a mess, two or three drinks away from hurling. She called him a prick, and her friend dragged her away.

Chink smirked and finished his cigarette. His patience paid off. A woman walked towards the bar, surrounded by friends. He smirked again, allowed her to enter, and followed.

Naomi swept through the club like she owned it, curves hugging the fitted black dress she wore, eyes fierce and lips full. Guys tried talking to her, but she ignored them.

'Lots of fellas in here tonight,' said Adele. She was pretty in her own right, but her beauty paled next to Naomi's.

'Bunch of posers, nothing worth hyping about.' Naomi turned to the bar to order her drinks. Before she could, the barman placed a bucket with a bottle of champagne in front of her.

'Who is this for?' she asked.

'I was told to give it to the beautiful lady in a black dress,' the barman grinned. 'I think that's you.'

'Who sent it?'

'Dunno where he's gone. Gave me one hell of a tip, though.'

'What did he look like?' Naomi glanced around.

'I don't check out other dudes. I'm about women.' The barman licked his lips like *LL Cool J's* long-lost brother. 'Speaking of which, why don—'

Naomi turned her back, dismissing him. Adele and the others had poured themselves glasses of champagne by now.

'Thanks, Naomi! Didn't know you were planning on buying champers.'

'I didn't,' she said. They weren't listening. She noticed a man watching her. Straight away, she sensed he had bought the champagne. His hair was styled in a disconnected undercut fashion, his eyes hard, a smirk permeating his lips. He held a glass, standing still as people danced and chatted around him.

Naomi felt like the only girl in the room. She smiled, and he drained his drink and walked towards her. She studied him. He wore an open-collar charcoal shirt, jeans and shoes. She noted the Breitling watch on his wrist.

'I guess I should thank you for the champagne,' said Naomi when he was closer.

'You don't need to.'

'Good, don't think you can win me with some bubbly.' Naomi expected him to wither and slink away, but he laughed.

'What would it take to win you over?'

'If I told you, it'd be no fun now, would it?'

'Good answer.' Chink held out his hand. 'My name is Xiyu.'

'That's an unusual name.'

'I've been told that before. What's yours?'

'Naomi.'

He took her hand and led her away from the dancers. She didn't resist.

'Where are you taking me?'

Ignoring her, he led them to an empty booth, signalling the bartender and ordering more champagne. His assertiveness impressed Naomi. His tone and the way he carried himself was a big turn-on. For the next half an hour, they learned more about each other. Chink told her about himself, most of which was nonsense. It worked, though. Women like Naomi always had guys trying to get them into bed, so Chink disregarded that and focused on her mind. He was skilled with wordplay; one minute, he stared into her eyes and smiled when she spoke, the next, he was reserved, staring into space. Finally, she'd had enough.

'What is it?' she asked.

'What's what?'

'Do you like me?' Her cheeks burned.

'Yeah. I think you're cool.'

'That's not what I meant. I meant do you *like* me?'

'I think you're spectacular. But,' he hesitated, shaking his head. 'Forget it.'

Naomi sat up. 'What?'

'It's not important.'

'I want to know. Please.'

He pretended to think it over.

'I think you're high-maintenance.'

'You what? I'm not high-maintenance!' Naomi's jaw clenched.

'It's just an opinion. I've only known you a short amount of time.'

'You're up your own ass,' said Naomi. To her surprise, he grinned.

'You're not wrong. I'm confident, I won't deny that. I'm my own man, and I call things as I see them. Not everyone can handle that.'

'What happens when they can't?'

Chink looked into her eyes, his expression becoming sombre.

'They miss out.'

'I'm sorry I said you were up your own ass, Xiyu. I lash out sometimes.'

'Why?'

'Why do I lash out?' Naomi struggled to keep up.

'Yes. Did someone hurt you?'

She turned away. 'No one can hurt me.'

'Because you distance yourself, avoid getting close?'

'Is that what you think?'

'I watched you swanning around, ignoring people. You don't want anyone to get close. I think it's because you were hurt.'

Naomi took a quick, sharp breath. This never happened. She called all the shots, did everything on her terms, but now here she was, desperate to make him like her. She stood, her head spinning.

'I should go.'

'It was nice meeting you.' Chink picked up his glass.

'Is this fun for you? Are you trying to mess with my head?' Naomi spat.

'Not at all. I want to know what makes you tick, what inspires you. I want to learn it all,' said Chink. Naomi took her seat. She wanted to believe him, but it was complicated. Things were happening in her life. Some she had control of, most she didn't.

'Why couldn't you want to fuck me?' She smiled.

'Who said I don't?' replied Chink. They laughed. He slid his phone towards her. 'Put your number in there.'

———

LAMONT ENTERED HIS HOME, bone-tired from the day's excursions. Neither he nor Chink could get hold of Winston Williams. He'd checked with a few associates, but none had heard from him. He needed Winston before he approached Delroy. Delroy was the leader, but he was much more level-headed than his father. He could bridge the gap.

Not wanting to overthink things, Lamont traipsed upstairs and was about to lie down, when his phone vibrated. When he saw the number, he sighed, knowing his night wasn't over yet.

Jukie's was heaving when he entered. He kept his head down,

dodging the locals. The man he'd come to see hunched over his drink in a corner. Lamont took a seat.

'Are you drinking?' Marcus didn't look up.

'No. What's so urgent?' It irked Lamont that he was drinking around the corner from the spot where he had almost killed a man. Marcus looked up, his huge scarred hands dwarfing the glass of Hennessy. He wore a grey t-shirt, stretched tight over his muscles, cargo trousers and boots, his leather jacket slung over the back of the spindly wooden chair.

'You're pissed off, aren't you?'

'Disappointed.'

'That's worse. Had to be done, though. Mack took the piss,' said Marcus.

'It did not have to be done. You should have discussed it with me.'

'There's time for talk, and a time for action. You would have talked us down.'

'That's because I look beyond pointless violence.'

'And we don't?'

People glanced at the pair, but turned away.

'If you did, Mack and his fool nephew wouldn't be in hospital.'

'No, they'd be planning to take you out. These aren't local wannabes. Mack is a force, and you needed to take him seriously.'

'You think I didn't?' replied Lamont.

'Course you didn't. You think you can sit and talk like a damn diplomat.'

'My talking has got you out of plenty of spots in the past, or have you forgotten?'

'No I haven't. I think you've forgotten all the times my fists have helped you, though.' Marcus drank more of his drink.

'Bullshit. All I want is to profit. Everything with you and Shorty is about protecting rep. Mashing up Mack wasn't about me; it was about your egos, and now I have to pick up the pieces. I have to placate Delroy, which means he has the advantage.'

Marcus rubbed his eyes, breathing hard now. Lamont fiddled

with his watch and resisted the urge to continue. After taking him and Marika in, Auntie had filled her pockets even more as a foster carer. A rough kid named Marcus Daniels had been her first and only case. He was uncontrollable, prone to fits of rage, with eyes that unsettled even the most experienced care workers. When he had first joined them, Marcus wouldn't speak or play. He only ate and slept. Lamont recalled the day they got along:

SCHOOL HAD FINISHED *for the day, and Lamont had done his chores. He was about to read a book when he heard a piercing scream from upstairs.*

Marcus had Marika against the wall, his hand around her throat. He was screaming in her face.

'Oi! Get off her,' said Lamont.

Marcus whirled around. The look in his eyes was one of utter lunacy. Lamont held his ground.

'She's a thief.'

'What did she take?'

'Something that didn't belong to her.'

'I said let her go. We can talk about this,' said Lamont.

Marcus released her, giving him his full attention. He was twelve and already built like a grown man. Lamont had heard him at night doing press-ups when he thought everyone was asleep. Marcus stepped towards him.

'It's nothing to do with you.'

'That's my little sis,' Lamont turned to his sister. 'Say sorry.'

Marika had recovered. Her face twisted with rage.

'He's crazy. All I did was look at that silly photo of his ugly parents.'

With another snarl, Marcus lunged for her. Lamont tried to get him in a headlock and was shrugged away like a dandruff flake. Marcus swung for him, but he ducked and hit him in the stomach. He doubled over, and Lamont struck him in the back of the head. With a mad yell, Marcus took him down, swinging wildly. Lamont kept coming back. Marcus was too strong, though. He hit the floor hard and didn't get back up. Marcus stood over him, wheezing.

'You're crazy.'

'That's my sister.' Lamont lifted himself, wincing. 'She's all I've got left.'

Marcus thought this over for a moment. He held his hand out. Lamont shook, and from that day forward, they were the best of friends.

'Say the word, and I'll bring you Delroy's head.'

Marcus brought Lamont back to reality with that statement. He was serious too. He was capable of a level of violence Lamont had never seen in another person. Marcus dominated on a good day. On a bad one, the results were downright frightening.

'That's unnecessary,' he said. Marcus drained his glass and stood.

'Make sure you're ready when it pops off. I will be.'

He left, leaving an annoyed Lamont behind.

CHAPTER TEN
WEDNESDAY 14 AUGUST, 2013

CARL AND TC sat in Shadwell. Across the road from them was a pristine apartment building. In the car park, they saw Chink's grey Jaguar.

'Nice area,' said Carl. He was a short man with light brown skin and a jovial attitude. 'Bet Chink's sitting on bare money. I've heard he's got a place in town too. Park Row or summat.'

'Who gives a shit? Let's go get the little Chinese fuck.'

'Cheer up.' Carl didn't like the way TC spoke to him. He was always on edge, and since the word had come down about the problems between Delroy and Teflon, he was even worse. Carl respected him, but didn't like him.

They climbed from the car and hurried across the road. The main door was locked. Minutes later, they'd broken in. They traipsed the stairs, approaching Chink's door. They were armed, but the guns were only to scare him. Their orders were to kidnap and work him over, sending a message to Teflon and the streets that they played for keeps.

After breaking in, the pair tore through the flat. Chink was nowhere to be seen.

'Shit. Where the fuck is the little prick?'

TARGET

'I'm right next to you. How would I know?' Carl's reply was flippant. TC ignored him, distracted.

'C'mon, let's go tell Ricky. He's gonna flip.'

―――

Chink watched from his vantage point as Reagan's soldiers hurried back to their car. He had rented another flat in the building opposite his, one of his old flings staying for appearances. Reagan and his team were after him, and he understood their thinking. He was the easiest of Lamont's inner circle to capture. It would send a message if they could take him out. He had a better plan.

'They're pulling out now,' he said into the phone. 'Follow them. I want to know where they go, and who comes and goes.' He hung up, observing Reagan's men driving away, Polo now on their tail.

―――

Shorty was at Amy's house. It was risky to come and see Grace with a war brewing, but he had two of his guys sat outside just in case. He'd dozed off whilst putting Grace to sleep. After shaking himself awake, he padded downstairs.

Amy was washing up in the kitchen, humming a tune he couldn't recognise. Desire skittered in his belly. He slipped his arms around her waist and kissed her neck. She shuddered and leant into his embrace, then composed herself and pulled away, leaving soap suds on Shorty's top.

'Shorty, not now.'

'C'mon, Grace is asleep.' He moved towards her again, but Amy held off.

'We can't keep doing this.'

'What do you mean?'

'You can't try it on with me every time you come round. I'm not just some plaything for you to mess about with.'

'Amy, why are you getting serious? This is how it is with us.' Shorty forced a laugh.

'Maybe that's the problem.'

'Amy—'

'No. Shorty, I love your bond with Grace, but I won't be like your other baby mother. I have other options.'

'What options?'

'Chris.'

Shorty gritted his teeth. Chris Hart had been smitten with Amy since day one. Even after Shorty had impregnated her, he still hung around on the friendship tip. Shorty detested him because he was competition. He told Amy all that empowering crap about herself, and then Shorty would have to talk her around when she talked shit.

Like now.

'So that's how it is then? He pays you attention, suddenly you're too good for me?'

'No, Shorty, it's—'

'Fuck it. I don't have the time.' He stormed off.

Lamont was sleeping the morning away when his phone rang. He ignored it until it stopped ringing. There was no reprieve, though. As soon as it stopped, it started again.

'Yeah?' he said, picking up.

'It's me,' said Chink. 'I need to see you. Now.'

'Okay. Come through.' Lamont tossed the phone and hurried to shower. He was on his second cup of coffee by the time Chink arrived with Polo. It was the first time he had met the goon, and he felt an instant unease. By the frown etched on Polo's face, he felt the same. Chink turned to the guard.

'Wait outside,' he said. Polo complied.

'Drink?' Lamont asked. He shook his head.

'Reagan's people were at my place.'

TARGET

'How do you know?'

'I recognised them. It was TC and that goofy one that drives them around.'

'So, where were you?' asked Lamont.

'Nearby. I expected this. I'm the obvious target.'

'Is that why he's watching your back?' Lamont glanced at the door.

Chink nodded.

'He's useful. I had him follow them. They went to a house in Harehills. We've got eyes on them wherever they go now.'

'Good. We might have to use that. For now, I'll give you keys to a spot. You'll be safe there.'

'L, this isn't what we signed up for.'

'I know,' said Lamont, stifling a yawn. 'We're in it, though, so we have to control it.'

'It would be different if the *Dynamic Duo* took responsibility for what they did. This is their fault, and they don't even care.' Chink loathed Shorty and Marcus's attitude. They had been starting fires for years, and everyone allowed them to get away with it whilst putting out the flames. It was frustrating. Not only was Shorty refusing to accept responsibility, he wanted to escalate the beef.

'I had words with Marcus. He stands by what he did,' said Lamont with a sigh. Chink glanced at him.

'You look wrecked, L.'

'I'm fine. Just didn't sleep well.'

'Me neither. Did you hear about Reagan and Shorty getting into it in a club? I must have had calls from about twenty people. We need a handle on it—' Chink's phone rang. He spoke then hung up, 'That was one of Delroy's people. He wants a meet. Today.'

'Ring Marcus and Shorty. Tell them I want them here now.'

———

Delroy Williams hunched over a plate when Lamont entered the cafe, his security team posted around. Lamont slipped into the seat opposite him. Marcus and Shorty perched nearby.

'What the fuck, Tef?' Delroy got straight to the point, not even bothering to chew the egg in his mouth. He'd picked the table that allowed him to see the comings and goings. Lamont glanced at a menu smeared with something that looked like a cross between syrup and egg yolk. A grey-haired woman limped over, asking if he wanted to order. He shook his head.

'What am I supposed to say?' he said when the woman left.

'Did you allow them to go at Mack?' Delroy jerked his thumb at Marcus and Shorty.

'Yes,' Lamont lied. Delroy took a swig of his drink and carried on.

'That was stupid. You know I can't let that slide. There has to be a comeback.'

'Did you tell Mack to come into the barbers and make threats?'

'Course not. Mack went solo.'

'He threatened me on my turf, in public. How was I supposed to handle it? What would you have done differently?'

'You should have talked to me first.'

'How does me running to you look? It's all about reputation. I have to work on these streets too.'

'Fuck's sake!' Delroy shouted. He lowered his voice. 'I respect you. You know that. This is bad, though. Reagan wants your head. He wants to take out the lot of you.'

'Can you control him?'

It was a loaded question, and they both knew it.

'Can you control those two over there? These psychos we keep seem to do what they like. Reagan's hated you for years. He's been waiting for this excuse.'

'I'm not scared of Ricky. Do I need to watch my back with you?'

Delroy rubbed his face. 'Have you listened to a single word I've said? This isn't just gonna blow over.'

'I'm sorry to hear that. Let me tell you something, just so there are no misunderstandings: Send your people at Chink or *any* of my guys again, and I will take it as an act of war.'

Delroy's eyes narrowed. His mouth opened, but no words came out.

'You're gonna take it as an act of war? What do you call kicking Mack's teeth down his throat?'

'Retaliation. He made threats. There was only one response.'

Delroy pointed a shaking finger at him, struggling to hold back his anger. It was obvious he wanted to reach across the table and rip his head off.

'Tef, I respect more than anyone what you've carved for yourself. I've done this longer, though. I've had my back to the wall. Have you? I know you've had little beefs, but you've never been in *real warfare*. It's no picnic. Recognise,' he said, his Grenadian tones coming through now. Lamont didn't flinch.

'Mack violated. It's as simple as that. You wanna talk about warfare? There's a reason I never needed to. Just like there's a reason you made this little meeting rather than just striking. You don't want war.'

Delroy assessed his words.

'Give me ten grand. I give that to Mack, and maybe this thing goes away,' he replied

Lamont got to his feet. 'I'll get back to you. Take it easy, Delroy.'

CHAPTER ELEVEN
THURSDAY 15 AUGUST, 2013

'TEN GRAND? ARE THEY HIGH?'

Lamont, Shorty and Chink were back at the base. Marcus had gone to get his people in order.

'It's a fair deal. You and Tall-Man almost killed Mack. I'm surprised he didn't ask for more,' Chink said to Shorty, who snorted.

'He's stalling.'

Chink and Shorty paused, looking at Lamont.

'What do you mean?' asked Chink.

'The money is a diversion. It won't stop Reagan from coming after us, and Delroy knows that,' said Lamont.

There was silence as they considered his words.

'How do you know?'

'His body language.'

'So what now then?' Shorty piped up.

'Chink, stay out of sight and focus on the money. Shorty, you coordinate with Marcus. Get word to everyone to be on alert. After that, we wait.'

TARGET

'We need to move on them.'

Delroy and Reagan had been in deep discussion for the better part of an hour. Winston Williams sat in the corner of the office, texting on his phone.

'You think so?'

'I know so. We missed our shot with Chink, but we'll get him next time,' said Reagan.

'Chink is guarded now. Teflon didn't even bring him to the meet.'

'Someone else then.'

'I'm still thinking about it.'

'Mack's laid in a damn hospital breathing through tubes. Every second we do nothing, we lose respect,' said Reagan.

'We can't rush on this.'

'Rush on what? You're acting like we're warring with some equals. Teflon can't test us on the battlefield. You know the soldiers I'm rocking with.'

'You're underestimating them. Just shut up and let me handle it. Run your little team, and I'll continue steering the ship. I fucking told you last time, this is big. Akhan is big. We cannot piss him off.'

Reagan stared at his boss. Winston noted the rising tension and positioned himself. Reagan scoffed and slid to his feet.

'You handle it then, *Captain*.'

When Reagan left Delroy's, he wore a scowl. Delroy seemed to make little decisions more difficult.

The whole situation was spiralling out of control, and it was because Delroy was too indecisive. Reagan didn't care about Akhan or what Delroy thought he could do.

Reagan drove to a small house in the heart of Harehills. Ten minutes later, he was slouched on TC's sofa drinking Hennessy. When he brought him onto the team, the first thing TC did was get a place of his own. It wasn't much, but the rent was cheap, and it was his.

'What are you thinking then, T?' Reagan asked. He'd told him about his talk with Delroy.

'Simple. Let's get them.'

'Just like that?'

'Why sit around? If it was anyone else, we would've gone at them by now.'

'Exactly,' said Reagan. This was why he loved talking with TC. He cut through the bullshit.

'Teflon's got soldiers, but so do we. Let's bump. This sitting around shit is pointless. Makes us look soft.'

'I tried calling Marcel about that money he owes. It's been two days, and he hasn't called me back yet,' said Reagan. TC shook his head.

'People are thinking we're weak. It's gonna get worse.'

'Chink is out of sight now. We missed our shot.'

'Shorty's always with that dickhead K-Bar. He'll still be easier to get. Tall-Man's like the fucking wind,' said TC.

'Put two people on Shorty. Mack's people will help. They're pissed off about what happened. We'll watch him, then we'll strike. Get on it ASAP.'

―――

LAMONT STARED AT HIS PHONE, willing it to ring. Since Jenny's impromptu visit, they had messaged each other a few times. They would flirt, but she would pull back and leave him hanging every time it got to a certain level. It was a strategy, but with everything going on, he didn't want to play games.

With that in mind, he called her. She answered within seconds.

'Hey, Jen. It's me.'

'How are you, Lamont?'

'I'm fine. Do you want to do something tonight? We could go to dinner.'

'I'm busy tonight, I'm afraid. Someone else is taking me out.'

'Kate?' Lamont asked, wishing he hadn't. There was a moment's pause.

'No. Not Kate.' Jenny didn't have to say anymore. Lamont was smart enough to know what she was trying to avoid saying.

'I see. Well, enjoy your date,' he said.

'It's not a date, Lamont. It's—'

'You don't have to front.'

'I don't have time for this. I'll call you, okay?' Without waiting for him to reply, Jenny put the phone down. He fumed for a moment, then dialled another number.

'It's L. Listen, what are you doing tonight?'

THAT EVENING, Lamont led his date into Moreno's, a Moroccan restaurant on the outskirts of the city. They had stopped off at a bar in town for drinks. Lorraine was a gorgeous caramel-skinned beauty with a penchant for shopping and gossiping. The white dress she wore complimented her skin. As he pulled the chair out for her, she sat down with a smile.

As well as Moroccan cuisine, Moreno's served a plethora of steaks and fish, along with an excellent tapas bar. Stained glass light fittings hung from the ceiling. On the walls were several obscure paintings, the seating tables small and intimate.

They ordered drinks and studied the menu. The waiter brought over a bottle of red wine. Lamont tried a sample and nodded his approval. The waiter then poured two glasses and took their orders.

'You know your way around this place.' Lorraine tasted the wine. 'This is good.'

'I've been here twice. The service is always great.'

'Who with?'

Lamont impaled Lorraine with a look.

'Don't start.'

'Start what?'

'I've been here before. Let's leave it at that,' said Lamont. Their relationship was one of convenience. She did her thing on the side, and he never questioned her about it. He expected the same treatment.

'Fine. Whatever. I only asked a question.' Lorraine pouted. He shook his head. He never learned. She tended to start arguments over silly things, and he had no time for it.

'Let's forget it then. How are things? What have you been up to?' She continued.

'Same old. Are you still doing the modelling?'

'When I can. It's slow nowadays. I do lots of promos for clubs right now. How's Shorty?'

'Shorty's Shorty.'

'Is he still with his baby mother? I've got a friend he'd like. Is it true he has a tattoo on his dick?'

'It's not something he's ever mentioned,' said Lamont, avoiding the question about Shorty and Amy altogether. He almost laughed at the absurdity of this situation. Lorraine was cool, but he didn't have that kind of vibe with her, causing him to ask himself a tricky question: Why *had he invited her to dinner?*

Lamont watched as a staff member showed an attractive couple to their seats. The dark-haired woman looked familiar. As they drew closer, and she glanced in his direction, the penny dropped for both simultaneously.

Jenny looked sensational. Her hair was wavy and styled, and she wore a plum-coloured dress that clung. He couldn't tear his eyes from her. She regarded him for a second, then took a seat opposite her date. Lamont hated him already. He was average height, looked like he did yoga and seemed to have good fashion sense. His hair was ridiculous, though; the same bowl cut that Javier Bardem rocked in the movie *No Country for Old Men*. He gave Lamont a quizzical look, then turned back to Jenny.

'Lamont?'

He turned back to Lorraine.

'What?'

'What's up with you?' she asked.

'Nothing. I'm just hungry.'

He doubted he could eat anything. He wanted to ditch Lorraine and whisk Jenny away to finish what they had started last time. Most of all, he wanted her date to choke on the cork of the bottle of champagne the waiter was opening for them.

'I'm hungry too, but you don't see me snapping at you.'

'Sorry.' His eyes again darted over to Jenny's table. She was deep in conversation, a small smile on her face. *What was she playing at?*

'L?'

'Yes?' He fought to keep his voice sounding normal.

'Who is she?'

'Who's who?' He was still staring.

'That girl you can't take your eyes off.'

'Just someone I know. No big deal.'

'Do you like her?' Lorraine sounded hurt.

'I told you; it's no big deal,' said Lamont. She heeded his tone, falling silent until their food arrived.

———

'Who is he?'

Jenny resisted the urge to roll her eyes.

'Who?'

'That guy who keeps looking over.'

'What do you want me to say?'

'Do you know him?'

'Yes, I know him.'

'So, who is he?'

'He's someone I know. Just leave it.'

Max grumbled, but heeded her request. She sipped her champagne, debating whether to get steaming drunk to ease the awkwardness of the situation. After the way the conversation she'd had with him had ended earlier, she hadn't expected to see Lamont. Max was a friend who had tried to get a date with her for years. He was nice, but he didn't intrigue her the way Lamont did. Lamont had the potential to get close and turn her world upside down, which was hard to accept.

He looked good tonight, and she wondered about the attractive woman with him. *Had Lamont screwed her? Would he screw her tonight?* Jenny drank more champagne, wanting to avoid further thoughts.

———

SOON, Lamont was ready to leave. The food was excellent, but he didn't care. Lorraine did her best to make conversation, but his answers were curt. They ate, he left a generous tip with the bill, and they departed without giving Jenny or her date another glance.

———

SHORTY PULLED his car to a stop near some flats outside the Hood. He was in war mode, heartbeat racing. He suspected he was being followed, so he parked away from his base. Hurrying up the stairs to his flat, he unlocked the door and strode into the front room.

'Your fridge is empty.'

The overhead light switched on. Ricky Reagan aimed a gun at him.

'You meant to be some kinda Bond villain?' Shorty snorted. Reagan slid to his feet, never once taking his eyes from him.

'Cocky little shit, aren't you?'

Shorty shrugged, aware there were guns stashed all around the room. He just needed to get to one.

'Do what you're doing. I don't give a fuck.'

Reagan smiled. 'Course you do. You said you were gonna get me.'

TARGET

'Doesn't matter. You can't hide forever. My people will finish you.' Shorty needed to keep him talking.

'*Hide?* Who am I hiding from?'

'Tall-Man and K-Bar will wrap you and your shitty team up like Christmas presents.' Moving quicker than Reagan expected, he dove to the floor as bullets thudded into the wall behind him. This was his domain. As Spartan and impersonal as the space was, Shorty knew every inch. He was up now, gun raised, two shots in Reagan's direction, causing the man to take cover. He hurried to the back room, flinching as a bullet exploded into his shoulder. He staggered, searching for something he could use. It was one on one. Reagan had been stupid to take him alone. As he thought this, TC charged out of the backroom with his gun raised. He froze, trapped.

More gunfire erupted. Then silence.

CHAPTER TWELVE
THURSDAY 15 AUGUST, 2013

LAMONT BROODED in his living room, drinking and trying to read. Even after the disastrous evening, Lorraine still hinted at coming back with him before he put her in a taxi. He felt a buzz, the wine and brandy playing havoc with his stomach and senses. Being tipsy seemed more manageable than being sober. He needed to think clearly. He had the potential to lose everything, and yet he was lamenting over Jenny. It was ridiculous.

When the knock sounded at his door, he was so deep in his own world that he almost didn't respond. He rubbed his eyes and strolled to answer.

'Trying to surprise me again?'

'No need. I already did that earlier.' Jenny swanned inside, still wearing the purple dress. She sat without being asked.

'Where's that prick you were with?'

'If I didn't know better, I'd say you were jealous.'

'Jealous of what?'

'Are you going to pour me one?' She pointed at his glass.

'Do it yourself.'

Jenny smiled. 'You're in a proper mood, aren't you?'

'Don't flatter yourself. It's just been one of those days.'

She fixed herself a glass of Amaretto. 'In that case, I'm surprised your little friend isn't here relieving your tension.'

'I might give her a ring.'

'Oh, and she'll come running, will she? Real credit to the female race.'

'Maybe she doesn't believe in games like you do.'

'We all play games. Maybe she thinks you'll invite her to *Bachelor Heaven* if she plays nice.' Jenny motioned around the room.

'Maybe I will.'

'Maybe you should. Times like this, you need someone looking after you.'

Lamont tried hiding a grin at the thought of party girl Lorraine waiting on him hand and foot.

'About time you smiled. So, why isn't she here?'

'I didn't want company.'

'Do I not qualify as *company*?'

'You . . .' Lamont broke off, poured another drink.

'Me . . .'

'You intrigue me. You already knew, though.'

Jenny sipped her drink, watching him.

'Good.'

'What were you doing with that dickhead?' Lamont leaned back, hands behind his head.

'Same thing you did with that slut.'

Lamont chuckled, tickled by the speed of her replies. He recalled the last time she was with him, how she had left him hanging. He'd been consumed by the same lust now enveloping him, threatening to twist his usual logical thinking and make it cruder, sexual.

'How do you know Lorraine's a slut?'

'With a name like that, she's one.'

'Who was that moron you were with? *Cedric*? *Leonard*? *Paul*?'

'Max.'

'What a twit.'

'Max is okay. He's safe.' Jenny faltered.

'And what am I?' Lamont inched closer, his left arm grazing Jenny's shoulder.

'You're—'

Lamont pulled her close, their mouths meshing, driving his tongue down her throat, causing her to drop the glass with a loud crash. They paid no attention. She teased his tongue with her own, wondering what had taken him so long. This would be no repeat of last time. There would be no escaping, no games. And so she surrendered to every hot kiss on her neck, every soft caress, and when he peeled off her dress and pierced her with those fiery rosewood eyes, she was every bit as willing, every bit as ready as he was. He lowered himself onto her, and then his phone rang.

———

CHINK lay in bed smoking a cigarette. Naomi was next to him.

'Is this your thing then?' She took the cigarette and put it in her own mouth. 'Preying on innocent girls and getting them to sleep with you?' She exhaled.

'Depends what's on TV,' replied Chink. She giggled.

'You're shameful. I never thought I'd like a little posh boy like you.'

Chink took the cigarette back. 'You think I'm posh?'

'You talk like you're royalty.'

'I was born and raised in Meanwood. I'm anything but posh.'

'So you just talk posh?'

'Not posh. Educated. I grew up hard. Decided early on I wouldn't live like my parents. College and university were my way out.'

'I never expected that; you seem so in control.'

'I have to be.' His practised cool appeared to dissipate. 'Loss of control is a failure.'

Naomi snuggled closer. Chink was like her; guarded and putting up a front. There was more beneath the surface. She kissed his cheek and sashayed naked to the bathroom.

TARGET

K-Bar stood outside, smoking a cigarette and watching Lamont approach. It was late, but the night air was warm. He'd dressed quickly and regretted picking a sweater.

'Safe, family.' K-Bar flicked the cig away and greeted him.

'How's he doing, K?'

'Come and look for yourself.' Turning on his heel, K-Bar walked into the spot. Lamont followed, hearing loud music, the slamming of dominoes, and voices coming from the kitchen. The stench of weed stung his nostrils.

Shorty lounged in the master bedroom, smoking a spliff and watching TV. The vest he wore made it easy to see the stitching on his shoulder. He looked up at Lamont and nodded.

'Nice to see you, Bossman,' he said. Lamont regarded his friend for a second before speaking.

'Give us a minute, K.'

K-Bar nodded. 'I'll be downstairs.'

'What happened?' Lamont asked as soon as the door closed.

'What did you hear?'

'I heard Reagan blazed you.'

'Well, I'm still here.' Shorty pounded his chest for emphasis, looking higher than a kite.

'Reagan went after you, though?'

'Prick was waiting at one of my flats. Almost got me too,' Shorty yawned.

'Where is he now?'

'Underground. Guess shooting your boy in the head makes you wanna hide.' Shorty laughed.

'Run that one by me again?'

'Ricky shot TC in the head.'

'On purpose?'

'Course not. He tagged me on the shoulder, and I took off. TC jumped out the bathroom. They had the drop, but I was stumbling cause of the gunshot. Ricky's next shot missed me, caught TC right in the face.'

'Are you serious?'

'Always. He put him down for the ten count. I jumped out the bathroom window and dipped.'

'Sounds like you got lucky.'

'For real. I sent a man to clean up. A Professional.'

'Is the flat in your name?'

'Don't be daft. One smoker in the Hood rents it.'

'Will they be a problem?' Lamont was in damage control mode.

'He's tight. Don't worry.'

'Shorty, they tried to kill you.'

'Yeah, but they failed. We won't. TC and Carl are down; Ricky's gonna follow.'

'Carl? What do you mean Carl's down?'

Shorty smiled. 'Didn't you hear?'

MARCUS TRAIPSED the roads of Harehills with purpose. It was late evening, and he watched for anything out of the ordinary. It was his way of ensuring he made it home when the job was done. He stopped outside a house. The gate looked like it would make a noise if he touched it, so he scaled the fence, heading to the back of the house. He broke in with minimal effort. It was a skill from his robbery days that had always served him well.

The house was quiet apart from noise coming from upstairs. He followed the sound, which became clearer once he reached the top. It was the exaggerated noise that came from bad porn movies. The door was ajar. He tiptoed into the room, gun at the ready.

An overweight black man perched on the edge of his bed, staring at the screen, pants around his ankles. Marcus crossed the room and put his gun to the man's head.

'Enjoying it?'

Carl froze. His right hand was still wrapped around his shrinking penis, but he didn't dare let go.

'You understand why I'm here?'

Carl was too scared to speak.

'Nod if you understand me.'

He nodded.

'Do you realise why this is happening?'

He nodded again, tears streaming down his face now.

'I won't explain then.' Marcus pulled the trigger twice. He crashed to the floor. He was dead on impact, but Marcus fired twice more to be on the safe side, then left the house and climbed into a waiting car.

THERE WAS a knock at Lamont's door early the following day.

'Lamont Jones?' Two suited men stood there. *Police.*

'Who wants to know?'

'We're just here to talk. This is DS Myers, and my name is DS Sinclair,' Both men showed identification. 'Can we come in?'

'Am I under arrest?' asked Lamont.

'This is just a chat,' said Sinclair. His tone was soothing.

'Do you have a warrant?'

'No.'

'Then, to answer your question, no, you can't come in.'

Sinclair shrugged.

'We can do it here then. I assume you heard about Tommy Carter's murder?'

'Sorry to hear about that. I don't know them, though.'

'You might know him by his street name. *TC.*'

'Doesn't ring a bell,' said Lamont, looking the officer in the eye as he did so.

'I'll enlighten you then. TC works for Ricky Reagan.' Sinclair paused, expecting a reaction. He continued, impressed with

Lamont's composure. He was up to his neck in street beefs, but he hadn't even blinked. 'There was a big shootout last night.'

'This is a fascinating story, Mr Sinclair. Why share it with me?'

'Wanna play dumb? Your choice. We know what's going on. Mack threatens you, the next day, he ends up in intensive care. Ricky shouts his mouth off about your crew. Suddenly, two of his people die. This is bold stuff, *Teflon*. Do you think you can take on Delroy Williams? You think he's just going to roll over?'

'*Delroy Williams;* is he a footballer?'

'You think you're so fucking clever, don't you? Do you think we'll lift a finger when Delroy sends a team to murder you? I'll shake that fuckers hand myself. I promise you that.' Spittle flew from Sinclair's mouth.

'Gents, this has been awesome, but I'm afraid I have a busy day ahead of me. You should write that tale you told me. You could sell it and make us all rich.' Lamont closed the door with a smile. He needed to shower and wake up. Police attention was never good. Trouble was on the horizon.

'Reagan needs to fucking go, L.'

Shorty, Lamont and Chink were in a safe house. It was a little spot they had in Calverley. Shorty's stitches were holding well, but he was irritable and out for blood.

'I don't even know why we're discussing this. The motherfucker tried killing me in my spot. I'm not taking that.'

'He tried getting me too,' Chink said to him. He kissed his teeth.

'Fuck Delroy. Let's fucking drop him too and end this shit instead of giving them time to reorganise.'

Lamont still hadn't said a word. A cup of coffee was in front of him, untouched, as he went over the variables in his head.

'L?'

Lamont looked at Shorty.

TARGET

'What the fuck? Are you gonna sit and stare into space, or are you gonna give us some guidance?'

'You don't want guidance; you want me to tell you it's okay to kill Reagan,' said Lamont.

Shorty shrugged. 'So what? Am I wrong to?'

'Yes.'

'For fuck's sake.' Shorty flung his arms in the air, wincing from his wound. 'What are we even doing here? We're at war, and we need to strike back.'

'We are striking back. Why don't you calm down and stop screaming and shouting? Listen for once.'

Shorty grumbled, but held his tongue.

'Reagan will expect us, you, to retaliate. It's a foolish tactic.'

'Do you have another way?'

'I do. Me and Chink have already worked on it,' said Lamont.

'You and *him*?' Shorty jerked his thumb at Chink.

'Chink, tell him about your new friend.'

Chink did as he was bidden with a smile.

'I've been banging Reagan's woman.'

'Since when?'

'L told me to pursue her a while back.'

'And you got her, just like that?'

'You think you're the only one who can get girls?' Chink sneered.

'This isn't important. The fact is, Reagan went too far, so now we destroy him,' said Lamont.

'But, you said—' Shorty started.

'Not by shooting him. Follow what we're saying. We'll destroy his reputation.'

'What the hell will that do? This is the streets, fam. No one cares about stories.'

Lamont and Chink shared a look.

'Do you trust me?' Lamont asked Shorty.

'Course I do.'

'Then relax, heal that shoulder, and let us handle it.'

THE VERY NEXT DAY, the games began. Lamont instructed Chink to ring a well-placed source in the Hood. That source went to several barber shops, then to Jukie's, then the streets, telling stories about Ricky Reagan.

Within hours, the streets were ablaze with tales he had murdered his comrades after refusing to pay them, plotted against Delroy Williams, and that he was financially crippled. There were elements of truth, which had the desired effect. In no time, Reagan's credibility plummeted.

'WINNIE, fucking ring me back when you get this. We need to talk.'

Reagan flung the phone on the sofa next to him. He was sure Teflon's people were behind the rumours, but he couldn't prove it. He couldn't believe anyone would think he would murder his own team. He and TC had been like brothers.

Reagan had been in hiding ever since the shooting had gone wrong. He blamed himself. He had had the element of surprise, but Shorty's lack of fear had surprised him. Now, his name was mud. No one in Delroy's organisation would speak to him.

'They'll fucking pay,' he mumbled, sipping a bottle of Red Stripe. 'No one fucks with me like this.'

As sure as he was of Teflon's involvement, there was no proof. The smearing was flawless, and the lies ingrained at street level. No one could say for sure where they had generated. He was, in fact, broke. He hadn't publicised it, but he lived move to move and never thought of saving. Whilst in hiding, he couldn't hit the streets to make money, and if that fat bastard Delroy and his links were turning their backs on him, it would be an absolute catastrophe.

Reagan's phone rang. He snatched it up, hoping it was Winston or Delroy, but didn't recognise the number.

'Yeah?'

TARGET

'Go on Star's profile on Facebook.'

'Hold on, who's this?'

The person had already hung up. Reagan logged into a fake account and typed *D.J. Star's* name into the search bar. He was directed to his page, and when he saw the latest photo they had posted there, it stunned him. Chink was in the photo, dressed in his expensive clothing. Reagan had assumed Chink was gay, but in the picture, he was draped all over Reagan's girl. His eyes narrowed as he saw Chink with his arms around Naomi, kissing her neck. His blood boiled. She didn't look distressed in the slightest. Her eyes shone as she looked into the camera, and she appeared at ease.

'Bitch!' He flung the phone across the room. He had poured money into her pockets, and this was how she'd repaid his love.

Reagan was beyond furious now. The picture had told him all he needed to know. Teflon and his team were behind this, and they would pay.

CHAPTER THIRTEEN
FRIDAY 16 AUGUST, 2013

FOR JENNY, work had been one disaster after another. She'd kept her composure, but now, nestled in the safety of her own home, she was happy to let the stress overwhelm her. As she placed her cup on the table, a sharp knock at the door surprised her. She unlocked it and stared out at Lamont Jones. He was smiling, smelt good and wore a fitted navy sweater, corduroy trousers and clean trainers.

'Can I help you?'

'May I come in? I'm not accustomed to doing business on the doorstep.'

Jenny shrugged, allowing him in. He took his off trainers and sat down in the living room. It was spacious, with various shades of red furniture and white porcelain furniture. Similar to his own place, there were books and papers resting on the cherry oak coffee table. He placed his phone and wallet on the papers, leaned back and steepled his fingers. She watched, amused.

'Can I get you a drink?'

Lamont gazed at her, lingering on her body. Her face grew warm. Apart from a hasty apology, she hadn't spoken to him since he'd all but forced her from his house.

'Jenny?' Lamont's voice brought her back to earth.

'Sorry. Did you say something?'

'I asked what the choices were.' He met her eyes.

'Choices for what?' Jenny's fingers tingled, her knees loosening. Lamont smirked.

'You offered me a drink. I was enquiring what was available.'

'Right. Juice. Tea. Coffee. Water. Wine.'

'Do you have green tea?'

Jenny nodded.

'I'll have some of that, please.'

She headed toward the kitchen. His words stopped her.

'I guess you were right.'

Jenny turned. 'About what?'

Lamont was in front of her now. He drew her in close, kissing her skilfully. She allowed the moment to continue, kissing him back harder. Lamont broke the embrace.

'You learn more about a person when you turn up randomly.'

'I'm glad I inspired you.' She kissed him again. The pair swayed in the middle of the room, green tea and other troubles all but forgotten.

Later, they lay in bed amongst messy, damp, sheets.

'That was unexpected.'

'Was it?' Lamont's cocky response tickled her. She poked him in the ribs.

'There's no way you knew what would happen.'

'I'm a man of many talents, Jen.'

'Pity sex isn't one.' She giggled at Lamont's splutter. 'Kidding. Maybe.'

'That was low,' he laughed, squeezing her. 'You're gonna give me a complex.'

'I'll try not to. How did you find my address?' Jenny asked.

'Like I said, many talents.'

'I'm serious. You weren't having me followed, were you?'

'Course I wasn't. Kate told me.'

'What happened last time? Why did you leave?'

'Business.' Lamont's manner instantly cooled.

'*Business* could mean a lot of things.'

'True. I can't say anymore, though.'

Jenny had so many responses ready. He seemed to turn his emotions on and off. She felt as if she was playing catch up. The pair were engaged in a game, and for the first time, Jenny wasn't sure she was winning.

'Fine. Keep your secrets.' She nibbled on his bare chest, closing her eyes.

'We do what we need to, to keep the intrigue alive,' said Lamont. The low rumble of his voice made her shiver.

'Is that what we're doing?'

'I think we're trying to analyse a situation that is still morphing and changing for the pair of us.'

'Where is this situation at the moment?'

'With me and you?'

'Yes,' said Jenny.

'I think we're good together.'

Jenny smiled, ignoring the warning at the back of her mind. He had a reputation, and she didn't want to be involved in a messy situation. She trusted her gut, though, and it was telling her to see where this went.

'I'll make you that drink now.' Jenny tried to get up, but Lamont stopped her, his mouth claiming her own.

'I'm not thirsty. Yet.'

Since his trouble, life had changed for Terry Worthy. After his disastrous dealings with Ricky Reagan, and Carlos falling out with him, he had become withdrawn. As a peace offering, Lamont had given him some drugs at a knockdown price, allowing him to make a decent profit.

Back in the day, Terry would have done the rounds, buying champagne and entertaining whatever gold-diggers were swayed by his wallet. Now, he was deflated after being ripped off by kids, almost killed by a maniac, and Carlos' termination of their friendship. Terry had fallen out of love with the game. He had no other skills in life, though, and lacked the drive and ambition to start again.

On this night, Terry had come from the pub. He was almost at his front door when there was a flurry of footsteps, and someone pressed a gun to his back.

'Open the door,' muttered Reagan. He complied. Reagan pushed them in, locked it, then frogmarched Terry to the sofa. 'Sit down.'

'W-What's this all about, Ricky? I thought we were cool.'

'Shut up, before I smack you up again,' said Reagan. It surprised Terry how rough he looked. His hair was tatty, there were noticeable circles under his eyes, and his clothing looked rumpled.

'You're gonna help me with summat,' Reagan started. He rubbed his nose before continuing. 'I've got two boxes of white. You're gonna sell them for me.'

'Why?'

'Because I said so, that's why. You tried to fuck me over, and I ain't forgotten that.'

'I paid you. I gave you the money.'

'Did you hear what I said?' Reagan's voice rose. He swallowed and nodded.

'Good. Shut up then. I don't give a fuck what you or that fat bastard you were with last time says. You work for me now.'

———

TWO DAYS PASSED by in a cocaine and weed-fuelled haze for Reagan. Before meeting Worthy, he'd robbed one of Delroy's smaller spots, stealing the two kilos of cocaine he'd given Worthy. After getting away, he'd been on the move ever since, never staying in the same spot for longer than twelve hours. He was crawling up the walls, but it was a temporary measure.

When he got the money back from the drugs, he would take it and leave Leeds. The more time spent running, the less time he had to plan. Reagan would build up and then rain down on anyone who doubted him.

By the time Terry Worthy got in touch, Reagan was slouched on the sofa with his eyes closed, listening to an old *Mobb Deep* album with a loaded gun digging into his hip. Without even turning the music down, he picked up the phone.

'What the fuck took so long?'

'Sorry, mate. This wasn't easy. It's proper hot out here, and—'

'Have you got it or not?' Reagan cut him off.

'Yeah, I've got it. Shall I come to you?'

Reagan considered this. He didn't want to leave his latest hideaway, but he also didn't want him knowing where he laid his head.

'No. I'll come to you. Make sure it's all there.' After Worthy gave him the address, he hung up and headed out the door.

'WHERE THE FUCK IS HE?'

Marcus Daniels stewed in the passenger seat of a stolen 4x4. He had two of his guys in the back. From their position, they could see Terry Worthy's Audi. It was late evening, and the night was a warm one. They had been sitting in the cramped car for over an hour and were sick of waiting.

'Check with the other guys,' said Marcus.

'Sharma, can you lot see anything?' Victor, the driver, spoke into a disposable mobile phone.

'Nah, it's clear down here,' Sharma's voice spoke back, a slight static in the background.

'Worthy must have fucked it up, the useless prick.' Marcus snorted as his phone rang. He answered, but sat up in his chair after listening for a few moments.

'I'm on my way.'

TARGET

Lamont Jones sat in his office in the barbers, poring over legal documents. He'd procrastinated for over a week, and the massive pile in front of him was his legal partner's way of sticking it to him. The boxy room was quiet, save for the soft Motown hits playing in the background. He kept checking his phone, waiting for confirmation the job was complete. He took a deep breath. Marcus always got results in this line of work. It was the one certainty the behemoth shared with Shorty.

The main room was silent. He assumed Trinidad and the other cutters had finished. He cleared his mind and worked through the paperwork, filing it away in his drawer. He would have a copy sent to Martin in the morning.

Downing the coffee, he washed out the flask and left it to dry in the kitchen. He yawned as he strolled to the main floor, then reared backwards in shock.

Trinidad lay motionless on his stomach, hands secured behind his back. The shutters were down, and he saw the key in the door.

'Just the man I wanted to see.'

Ricky Reagan sat in one of the leather barber chairs as if waiting for a haircut. His eyes glittered as he stared Lamont down.

'Shut that door behind you. We need to talk.'

Lamont hesitated as he saw Reagan's gun pointed at his chest. A fresh jolt of fear resonated through him.

'Just me and you, Tef; How does that make you feel?'

Lamont tried to marshal his fear.

'Did you kill him?' He pointed to Trinidad.

'Fuck the old man. This is about you. Thinking you're the smartest guy on the planet. Did you think you could get the drop on me?' Reagan's wild hair was nappier than normal, and his clothing looked slept in. He was a killer, though, and Lamont had no doubts about the man's ability to pull the trigger.

'Am I supposed to understand what you're talking about?'

'Don't play dumb. That snivelling little shit Worthy contacted you after I threatened him. I counted on that. Who's waiting for me at the bullshit meeting? Shorty? Tall-Man?'

Panic rose in Lamont.

'You left yourself open, didn't you? You've never taken this shit seriously. Always left it to those pieces of shit working for you,' Reagan spat the words out. His hand shook. Lamont considered charging at him, but knew it wouldn't end well.

'Now, I get to take my time with you.' Reagan placed his gun on the counter, never taking his eyes from his. 'This has been a long time coming.'

Lamont turned to escape through the back, but Reagan was faster. He grabbed him by the back of his top and flung him toward one of the barber chairs. His back hit the chair, and he fell to the floor.

'Fight back, you pussy,' grunted Reagan. He struck Lamont in the face, sending him skidding along the wet floor. Lamont eyed the mop and bucket in the corner. Trinidad must have been cleaning when Reagan took him out.

Reagan drew back his foot to kick him, but he grabbed his leg and took him down to the floor. He hit the lunatic once before Reagan head-butted him. Lamont reared back, one hand to his nose, trying to stem the sudden flow of blood. Reagan kicked him in the chest and straddled him, hitting him with slow, deliberate punches to his unguarded face.

'You're a pussy,' Reagan hissed. 'You've always been a pussy. Even back in the day.' He hit him again, panting now, undisguised relish in his voice. 'You're nothing without your people. When I'm done with you, I'm gonna split, and everyone will know.'

Lamont was dazed and bleeding. He couldn't afford to lose, but each blow weakened him. Reagan stood in front of him, smug, self-satisfied. He was gearing himself up to finish this, Lamont could sense it. Heart pounding, with nothing to lose, he charged Reagan, slamming the maniac into the main worktop, causing him to cry out in pain.

This was Lamont's chance. He groped, fingers closing around a

TARGET

straight razor. He jammed it into Reagan's leg just as the man straightened up. He screamed. Lamont didn't let up as he pulled the razor from his leg and thrust it into his stomach with the last of his strength. He fell back, spent.

Reagan's eyes bulged. He spat out blood, trying to stem the torrents of blood billowing from his stomach. Lamont watched, panicking, terrified he hadn't done enough. Reagan's eyes met his for a moment. He jerked and was still.

MARCUS DIDN'T KNOW what to expect as he pulled up to the barbers. He hurtled to the back door and wrenched it open, gun by his side as he cut through the makeshift kitchen to the main floor. Marcus paused then, his mouth agog. Usually tidy, there were various shavers, hair products and wires all over the barbershop floor. Trails of blood led to the prone body of Ricky Reagan.

Marcus's eyes flicked to Lamont. He slumped in the corner, drinking from a bottle of Red Label whisky. His clothing was speckled with blood, and his face was bruised.

'Your first?'

Lamont nodded.

'Thought Shorty might have brought you in on one of his jobs,' Marcus continued. 'You did good.'

'It's nothing to be proud of.' Lamont wiped his mouth and took another drink.

'Reagan had to die.'

Lamont stared at the blood on his hands, then at the majority tarnishing the floor. It was revolting. He could smell the stench of death. Marcus had his phone out, telling someone they had a *situation*. He hung up, glancing at him again.

'Get undressed. Take everything off.'

Lamont stripped to his boxer shorts, wincing as he took his shirt off. Marcus glared at him.

'I said everything.'

Lamont removed his shorts, covering himself. He didn't argue. He was in Marcus's world now.

'Do you have any spare clothes here?'

'No.'

'We'll get some brought over. Until then, go sit in your office,' Marcus noticed Trinidad slumped in the corner. 'Is he alive?'

'Reagan knocked him out.'

'Little prick. Sharma and them lot are still waiting at the lockup. I'll let them know about the change of plan.'

'Keep my name out.' Lamont didn't want everyone knowing what had transpired.

'Why? You should be proud, L. Reagan was a prick. He fucked a lot of people. Hold up your head, man.'

Lamont knew he meant well, but he took no pleasure in what he had done. He'd hated Reagan for years, but ending his life felt dirty, like the despicable acts he'd tried his hardest to pretend weren't associated with his world. He kept telling himself it was necessary.

'No one can know, Marcus. I mean that.'

Marcus shrugged.

'It's your call,' He looked to Reagan. 'We need to sort this quick, though. Trinidad was a witness. What are we doing about that?'

'What do you mean *what are we doing*?' Lamont's eyebrows rose.

'I mean, if you don't think he'll stay quiet, we can clean up two bodies.'

'We're not killing Trinidad. I'll talk to him.' Lamont was horrified at the suggestion.

'Fine. Whatever. Go to the office. People will be here soon.'

CHAPTER FOURTEEN
MONDAY 19 AUGUST, 2013

DELROY SAT IN HIS KITCHEN, annihilating a plate of food. His wife had left early without saying where she was going. Delroy hadn't complained. He had a lot on his mind.

The streets had been in absolute chaos. The Lamont situation was bad. His people were looking at him sideways over his lack of counter. Lamont and his team had stepped up, and with Akhan in his corner, his hands were tied. To add to a torrid situation, Reagan's name had been in the streets, connected with everything from TC's murder to a run for his crown. Reagan hadn't helped when he had robbed one of his stash spots a few nights back.

Delroy had a team looking for him, with orders to put him down. He hadn't surfaced, but Delroy remained confident, upping his home security and placing guards around his multi-million-pound home.

After finishing his meal, he was about to summon his driver, when his phone rang.

'Yes?'

'We need to talk.'

'Tef?' Delroy's grip on the phone tightened.

'The green place. One hour.' Lamont hung up. He stared at the mobile in disbelief. He didn't know why Lamont was calling, but he knew he wouldn't like it.

———

'THIS MUST BE HIM.'

Lamont and Chink stood in the park, watching Delroy and Winston make their way towards them. Delroy looked as imposing as ever. As he drew closer, Lamont sensed in his eyes what he'd noticed when they were at the restaurant with Akhan; uncertainty. They shook Lamont's hand. Both ignored Chink.

'What do you have to say?' asked Delroy.

Lamont looked at Chink before he replied.

'Reagan isn't coming back,' His words were blunt and had the desired effect. Winston glanced at his father. Delroy's eyes hadn't left Lamont's.

'Why are you telling me?'

'This thing we have going on. It's over.'

Delroy's eyes narrowed. He didn't like the authoritative tone he was taking with him.

'Tef, who do you think you're talking to?'

Lamont stared him down. Something had changed. His face was bruised, but it wasn't that. He seemed surly, more aggressive than he had previously.

'I understand you lost two boxes of food,' said Lamont. 'Later, my people will ring Winston and arrange for someone to pick them up. There's no need for further conflict.'

Delroy weighed up his words before he responded. Reagan was dead. Lamont was dealing from an option of strength, and Delroy found that more galling than anything.

For a fleeting moment, he wondered if Lamont had killed Reagan, but dismissed this. It was impossible. He had killer instincts, but he didn't have the nerve or the skill. No. It was likely Marcus. Or Shorty. Getting the drugs back would help.

'And if I feel otherwise?' He asked. Lamont walked away.

TARGET

'You don't. Be easy, Del.'

———

MARRION BERNETTE LEANT against the hood of his rented Volvo, adjusting his shades as he let the intense heat from the sun waft over him. In the driver's seat, Antonio sat with the car door open. He checked his phone, mumbling to himself.

A short while later, a blue Ford Focus rolled into view and pulled up a few yards away from the Volvo. Shorty glided from the car with his usual swagger. He wore a heavy chain over his crisp, white t-shirt. Blakey remained in the vehicle.

'You good?' asked Shorty, slapping hands with Marrion.

'I'm living. Have you got that?'

'Wouldn't be here if I didn't.' Shorty signalled to Blakey, who climbed from the car clutching a Morrison's carrier bag. He handed it to Antonio.

'If this is like the last batch, you'll need to return quick. That's my word,' said Marrion.

'Cool. Ring me or Blakey. We've got it to give.' Shorty's eyes darted around the quiet backstreet as they spoke.

'Listen, I can help with street stuff too. I've got people of my own I can call up to do the dirty work. No cost to you or Teflon.'

Shorty considered his words.

'We've got that end covered, bro. Ain't no more warring. Get at me when you want more.' He nodded at Antonio and ambled away.

———

ANTONIO AND MARRION drove back to the base. They stuffed the drugs under Antonio's seat. He held the wheel one-handed and put a CD on, which Marrion turned off. He frowned.

'Shorty's a cold bastard, man.'

'Shorty's mellow. His boss is the cold one.' Marrion glanced out of the window as they drove down Chapeltown Road. As he watched the usual's congregating outside the Landport building, he felt a longing for his own Manchester streets.

'*Boss*? Thought they were partners?'

'Teflon keeps them close, but he's in charge.'

'Why do you think he isn't keeping you close?'

Marrion scowled. 'Fuck knows. Either way, we're making money.'

'We could make more, though. Those lot are killing it. Do you think it's because you're banging his little sis?'

Marrion shot his friend an angry look. Antonio was oblivious.

'How did you get in with her, anyway? You kept that on the low for ages.'

'No one needed to know,' replied Marrion. 'I met her on a night out ages ago; we chilled, and shit grew from there.'

'You like her then? Usually, you're gone by now.'

Marrion didn't reply. He did like Marika Jones. It had started as something physical, but she was as stubborn and strong-willed, different to the norm. His brow furrowed as he thought about Antonio's words. He was being kept in the cold. The product was off the scale. People couldn't buy enough. Chink had told him he would grow rich moving to Leeds, but this had never seemed truer than it did now. There was more to earn, though, and he wanted all of it.

Marrion's phone vibrated. He read the text, smiling.

'Brownie said Timmy got that chain I copped for him.'

Antonio made a derisive noise and kept his eyes on the road.

'You got something to say?'

'I don't get what you see in that kid.'

'He's got potential.'

'Potential to do what?'

'He comes from a solid bloodline. He's got skills we can use.'

Antonio shook his head. 'I don't see it.'

'I didn't ask you to. Just drive the car and leave the thinking to me,' said Marrion. The rest of the ride continued in stony silence.

TARGET

After meeting with Marrion, Shorty dropped Blakey off, then headed to Chink's Shadwell apartment. It was decorated similarly to his town place, but to Shorty, seemed over the top.

As he walked through to the main room, he saw Lamont standing on Chink's balcony, looking out. Lamont turned, holding a glass of wine in his hand and nodding at his comrade. He wore a tan short-sleeved shirt, chinos and a pair of tasselled loafers. Shorty spotted the slight bruising around his eye and mouth. He didn't comment.

'Drink, Shorty?' Chink called from the kitchen.

'Yeah, go on then.'

Chink brought him a glass of white wine. Shorty shook his head.

'Ain't you got any beer or brandy?'

'I'll remember for next time,' said Chink.

'Whatever. I dropped a box on your boy from Manny.'

'A full box?'

Shorty nodded. 'He's getting quick with the return too.'

'He does a lot of business outside the Hood.' Chink was fully aware of Marrion's moves.

'If he's opening new markets, maybe we should give him more work.' Shorty considered his pockets. He received a healthy share of profits, but wanted more.

'It's worth talking about.' Chink straightened.

'What are we doing about Terry?' Shorty steered the conversation to other business.

'He's now part of the team.' Lamont glanced over the balcony again. Shorty glared. He was pleased Delroy had backed off, but didn't like the sneaky way they had gone after Reagan.

'You what?'

'Nothing major. He's gonna be in charge of a team and report to you.' Lamont faced Shorty again.

'You've gotta be kidding. Why would we want that loser on our squad?'

'He could be an asset. As long as he's working for someone, he's fine. Keep your foot to his throat, and he'll make us money.'

'He's loud, and he knows too much about the setup. We need to eliminate him. I'll handle it if you don't wanna be involved.'

Lamont him Shorty off.

'Forget him. I've got other news to share.'

'Cool. Afterwards, though, we're gonna talk more about this Terry situation.'

Lamont took a deep breath. It was time.

'I'm walking away.'

Silence ensued. Chink chuckled. Shorty's mouth fell open, his expression dazed.

'From what?'

'This. What we do.'

'What are you talking about? You can't walk away.'

'By the time Carnival ends, you two will run the show.'

'You've squared it with Akhan?' Chink spoke up.

'Fuck that,' Shorty turned on Chink. 'You can't agree with this. He's talking about breaking up the team!'

'L's a grown man. We can't talk him out of something when he's made his mind up.'

'Fuck you too then. You're a punk. When we started, you were too pussy to even join us.'

'You're mad at me for getting an education?' said Chink, laughing.

'Don't flip this.' Shorty whirled back to Lamont. 'This is about you. This got anything to do with that girl you met at Tek's; the one you're grinding?'

Lamont gazed at his friend, his expression neutral.

'This is nothing to do with Jenny.'

'Bullshit. It's always about some girl with you. Ever since we were young, you've always lost your shit over some female.'

'I told you it's nothing to do with her. I've wanted this for a long time. You should see it as an opportunity to grow.'

'You wanna sell out for pussy, fine. Don't make out like you're doing me a favour.' Shorty stomped away.

Lamont sighed and poured himself another glass of wine.

'That could have gone better.'

'I'd say it went just as expected.' Chink surveyed him. 'You're doing the right thing. You don't look as haunted anymore.'

'I feel better,' Lamont admitted. What he'd done to Reagan was front and centre in his mind. It was self-defence. Reagan had tried killing him, and he'd defended himself. The world was better without him. Lamont had spun a story to Trinidad Tommy about an argument growing out of control. He suspected he knew he was lying, but the old man had nodded and gone along with it.

'I'll sort things with Akhan. Shorty will be fine when I'm gone.'

'You think so?'

'I hope so.' Rubbing his eyes, Lamont took another sip.

Marcus Daniels sat in Jukie's spot, sinking glasses of white rum, soaking up the smoke-filled hangout area. He'd tried his hand on the card tables earlier, losing a few hundred. After sorting Lamont's mess, he'd slept for a full day. When he'd got up, he had come to play. Now he was getting bored. He drained the glass and climbed to his feet, unsteady for a second. After he collected himself, he headed out and clambered into his ride.

He'd only driven a few streets from Jukie's when he was surrounded by flashing lights. Tempted to bulldoze his way through, he calmed down when he realised he had no weapons in the vehicle. He assessed the surroundings. There was a police van and two Corsa's. A legion of officers had climbed out.

Unafraid, Marcus stared at them. Two of them appeared at either door, cutting off the possibility of escape.

'Marcus Daniels?' One man asked. He was broad with a pencil-thin moustache and dry lips.

'Who the fuck is asking?'

'We need you to come to the station and answer questions.'

'About what?'

'Climb from the vehicle, and I'll tell you.'

'I'm tired. Maybe next time.'

'You're being charged with murder, so that will not happen. Marcus Daniels, you do not have to mention when questioned . . .'

Marcus shot daggers at the officer as he read the rights, the raging inferno in his eyes making the man step back. He climbed from the ride, eyeballed the contingent of officers, then put his massive hands behind his back.

CHAPTER FIFTEEN
WEDNESDAY 21 AUGUST, 2013

CHINK RECLINED AT HOME, drinking a bottle of water. He was reading over the specs for a potential investment and thinking about his future. He'd earned a lot of money over the years, but once he stepped into Lamont's shoes, this would skyrocket.

The only problem was Shorty. It was clear from his reaction he didn't want to work with him. The idea didn't please Chink either. Shorty was stubborn and brutish. Without Lamont to guide him, he didn't see how it would work. For now, he was focusing on his profits.

'Wow, that painting looks old!'

Raised voices startled Chink from his papers. He frowned as Naomi and another girl staggered into the room, laughing.

'Oooh, is this him then? You've done well, Naomi. He's gorgeous,' the girl slurred. She was an attractive pecan-skinned girl with sultry lips and hazel eyes. Her crooked eyebrows looked ridiculous, though, and once he saw them, he couldn't take her seriously. He turned to Naomi, who leaned against the wall, giggling. The stench of vodka, weed and cigarettes filled the room. Chink wiped his nose.

'What are you doing here?' he said to Naomi. Her dress clung to her curves but was too short for his liking.

'Town was dead, so we thought we'd have a few drinks here.' Naomi sashayed to the kitchen. She returned with a bottle of red and two glasses. 'This is Adele, by the way. Adele, this is my boo, Chink.'

'Nice to meet you. You're fit,' Adele said.

Chink nodded at her, his eyes boring into Naomi's.

'You never said you were coming.'

'You're my man. I shouldn't have to say when I'm stopping by. You got another woman here or something?'

Chink shook his head. 'Don't be silly. I'm working, and I didn't expect to see you tonight.'

'Oh, crap.' Adele had opened the bottle, which slipped from her grasp and spilled on the plush cream carpet, staining it scarlet.

'You clown,' Naomi giggled again. Chink whirled on her so quickly that she took a cautionary step back.

'What is so bloody funny?'

'She's an idiot. She's always doing stuff like this.'

'I want her gone. Now.'

'Wait a second—' Adele started. Naomi stopped her.

'I'll sort it, 'Dele,' she glared at Chink. 'That's my best friend. She goes, then I go, and you'll never see me again.'

Adele smiled at Chink, drinking wine from the bottle. The smile vanished when he took her by the arm and ushered her from the apartment. He slammed the door and faced Naomi, bristling.

'What are you doing? Go let her back in.'

'She never comes again. In fact, as long as you're here, never bring anyone you associate with again.'

'*Associate with?*' Naomi's face twisted. 'Listen, you don't tell me what to do. I'm leaving.'

'Sit down,' said Chink. Naomi glared. Shaking her head, she moved to push past him. The crack as his palm lashed her cheek was like a gunshot. She toppled to the floor, shocked. He was so slender she hadn't expected him to pack so much power. With shaking legs, she stared up at him.

'You don't come into my home with degenerates and make messes. Remove that dress, then clean this carpet.'

Naomi's mouth hung open. She wasn't seeing the generous, attentive man she had been sleeping with. His face was red, his eyes bulging, and his fists clenched. Naomi was a warrior. She had allowed no guy to dominate her, but at this moment, she didn't want to try Chink. She slunk from the room to do as ordered.

MARCUS SAT in the interview room, glaring at his arresting officer. He wanted to rip his head from his shoulders, but calmed himself. Sitting in the police station for over twelve hours was cramping his style.

The police had arrested him in connection with the murder of Carl Coleman. Marcus didn't know how they'd linked him to the crime, but the police had ways.

The solicitor Lamont hired looked confident, which reassured him. He'd refused to answer their questions when they had booked him. They had sent him to a cell, and now they were trying again.

'Interview recommencing at eleven eighteen am. Present are DS Sinclair, DS Myers and the suspect, Marcus Daniels and his legal counsel.' Sinclair assessed Marcus, searching for weakness. He was a closed book. He put out a powerful vibe, and Sinclair resisted the urge to shrink back. Sinclair knew Marcus Daniels was legendary in the Hood, and had been on the police radar since his teens. Sinclair had heard the stories, the rumours of murders he had committed, people he'd had maimed. If they could put him away, it would be a powerful statement.

'Marcus, can you please confirm your whereabouts on the night of Thursday, Fifteenth of August, 2013?'

Marcus didn't take his eyes from Sinclair. 'No comment.'

'Do you know a man named Carl Coleman?' Sinclair tried again.

'No comment.'

'Do you know a man named Ricky Reagan?'

'No comment.'

'How about Delroy Williams?'

'No comment,' drawled Marcus.

Sinclair paused again.

'How long have you been friends with Lamont Jones?'

'No comment.'

'Is Lamont your boss?'

'No comment.'

'Did Lamont give the order for you to murder Carl Coleman?'

'No comment,' said Marcus.

'Did you murder Carl Coleman?'

Marcus hesitated. Sinclair thought they had him, but a second later, he was proved wrong.

'I don't know Carl Coleman. I don't know Ricky Reagan or a Delroy Williams. Anything that might've happened is not my business. That's all I'm gonna say.'

'If you didn't murder Carl Coleman, would you be able to say who did?' Sinclair was reaching, and he knew it. The solicitor answered before Marcus could.

'My client has asserted his innocence, and I am recommending for the record he make no further comment during this interview.'

'Do you sell drugs for your friend, Lamont Jones?' Sinclair ignored the solicitor.

'No comment.'

'Has Lamont fallen out with Delroy? Is that why Carl was murdered?' asked Sinclair.

'No comment.'

'Where is Ricky Reagan?'

'No comment.'

Sinclair shared a look with Myers. It had been risky to bring

TARGET

Marcus in, but they had hoped to get lucky. He wasn't breaking. They would have to find another angle.

'Interview ended at eleven thirty-six am.'

———

'Keyshawn!'

Marika's son hurried into the living room at the sound of his mum's voice. She held his Xbox 360 controller, scowling. Marrion, his mum's new friend, lounged on the couch. He held out his fist, and Keyshawn touched it in greeting. Keyshawn liked Marrion. As far as his mums' friends went, he was an okay dude. He never tried telling him what to do, and he treated his mum nice. He'd even bought him a new game for his computer.

'Don't you hear me talking to you?'

'Sorry,' said Keyshawn, not meaning it. He didn't understand why his mum was like this. Even when she had company, she still yelled at him.

'Why is this pad lying around? What have I told you about tidying up after yourself?' Marika flung the pad at him. He caught it before it could hit the floor.

'Careful! That's expensive.'

Marika narrowed her eyes.

'You're telling me it's expensive like you paid for it. You don't pay for shit, so next time just do as you're told and stop leaving your fucking things around the place, or you'll find them in the bin.'

'I didn't leave it down here. Bianca must have moved it from my room.'

'I don't care who moved it. Get it out of my sight and stop answering back,' said Marika. Keyshawn glanced at Marrion, who gave him a sympathetic look. Turning on his heel, the little boy stomped from the room.

'Make sure your room is tidy too,' she yelled after him one last time. Marrion chuckled, causing her to turn on him.

'What are you giggling at?'

'You. Why are you flipping out on your kid like that? All he did was leave a pad on the floor.'

'I didn't ask you for your opinion, so just stay out.'

'I like to have an opinion.' Marrion's smirk infuriated her more. She trembled with rage. Lamont had always told her she had an anger problem, but she never paid attention. The world couldn't handle strong women.

'I don't need you to have an opinion on me or my kids.'

'Well, I'm going to. Deal with it.'

Marika shot him her most withering glare, but it seemed to have no effect. She looked him up and down. It annoyed her she couldn't get him to bite. Every time she snapped, he never rose to it. As much as it aggravated her, she knew it was one of the biggest reasons she was still interested. She had a low attention span with men. If they couldn't provide, they were useless and sometimes, even when they could, she was happy to back off when it became too real.

Marrion was different. He was making strides in the game, and he was strong. Marika hated bitchy men. He had no interest in arguing with her, but he was decisive.

Marrion stared at her with a half-smile on his face. Marika Jones was the sexiest woman he knew. It was more than just looks. She was a tiger. She didn't back down, and she always had an opinion, a refreshing change from the wishy-washy women he dealt with. You received what you expected with her, but underneath she had a vulnerable side. It was worth braving the volcano for the warmth within.

'Why are you always so highly strung? Come here and relax,' he said.

'No, I'm not gonna relax.'

Marrion stood, towering over her. She scowled, pissed off yet pleased with the image her man presented. His clothes hung just right, and she knew what was underneath was even better. She allowed him to kiss her on her neck. It was a sloppy kiss, but she was wound tight and, in her state, was enough to do the trick.

Soon his hands roved all over her body, and Marika couldn't even remember why she was so mad. She almost told him to slow down, in case Keyshawn walked in, but once she felt his arousal, she decided against it and pushed him towards the sofa.

'WHAT DID THEY SAY?'

Shorty, Marcus and Lamont were in Lamont's office. They had released Marcus on police bail. He wore the same clothes they had picked him up in. His face was lined, and his eyes were bloodshot, but alert.

'They were asking if I knew Carl, Reagan's boy.' Marcus lit a cigarette.

'Someone's talking then,' Shorty spoke up. 'How else would the Feds make that connection? You wore a mask, right?'

Marcus's silence answered the question. Shorty shook his head.

'Are you for real? How could you go barefaced?'

'I wasn't planning on leaving witnesses.'

'Doesn't matter. You wear a mask so little bitches that see you, can't run to the police and tell them. That was stupid.'

Marcus cut his eyes to him. 'I don't need a lecture.'

'I'm not giving you one; I'm telling you you're an idiot.' Shorty didn't hold back. Marcus's eyes blazed with anger, but he remained seated. Shorty was right. In the heat of the moment, he hadn't considered covering his face. He hoped the mistake wouldn't cost him his freedom. Whilst they argued, Lamont stared ahead, not getting involved in the conversation.

'I'll handle it. Don't worry,' said Marcus.

'You better do.' Kissing his teeth, Shorty stood. 'I swear, it's like I'm the only guy keeping it real.'

'What's up with him?' Marcus asked Lamont when he'd left.

'He had bad news.' Lamont filled Marcus in on what he had told Shorty and Chink.

'How the fuck can you be ducking out?'

'That's not important, Marcus. We need to focus on keeping you out of prison.'

'I'm not going to prison,' said Marcus.

'Did they mention Reagan?'

'They'll never find him,' said Marcus. 'I wanna hear more about your plan, and I wanna meet this girl of yours too.'

'Marcus—'

'Tonight. Just for one drink. I'll bring Georgia.'

Lamont didn't want to go. Shorty had already fallen out with him, though; if a few drinks kept Marcus sweet, it was a small sacrifice.

'Tonight it is then.'

THAT NIGHT, Lamont and Jenny met Marcus and Georgia at a bar near the train station.

'He's massive,' Jenny whispered to Lamont. They waited as Marcus and Georgia walked across the room towards them.

'You're the girl who won my brother's heart then?' Marcus said to her as a greeting.

'You can just call me Jenny,' she said, laughing. Marcus hugged her, Georgia by his side. Lamont had met her several times, and found her nice enough, but quiet. She was short, blonde, blue-eyed, and curvy. She and Marcus had been on and off for almost ten years. He made small talk with her, and then the four of them sat in a booth in the far corner of the room, ordering drinks.

'Where did you two meet then?' Georgia asked Jenny, whom she'd swiftly formed a bond with.

'We met through friends,' said Jenny with a smile, sharing a look with Lamont. He grinned and sipped his gin and tonic.

'You're feeling her, aren't you?' Marcus said to him. Lamont nodded.

'She's a special woman.'

'Is she the reason you're quitting?'

'I don't know.'

'You'd walk away over a chick?'

'I'd walk away if I thought it was the right thing to do,' Lamont corrected him. Marcus was about to reply when his eyes narrowed. Lamont turned, noticing two dudes walking in their direction. They were young, well-dressed, laden with jewellery, and flanked by an entourage consisting mainly of women. One youth was stocky, dark-skinned and bullet-headed. The other was the same height, but chubbier. As they walked by the booth, the bullet-headed one grinned at Georgia. She didn't respond, but Marcus picked up on it.

'Oi!' he called, half the bar now staring.

'You talking?' Bullet Head asked, looking back.

'Don't scope my girl like that.'

'Don't tell me what to do.'

Marcus was on his feet. 'Are you on something?'

'Are *you*?' Bullet Head wasn't backing down.

'Marcus, chill.'

He ignored Lamont and focused on Bullet Head.

'Little man, don't try me.'

'Whatever, *old man*. Step off before you get hurt,' taunted Bullet.

'Who's gonna hurt me? You?'

Bullet Head shrugged. Marcus moved towards him, but the bouncers were all over it, swooping in, trying to calm the situation down. Marcus yelled at Bullet Head to follow him outside while Bullet Head and his people shouted insults at him. Lamont helped the bouncers calm Marcus, who had gone ballistic. They got him outside.

'I'll fucking kill them. I swear down I'll fucking kill them.' He punched the wall, cursing out loud one minute, mumbling under his breath the next. Lamont was stumped.

'Marcus, let's forget it and go,' he said, still trying to talk sense into his friend.

'Lemme back in there.'

'Marcus, please. Just forget them and go. Please, baby,' Georgia pleaded.

'Lamont, please take me home,' Jenny whispered. She shook with fear.

'Marcus, c'mon, we're going. Get in a taxi with us.'

Marcus took one last look at the bar, kissed his teeth and followed him.

CHAPTER SIXTEEN
WEDNESDAY 21 AUGUST, 2013

LAMONT AWOKE THE FOLLOWING DAY, tangled up in a mix of sheets with Jenny. He tried kissing her neck. She skated out of his reach and got to her feet.

'What's wrong?'

'What happened last night?'

'Don't worry about that. C'mere.'

'L. Your friend needs help.'

Lamont sat up and sighed.

'Marcus is just Marcus. He overreacted.'

'Overreacted? He was ready to fight all those men by himself because one of them looked at his girl. How primitive does that sound?'

'Jen, you wouldn't understand.'

'Course not. I don't even understand you, and you're meant to be normal,' said Jenny. Lamont's eyes narrowed.

'What do you mean by that?'

Ignoring him, she grabbed her clothes, hurried to the bathroom, and shut the door.

Lamont rubbed his forehead. Marcus was too much for most

people. He was intense. He should have prepared Jenny for it rather than assuming she would be all right.

'I'm sorry,' he said through the door. There was no reply.

'I'm not the most forthcoming guy, and my friends are fucked up. Me and Marcus grew up together, though. He's just stressed.'

Nothing. He shrugged, then headed downstairs and made himself a cup of coffee. Jenny came downstairs a while later, her hair still damp from the shower. She sat down, and he poured her some.

'Are you hungry?' He asked. She shook her head.

'I'm trying, Jen. I know it wasn't ideal for you last night, but I promise you, Marcus just had an off night.'

Finally, she smiled. 'Your lifestyle just worries me. I try not to let it, but I can't help it.'

Lamont pulled Jenny to him and kissed her on the head. He hadn't told her of his plans yet.

'Are you busy tonight?'

'No. Do you want to do something?'

'A friend of mine is holding a fundraiser. Want to come with me?'

'I'd love to.'

He grinned, pleased she'd said yes.

'I'll pick you up about sevenish then.'

'You sure this is the spot?'

It hadn't taken long for Marcus to track down the perpetrators from the club. The mouthy one was a dude on the rise known as *Maverick.* The other was known as *Scheme.*

'Yeah, boss,' said Victor. He was a rough-looking meathead loyal to Marcus. 'This is where they base. You wanna rush it?'

'We don't need to.' Marcus pointed out of the window. Maverick strutted down the road towards the house, looking pleased with himself.

'Wait here.' He climbed from the ride and approached Maverick.

'Still wanna talk shit?'

'You again. What the fuck do you want?' Maverick snorted, eyeballing him.

'Do you know who I am?'

'You're that washed-up knucklehead from the Hood, so what? You and your whack crew had your time, and this is ours.' Maverick held his ground. Enraged, Marcus struck, almost taking his head off with an uppercut.

'Still wanna talk shit?' he repeated. He punched him in the mouth.

'Fuck you, you're a fucking joke.' Maverick spat blood on the floor. Marcus kicked him in the head, knocking him out.

'Now who's the fucking joke?' He stalked back to the ride rubbing his knuckles.

―――

The fundraiser took place in the Town Hall, in the heart of Leeds city centre. The organisers, hoping to attract deep pockets, spared no expense. It had a smart-casual dress code, and was invite-only.

Jenny and Lamont entered after the party started, accompanied by Lamont's business partner, Martin Fisher, and his fiancé. Jenny liked the vibe. From the moment they arrived, people clamoured towards Lamont, and he'd handled them with a lot more tact than she expected. He could be cold and just switch off, but he seemed in his element tonight. She remained by his side, sharing in this energy. For almost an hour, they navigated the crowds, talking to people from different walks of life. He'd gone with Martin to get drinks when she became distracted by shrill laughter.

Ignoring the rumbles from the crowd, Jenny looked over, seeing a group of women laughing at something a stocky man in a tight shirt and jeans had said. The man glared at her with sullen eyes.

When he did, she realised it was Lamont's friend, Shorty. She smiled, then frowned when he shot her a hateful glance.

'Here you go.' Lamont handed Jenny her drink.

'Thank you. Your friend is here.' She motioned towards Shorty.

'Oh yeah. So he is,' said Lamont. He and Shorty eyed one another now. Both men nodded. Jenny watched, enthralled.

'What was all that about?'

'You'll have to be more specific.' Lamont sipped his drink. Martin and his lady were talking at length to another couple, so Jenny gave him her full attention.

'Have you fallen out with him?'

'Shorty? Nah, we're just going through some stuff,' said Lamont. It was a vague answer, and she found it unsatisfying.

'What kind of stuff?'

'Differences in opinion.'

She glanced back over at Shorty, who was shooting Lamont looks so ugly, they sent a shiver down her spine.

'He looks like he hates you.'

'Shorty's intense.'

Jenny frowned, forcing her mouth shut. Lamont surrounded himself with dangerous people, then seemed to placate them when they displayed any signs of aggression. She wondered if he feared his friends. Before she could retort, however, a thin, dreadlocked man in a blue shirt and trousers seemed to materialise out of thin air.

'You weren't even gonna say anything, were you?' The man said to Lamont. Jenny clutched his hand.

'I figured you'd drag yourself over here,' replied Lamont, his eyes as hard as the man's. Jenny held her breath. A moment later, she gaped as they both laughed.

'It's good to see you, L! For real. Didn't think you'd come tonight.'

'I wouldn't have missed it,' said Lamont. The man turned to Jenny.

'L's not going to introduce us, so I guess it's up to me; my name is Kieron. Everyone calls me *K-Bar*.'

'Nice to meet you, Kieron. I'm Jenny.'

'Likewise. Jen, I'm just gonna borrow L for two minutes if you don't mind?'

'That's fine.' She watched K-Bar lead him over to Shorty and his harem of women. It seemed frosty, but they touched fists, K-Bar smiling in approval. She turned to Martin, leaving him to his business.

———

'Guess who I found?' K-Bar interrupted Shorty as he whispered in a woman's ear.

Shorty and Lamont regarded one another. They hadn't spoken since he had shared his news. The girl Shorty had been flirting with, still stood there.

'Leave,' K-Bar told her. The girl made a derisive noise and didn't move. K-Bar's eyes darkened. 'You don't want me to repeat myself.'

The girl cut her eyes and stomped away. Lamont and Shorty half-glared at one another. K-Bar smiled at their stubbornness.

'I dunno why you two are fronting, acting like you ain't got love for one another. Bury this and move on.'

'He'd know all about moving on.' Shorty jerked his head towards Lamont, who smiled.

'Shorty, we're family. Even if I'm not in the mix, I'm always gonna be around.'

'It's not the same. You're leaving us to struggle, L. For a chick.'

'Struggle? Shorty, the team is stronger than ever. You have the best product, no Reagan or Mack to handle. Work with Chink, and you will prosper.'

'Fuck Chink.'

'He's one of us, and he worked hard to destroy Reagan. You owe him respect for that, if not anything else.'

'I don't owe him nothing. I've been watching out for his sneaky ass since day one. He owes me,' said Shorty.

Lamont rolled his eyes. He was about to return to Jenny when he noticed Marrion Bernette, followed by Timmy.

'What the fuck is he doing here?' said Shorty.

Marrion ambled over, Timmy trailing behind.

'Why are you here?' Shorty said to his cousin.

'He came with me, bruv. Hope that's not a problem,' Marrion spoke first.

'Get outside now. I want to talk to you.' Shorty ignored Marrion and addressed Timmy.

Timmy headed outside as Shorty stalked him. Marrion looked tight at being snubbed, but hid it well.

'What was that?' he asked Lamont and K-Bar. They shrugged.

'Shorty looks after his cousin,' said K-Bar, as if that explained everything. His lip curled as he stared Marrion down. Lamont noted this as Marrion turned to him.

'Can we talk?' he asked.

'The floor is yours,' said Lamont. Without being asked, K-Bar left.

'You don't like me, do you?' said Marrion.

'That's irrelevant.'

'That's a yes then?'

'Like I said, it's irrelevant,' replied Lamont.

'Things could have been different with you and me, and I should have stepped to you like a man about your sis. I do care about her, though.'

'It's nothing to do with me.'

'You're Rika's older brother. I've got sisters back home, so I get the role. I don't wanna step on toes; I just want to be with her.'

'Then be with her, and leave me out of it.' Lamont headed over to Jenny, now standing by K-Bar. Marrion watched, fury etched in his face.

TARGET

'WHAT'S WRONG WITH YOU?' Timmy said to Shorty. They stood at the bottom of the concrete steps leading up to the building.

'I'm doing the talking. Why are you here?'

'Marrion invited me. What's the problem?'

'You've got no business being around Marrion. You don't know him.'

'I know him more than you. He treats me like family. You treat me like I'm an outsider.'

'I'm not debating with you. Go home. Now.'

'No,' said Timmy, squaring up. Shorty slapped him in the mouth, stunning him.

'Recognise who the fuck I am and go home before I leave you laying here!'

Timmy wiped the blood from his mouth and glared at Shorty for a moment, then stormed off.

MARCUS SMOKED A SPLIFF, a slow, heavy rap track playing in the background. He'd been stewing all evening, ignoring his phone and brooding over Maverick's barbs. Since childhood, he'd grown used to people fearing him. Now, Maverick had squared up, unintimidated, and it wasn't sitting well.

Marcus wasn't like Lamont. He didn't have portfolios and investments. He spent money as it came in, and for the first time, he was worrying about his future. Over time, his money streams were drying up. It was getting harder to extort money from people, and everyone and their mother seemed to do loans. It made more sense to take a chance with one of the less experienced loan sharks than someone with his violent reputation.

In the back of his mind, he knew if he told Lamont he was struggling, he would give him the money in an instant. Pride stopped him. Marcus had always looked after himself, however. He couldn't let Lamont see his weakness.

'Can you turn that noise down please?' Georgia wrinkled her

nose at the pungent stench of weed. She stood in front of him with her hand on her hip. He ignored her, placed the joint in a nearby ashtray, then closed his eyes.

'For God's sake, Marcus; couldn't you open a window?'

Marcus again disregarded her. She meant well, but he was in no mood for her nagging. He had his own place, but when he wasn't working, he spent most of his time at Georgia's.

'I'm talking to you.' Georgia raised her voice.

'Piss off. I'm not in the mood.' He waved her away.

'This is my home, not yours. I've had a hard day and if you can't respect that, leave.'

Marcus snarled. Moving swiftly, he backhanded her with enough force to lift her off the ground. She crumpled in a heap, tears of shock and pain filling her eyes.

'I told you I wasn't in the fucking mood.' Marcus scowled as if it was her fault, before storming out. She touched her bloody mouth as the door slammed, crying now.

CHAPTER SEVENTEEN

THURSDAY 22 AUGUST, 2013

TIMMY HEADED to Ben's house in a taxi. He plastered a smile on his face when his mother answered the door.

'Timmy! You okay?' She swayed on the spot.

'Yeah, Mrs Skelton. Ben about?'

'He's upstairs. Go on up,' she slurred. Timmy stomped upstairs into Ben's room.

'Yes, Tim.' Ben was on his bed smoking a spliff. Jerome sat on a nearby chair, pouring Alizé into a paper cup.

'Where are you coming from?'

'This thing in town,' replied Timmy.

'Should have brought us in.' Ben held up the joint to him. 'What happened to your mouth?'

'Got into a little scuffle.' Timmy took a drag of the joint.

'Where d'you get that chain from?' Jerome noticed the heavy belcher piece around his neck.

'Marrion gave it to me,' said Timmy. The chain had been a random gift. The gesture touched him, and after the argument he'd had with Shorty, he wondered why he was even bothering to stay loyal to his cousin.

'That must have cost a bomb.'

'Marrion's loaded,' Ben piped up. 'He was paying for top-notch champagne and everything when we were with him.'

'Is he rolling like that?' Jerome had a greasy expression on his face. 'We should rob him and take his shit.'

'Marrion rolls with killers. It's not worth it.'

'Yo, fuck him and anyone else coming out of Manchester. This is Leeds, fam. I say we fucking kidnap him. Make his team pay to get him back, or we pop him.'

'You'd do that?' Timmy asked.

'Course. I've got a piece at home.'

'You try stupid shit like kidnapping, you'll have to kill Marrion and his team to survive.'

Jerome didn't like him disagreeing, and it showed.

'I ain't scared of that Manc prick,' he growled, frowning. Timmy saw how pointless the discussion was. There was a reason Jerome would never succeed; he was trapped at the bottom rung, and he didn't have the smarts to rise in the game.

'Do it, then.'

'Do what?'

'Kidnap him.'

'I will!' Jerome declared. 'Have you lot got my back?'

'I'm not robbing him. That's snake shit.'

'I see how it is; my man buys you a little chain, and suddenly you're on his dick? Fuck you then. I'm gone.' Jerome snatched the bottle of Alizé and stormed off.

'Should we go after him?' asked Ben.

'No. Let him cool off.'

―――

LAMONT SAT AT HOME, thinking about the loose ends he needed to tie up. Carnival was close, and he had everything ready. He always made money from the event, but he was taking it to an audacious level. On the legitimate front, he'd spent more time at the office with Martin, learning exactly where the money went. This also meant more sessions with his accountant, which he'd pencilled in.

Everything was well, yet he felt uneasy. His sleep had been reduced to two or three hours a night again if he was lucky, and no matter how much he analysed, he couldn't figure out where the feeling was coming from.

Lamont recalled the fundraiser, and how much he enjoyed being out with Jenny. He had felt almost normal. He only hoped he and Shorty would get back to their old relationship now.

A knock at the door interrupted his thoughts. He assumed it was Jenny and opened the door.

'Mr Jones.'

Lamont was startled for a second, but recovered.

'Saj, nice to see you again. Come in.'

Akhan's second-in-command followed him into the living room and perched on the sofa.

'Can I get you something to drink?'

'Some water, please,' said Saj. Lamont fetched him a bottle and sat opposite him. The indication was clear; Akhan was telling him they could find him.

'This is a lovely place.'

'Thank you.'

'Did you do the decorating yourself?'

'No, I paid someone.'

Saj smiled, placing the bottle on the coffee table.

'I'm here to talk about this conflict you are waging in the streets. Your altercations bring unnecessary attention. You see this.'

Lamont nodded. 'The conflict is over. Delroy and I have ceased our drama.'

'What about Marcus Daniels?'

Lamont's stomach fluttered, his body tensing. He'd had no idea anyone else knew of the arrest.

'Don't be surprised. We couldn't do our business if we didn't know everything about everyone. The police questioned Mr

Daniels about a murder. This is a worry.' Saj's tone remained solicitous.

'I appreciate the concern. Marcus is a rock, though. He won't talk. No matter what.'

'And you would put your reputation on the line to guarantee this?'

It took Lamont only a second to reply.

'Yes.'

'Why are you asking?'

Lamont was at Jukie's gambling spot. Once Saj left, he'd driven down to the Hood.

Saj's comments had triggered something. He'd learned titbits about the things Marcus was doing a while back and ignored them. He felt awful, but he had become immersed in Marcus's problems in the past, and he had no desire to do it again.

Jukie learned everything in his spot. Lamont's relationship with Shorty was tenuous at the moment, so he couldn't go to him. He and Jukie went back far enough for him to learn that he could speak to Jukie in confidence. A man in Jukie's position couldn't afford enemies like him.

'You're a pillar of the community. People speak around you.' He stroked the older man's ego, and it worked. Jukie nodded.

'Your boy is up to his neck in it.'

'How bad?'

'He's in here every night, L. Playing cards, betting big. High and drunk. He's—'

'How bad?'

Jukie swallowed. 'He's into me for fifteen grand. I don't know the ins and outs, but I'm not the only one he owes.'

Lamont gritted his teeth, annoyed at Marcus's carelessness. If he needed help, he could have come to him rather than gambling.

'Have you approached him about paying?'

TARGET

Jukie shook his head. 'You don't get heavy with Tall-Man like that. Last time he got in deep, he paid a few weeks later.'

Lamont digested the information. Marcus had always lived hand to mouth, and no amount of advice to save could dissuade him.

'L, are you that worried about him?'

'I'm not sure, Juke. Thanks for your time, though,' he said, handing the man some money.

'I don't need your money, L. The info's free.'

'Nothing is free. Take it.' Lamont didn't raise his voice, but there was an insistence that made Jukie take heed. He thanked him and limped inside.

'Fuck.' Lamont allowed his rage to take over. He had vouched for Marcus, but now there was more. As he started the engine, someone called his name. He cursed as he watched the person approach.

CHINK STOPPED outside Georgia's place and killed the engine. He checked his reflection in the wing mirror, then knocked on her door.

'Who is it?' She called. He didn't answer, knowing curiosity would bring her to the door.

'Xiyu? What are you doing here?'

Chink noted the bruise on Georgia's face she'd tried to cover with makeup.

'I've been trying to get hold of Marcus. Does he have a new number?'

'Not that I'm aware of.' Her voice shook.

'If you speak to him, tell him I'm looking for him.'

Georgia burst into tears, unable to maintain her composure.

'What's he done?' Chink led her into the house and closed the door. She was in near hysterics now, unable to answer. He made her a hot beverage and forced her to drink while he stood over her.

'T-Thanks,' she said when she'd calmed down.

'What did Marcus do?'

'He's been stressed. I pushed him too far.'

'Don't blame yourself. He's wrong,' said Chink.

'He does. It's just been hard for him.' Georgia felt compelled to defend Marcus. Chink didn't like it.

'Stop making excuses. Just stop it. You're better than that.' He sat next to Georgia, taking the half-drunk teacup from her hands and putting it down.

'Xiyu—' Georgia started. He hushed her with a finger to his lips.

'No,' he said. 'I love you, Georgia. I've always loved you.'

'Xiyu—' Georgia tried to stop him, but it was too late. He pressed his mouth to hers, and all the doubt and anguish seemed to leave her in a lustful rush. The walls she had built after straying the last time crumbled, and she kissed him back with fervent gusto.

'I love you,' he repeated, unbuttoning Georgia's blouse. Like the last time, she succumbed.

'LITTLE LAMONT,' said the man, shuffling towards Lamont's car. Old Man Charlie was one of Auntie's more prominent suitors. The sight of him filled Lamont with rage as he remembered the turbulent childhood and thoughts he hoped to forget:

LAMONT WAS ELEVEN YEARS OLD. He'd come home from school early. Auntie was in the living room, lording it up.

'What are you doing here?' Her words were harsh.

'I didn't feel well. Got sent home early.'

'Make yourself useful then. Go sweep your room,' said Auntie. He didn't move.

'Are you listening?'

'Why are you wearing that?'

'Wearing what?'

TARGET

Lamont pointed at the jewellery around Auntie's neck.

'None of your business.'

'It's not yours. That's my mum's necklace.'

'It was your mum's necklace. She left me in charge.'

Auntie's man bounded into the room. Charlie Mullen was overweight with bad breath, coarse skin and a rotten attitude. He glared at him like he was the intruder. Lamont's eyes shifted to his wrist, recognising the gold watch as his dad's.

'What are you looking at?' said Charlie.

'That's not your watch. That was my dad's,' Lamont told him.

'It's mine now. Get out of here. Your Auntie told you to do something.'

Again Lamont didn't move. Charlie's eyes narrowed.

'Did you hear what I said?'

Lamont continued to glare at Charlie, feeling an infusion of hatred towards him and Auntie. He couldn't tell him what to do. He was nothing.

'Lamont, Uncle Charlie told you to do something.'

'He's not my Uncle.'

Charlie's palm shot out, lashing against the side of his face. He tumbled to the floor. Charlie picked him up and hit him in the mouth. He tasted blood and felt the sting of salty tears falling down his face. Auntie watched, not saying a word.

'If I have to tell you again, I'm gonna give you something to cry about. Now go!'

'Look at you, boy; you got big,' said Charlie, exposing his worn teeth when he smiled. Lamont eyed him, self-consciously rubbing the watch on his wrist. 'Do you remember me?'

'How could I forget?' Lamont wound his window down, his voice dripping with sarcasm.

'Long time. You're not a little boy no more,' Charlie laughed, expecting him to join in. 'I'm in a bad way, champ. Don't suppose you could lend me something to get me back on my feet?'

Lamont's nose wrinkled.

'You've got to be kidding me.'

'I'm desperate, boss. I've got info. We could do a trade,' said Charlie, his words quicker now.

'You've got nothing I want. Get away from my car.'

'Lamont, let the past go. I gave you some licks, but they made you strong. Help me out.'

'Are you deaf?' Lamont's fists clenched.

'Levi. What about Levi? Are you interested in him?' Charlie had his attention. He froze, the name he hadn't heard in years triggering more memories he wanted to forget.

'What about him?'

'I'll tell you where he is, if you help me. Please, man. I'm sick.'

Lamont pulled out two twenty-pound notes.

'Talk.'

———

Marcus drove to Georgia's house, wiping his eyes and popping two pieces of chewing gum into his mouth. After leaving in a rage a few nights back, he'd holed up, smoking rocks with some delinquents from the old days. He had come to his senses that morning, when he awoke to find himself face down on a wooden floor, missing a boot and surrounded by fiends.

'Georgia,' he called. 'Let me in, please. I want to talk to you.'

'Bloody leave her alone!' The next-door neighbour opened her own door and poked her head out. 'She doesn't want you.'

'Fuck off, you fat bitch,' snarled Marcus. Georgia's neighbour, Mandy, was a squat woman with big hands who looked like she could handle herself. They had always hated each other, and for as long as he could remember, she had been trying to convince Georgia to leave him.

'You fuck off. I chuffing live here. I'll call the police if you don't leave.'

'Just because you can't get a man, doesn't mean you can interfere in my business.' Marcus was close to losing his top and head-butting her.

'I'd rather be alone than shackled to a loser like you,' said Mandy. He ignored her and knocked again.

'Please, Georgia. I want to talk.'

'Mate, I think you should leave,' A neighbour across the street weighed in. That was it. He was about to deal with the interferers, when Georgia opened the door.

'It's okay, Mandy; I can handle this.'

Marcus saw the bruise on her face and felt worse than he already did.

'Fine,' scoffed Mandy. Marcus waited until she was inside, then turned back to Georgia.

'I'm sorry,' he whispered.

'You can't keep doing this, Marcus. I don't deserve it.' She choked back a sob. He closed his eyes. The weight of his woes, the life he was living and the risk of prison all caught up with him. Tears pooled. He tried wiping them away but couldn't stop them falling.

'You're right. I need help. I need you,' he mumbled.

Georgia stared at him, and her heart melted. She had never seen him cry. This show of emotion, mixed with the guilt she felt over Chink, caused her to forgive him.

'If you ever hurt me again, we're through. For good. Okay?' she said. Marcus nodded, sniffing. 'Do you wanna come in?'

He nodded again and followed her inside.

LAMONT STOOD in front of a ramshackle house that wouldn't have looked out of place in 2003 Iraq. The grass in the garden was overgrown and littered with weeds and refuse. The front and upstairs windows were boarded. Two grubby-looking youths had watched him get out of his ride. He ignored them and knocked at the door.

A living corpse of a woman answered. She was thin, with lank blonde hair, dull eyes that were too big for her face, and dry lips. He resisted the urge to flinch as she glared.

'What do you want?'

'Let me speak to Levi.

'Who?'

'I'm an old friend.'

'Levi 'ant got no friends.'

'You know him then?'

While the blonde zombie verbally tripped over herself, a movement by the dirty window caught Lamont's attention.

'Move.' He pushed past the woman. The volley of curses thrown at him dissipated when he locked eyes with the man sitting in the middle of the derelict living room. *Levi Parker.*

'You got past Siobhan then.' Levi laughed so hard he coughed.

Lamont took a step forward but stopped himself. He was trying to spot the Levi he'd known; the carefree, well-groomed ladies' man. That image wouldn't stick, though. It never would again. Now, all he would see was the shrunken remains of his friend. Levi had lost a lot of weight. His eyes had that lifeless sheen Lamont had seen too many times before.

'L, man, you look good.' Levi finished coughing, speckles of blood around his mouth, and hugged him. He stank, but Lamont withstood it.

'Sorry, babe; this rude prick pushed past me,' said Siobhan, storming into the room. Levi cut his eyes to her.

'This is my oldest friend. Piss off upstairs.'

'But—'

'Just do one.' He didn't raise his voice. She flounced from the room, mumbling under her breath. A door slammed upstairs, followed by a shout.

'Sorry about her. She's a horrible cunt. Can't believe you're here. How's everyone doing?' He sounded like the animated kid Lamont once knew.

'Everyone's good.'

Levi grinned, showing brown teeth. 'You're killing the streets. Everyone knows your name.'

'I'm just living.'

'Bollocks. You're sorted. I saw your clothes, and the whip when you pulled up.'

'Things aren't always as they seem,' said Lamont. 'I can't live like this forever.'

'You're a fool. I could.' The hunger, the undisguised envy towards his friend's lifestyle was clear in Levi's voice.

'Why don't you?'

'What?' Levi was startled.

'Get straightened out. I'll pay. Get clean, then work with me.'

Levi didn't reply straight away.

'No. I'm not good enough.' He hung his head.

'If I can do it, you can.'

'L, look at me.' Levi grabbed his yellowing t-shirt for emphasis. 'I'm a pissing crackhead.' Tears spilled down his face.

'You can get help. I've got more than enough money.'

'No, I'm too far gone. I tried, L. It always wins.'

'Levi—'

'Just go, L.'

'Levi —'

'I'm serious,' Levi's voice was stronger. 'Go, man. Don't come back. Please.'

Lamont nodded. He reached into his jacket pocket and dropped an envelope on the coffee table.

'Use that. Buy yourself whatever you need.'

Levi snatched the cash and gave it back. 'I'm not taking your money, L.'

'C'mon, Levi.'

'No. I'm not taking it.'

Lamont stared, once again seeing the excitable, ambitious kid Levi had once been. The image faded to Levi's tear-streaked face the day his big brother had been murdered in the streets. He snapped back to reality, understanding how things could have turned out for them both.

'Take care of yourself, brother.'

They shook hands, two young soldiers of the street, cut from the same harsh cloth yet at two opposite ends of the crime pile. Lamont walked out. Siobhan hovered near the top of the rickety steps in the hallway and scowled at him.

Outside, he glanced at the window. Levi watched him. Not taking his eyes from his friend, he tossed the money onto the doorstep, climbed into his car and started the engine. A lone tear pooled in his eye. Brushing it aside, Lamont drove away.

———

JENNY HAD FINISHED work for the evening and was on her way to Lamont's. They had arranged to meet, but she hadn't spoken with him today. She saw his car parked in the drive, but the house lights were off. Her heart raced as she called his phone again. Still no answer. On a hunch, she tried the front door, surprised when it opened. The sweet sounds of *Stevie Wonder's Innervisions* album filled the house, and her insides shifted. Lamont was cheating on her. She wanted to flee, but she was stronger than that. She wanted to catch him in the act.

Storming into the bedroom, she stopped short. Like the rest of the house, the room was pitch-black, save for a small patch of light coming from the dashboard of an Mp3 dock. She switched on the light and noted with stunned relief that Lamont was alone. His eyes were closed, and turning the light on hadn't startled him.

'L?' she called. He opened his eyes.

'Hey,' he said.

'Are you okay?' she asked. It looked like he'd been crying. He sat up in bed, wiping his eyes.

'I had a rough day.'

'What happened?'

TARGET

'I ran into an old face. Someone I allowed myself to forget when I shouldn't have.'

'Who?'

'A friend. I abandoned him, Jen, and now he's a fucking drug addict.' Lamont laughed darkly. Jenny didn't know what to say. She had never seen him so unglued. It was strange to witness him lamenting over an addict, considering how he made his money.

'Levi and me were friends in our younger days,' Lamont carried on. 'His older brother sold weed. Offered to set us up.'

'Did you take the offer?' asked Jenny. He gazed into her beautiful eyes.

'My parents died when I was a kid. In a car crash. It's how I got this.' He pointed to a thin scar on the underside of his chin that Jenny had never noticed. 'After they died, me and my sister had to live with my Auntie.'

Jenny nodded, listening to the story.

'We were struggling, so I did what I needed to do.'

'Wait a second; you sold drugs because your parents died?'

'I did what I needed to do,' Lamont repeated. Jenny scoffed. She'd held back what she wanted to say about his life, and wouldn't anymore.

'How can you use your parents as a cop-out for doing something you know is wrong? It's illegal, L! You sell poison. The two areas do not mesh. How do you think they would feel? How would your parents feel if—'

'Who the fuck do you think you are?' Lamont hadn't raised his voice, but the effect was like a gunshot. Jenny's mouth snapped shut. He seemed to radiate some innate power. His rosewood eyes blazed. She froze.

'You . . . grew up in comfort. You don't have the slightest idea what my life was like, so don't you dare knock me for trying to survive.'

'I'm sorry, L. Please, tell me,' Jenny found her voice. He took a deep breath, then spoke again.

'Auntie betrayed us. The little money left to us, she spent on herself.'

'All of it?' Jenny gasped.

'I didn't realise straight away. She hated me. I was her slave. She abused me, her and whatever boyfriend was hanging about,' he said. 'I was sent to school in whatever clothes Auntie could scrounge up. I was laughed at, bullied and ostracised. We were broke, Jen. We went from happy to hell. Marika didn't remember. She was too young when our parents died. She grew up used to being poor.'

Lamont paused, then continued.

'I played it straight until my teens. I worked hard, wanting to get a good job so I could get us out, but I reached my breaking point.

'Levi's brother fronted us. We were up and running and making decent money. It didn't last. Levi's brother got into it with another crew. They murdered him.'

'Oh, God. That's awful.' Jenny's hand went to her mouth in horror.

'Levi attacked Leader, the head of the crew. Stabbed him. Ended up going to a young offender's prison. When Levi got out, he avoided us.'

'What about Leader?'

'What about him?'

'Is he alive?'

'No. Someone killed him,' said Lamont. Something about the way he said it sounded strange. His tone was the same as it had been when she'd confronted him about the bruises on his face a while back; vague, almost disconnected. She didn't dwell.

'What made you visit Levi?'

'Someone pointed me in his direction. He left Leeds after all that trouble. I wasn't aware he was back.'

Jenny sat next to him, holding his hand, having a broader understanding of him and why he did what he did. She stroked his fingers, enjoying the closeness.

'What now, Lamont?' She whispered.

'Now, I walk away.' Lamont's posture straightened, his eyes softening. 'The plan has always been to leave. I never wanted to do this forever. I was waiting for the right reason.' He gripped her hand. 'And I've found it.'

Tears of happiness sprang to Jenny's eyes.

'I love you, Lamont,' she let out the words she had been holding back. He blinked once before replying.

'I love you too, Jenny. You've saved me.'

They continued to hold one another then, having embarked on a new phase of their relationship.

CHAPTER EIGHTEEN
SATURDAY 24 AUGUST, 2013

SHORTY SAT in a club knocking back liquor, sad and angry. Earlier in the day, he had hosted a pre-carnival barbecue. It wasn't a huge event, but the turnout was always good. He and a few others cooked and played music while people hung out. Everything had gone ahead like clockwork, apart from the noticeable absence of Lamont.

For the past five years, he had run the event with Shorty. He had called the day before to apologise and say he couldn't make it.

It was a sign things were changing. Lamont was already making his transition. It was rarer to see him in the streets these days. Instead, he was with Jenny, or schmoozing potential business links at *Épernay* or other high-end spots.

Shorty wanted to be happy for him, but he didn't see how they would stay tight if they were in two different environments. To add to his mood, he'd taken Grace to Amy's after the barbecue, stunned when a man opened her front door. What hurt most was Grace yelling *Chris* and jumping into the man's arms for a hug. It showed familiarity, and he'd been forced to keep his composure in front of his daughter.

Everything was changing. Only Shorty remained the same.

TARGET

He shrugged away the thoughts and ordered a glass of tequila. Drinking and surveying the room, he spotted an old friend, Kimberley, from the roads. She seemed to be arguing with a group of girls. As he watched, the biggest of the girls slapped her. The rest of the girls attacked her before he hurried over and pulled the biggest one off.

'Oi, who are you?' She got in Shorty's face. He didn't recognise her but her accent was a Manchester one.

'She's cool. Fuck off and leave her alone.'

'Who the fuck are you, though?' The girl shoved Shorty. Part of him wanted to walk away, but the rest screamed for action. He stepped around the angry girl and helped Kimberley. She had a couple of cuts and scrapes, but apart from that, she looked okay.

'You good?' He asked, ignoring the hateful glares of the other girls. She nodded.

'I'm fine.'

'Come. Let's sit you down.'

'It wasn't my fault. They started on me. I've never met them.'

'You know what these out-of-towners are like,' said Shorty. They were walking away when the angry girl cut him off.

'Who are you, dickhead?' She was wild.

'Take your drunk ass back to Manny.' Shorty turned his back on her and led Kimberley over to his table. They had just sat down when she grabbed his arm.

'She's coming.'

Shorty watched her approach. She was bigger than him, her shoulders bouncing. He imagined she could hit hard.

'Go on, who are you?'

'You need to back off. I ain't gonna treat you like a woman if you start.'

'Fuck off.'

'I'm not gonna warn you again.' Shorty remained seated as the loudmouth stood over him. Her friends gathered around, giving her confidence. She raised her arm to strike him. A second later, he was on his feet, and the girl was on the floor, out cold. The punch had come out of nowhere, a blistering uppercut that had crunched her jaw, snapping her head back. He sat back down, picking up his drink without another word.

IN ANOTHER PART of the club, a gang of guys from Manchester were getting loose on Grey Goose vodka and other liquor. The leader of the group, a man named Solly, slouched in the middle of the booth. Solly earned good money in Manchester and had women queuing because of this. He was about to order more bottles when he saw one of his girls hurrying towards him.

'Solly, you need to handle one guy! He's going on reckless,' she said, getting the attention of the six-strong group.

'Zona, what are you on about?'

'This little guy knocked out Jasmine. She's out cold.'

'What?' Solly stood up. Jasmine was irritating, but she was from his area, and he was cool with her brother. 'Who hit her?'

'This cocky little fuck. We were just dancing, and he spazzed out.'

Solly flexed his muscles.

'Let's handle this dickhead. Show me where he is.'

'WE NEED TO LEAVE.'

Shorty ignored Kimberley. He wasn't letting his night get ruined by a couple of rude out-of-towners. He had no idea where they had taken the girl, but if he saw her again, it would be worse.

'We're not going anywhere. She started it.'

'I can't believe you hit her so hard.' Kimberley glanced at the dance floor, as if expecting to see the bully lying there.

'She deserved it. No one fucks with one of my girls.'

'Please, I haven't been your girl in a long time. You're Amy's property.' Kimberley shook her head.

'You must be high.' Shorty's feet shuffled. Before he could add more, there were loud voices, the women yelling and pointing in his direction, followed by at least half a dozen angry-looking guys.

'Oi, mate, what do ya think ya playing at?' The smallest guy started in a Manchester accent. He was stocky and looked like he could handle himself. His team surrounded him like bodyguards, each eyeing Shorty with dislike. The mouthy girls stood to the side, waiting.

'Do I know you?' said Shorty.

'Nah. You've been threatening my girl and her people, though. Think you're tough, sparking out a woman?'

'You've got it twisted. They jumped my girl. That other bitch tried swinging, so I sat her down.'

Solly looked to his people, annoyed at Shorty's complete lack of fear.

'Are ya taking the mick? Do you know who ya fucking with?'

'If you wanna do something, then let's do it.' Shorty stood. Solly looked to his people again, taking a step forward. He was about to rush Shorty when a voice halted him.

'What's going on?' Marrion Bernette strode over, flanked by Brownie and Antonio. His eyes assessed the situation. Shorty looked bored, Solly ready for combat.

'M, this dude's talking reckless. I'm gonna do him in.' Solly eyed Shorty.

'No, you're not.'

'You what?'

'You heard,' Marrion touched fists with Shorty. 'Sorry about this mess, fam. My guy's out of line, but he's all right.'

'He needs to watch himself.' Shorty's eyes remained on Solly.

Marrion nodded. 'You're right, fam. Oi barman,' he addressed the bartender who was bringing more drinks. 'Three bottles of champagne. Quick time.' He dropped a handful of notes in his hand. Shorty glanced at Solly and his people, but didn't gloat.

'C'mon, let's have a drink,' said Marrion.

'Fine. This is my home girl Kimberley.'

Solly watched as they drank champagne and chatted like the best of friends. Marrion was from his ends, and he was a big deal. Knowing he was around, Solly figured it would be a wrap for the cocky little prick. Now, not only was Marrion buying the bar with him, he had talked up to him. Shorty was a big deal, and this irritated Solly more. He grew angrier as he thought about the time they'd gone partying in Manchester. Marrion had bought one bottle of champagne for the group to share. Now, Shorty and his girl comfortably sat with three.

'Let's go,' said Solly.

'What?' Zona spluttered, wanting to see Shorty get his comeuppance.

'Now. Fucking come on.'

'Yo, sorry again about my boy.'

'It's squashed. Don't worry about it.'

Half an hour had passed, and Marrion was still trying to apologise. Shorty just wanted to drink in peace.

'Yo, I'm living good here. Last thing I want is some of my people from home fucking it up,' said Marrion. 'It's bad enough Teflon already doesn't like me. This is about money. I don't want anything to stop that.'

'True.' Shorty was half-listening.

'Teflon's cool, but he makes it tough, don't you think?' Marrion had been waiting for this opportunity. Chink had mentioned that Lamont and Shorty weren't clicking. 'I mean, I treat Marika good. She could be messing with some trampy dude who'd mess her around, but I've got her living pretty.'

'Yep.' Shorty sipped his drink.

'Trust. I mean, Tef can be a stuck-up little prick sometimes. He's lucky I—'

'You need to end it right there.' Shorty slammed down his glass.

'L's my brother. I dunno what you think is going on, but if you violate, it's a wrap.'

'I didn't mean it like that,' Marrion back-pedalled. 'He needs to chill.'

'Nah, *you* need to chill. You seem cool, but you're moving way too fast for some people. Furthermore, I'm not feeling the way you've got my cousin running around after you. Focus on your money moves, and when the time is right, you might get brought to the big table. Get me?'

'I get you.' Marrion gritted his teeth, but said nothing else. Shorty turned to Kimberley in time to catch her studying him. He moved closer.

'You want a top-up?' He motioned to the bottle.

'You had this mapped out, didn't you?'

'What are you on about? What thing?' asked Shorty.

'You knew your mate was here, didn't you?'

'I'm not a criminal mastermind. I didn't know he was in the club.'

'Whatever. Why else would you start with that guy and his people?'

'Because I'm crazy. Why else?' Shorty sized her up. Apart from the scrapes, she looked like pure sex in her wrap dress and heels. 'Fuck, you look good, Kim.'

'Don't start.' Kimberley couldn't deny the chemistry. Shorty was a thug, but you knew where you stood with him. He had earned big points with her too. He'd had her back and had even fought someone over her.

'I'm not starting, I'm *stating*. Drink up. It's gonna be an even longer night for you. I guarantee it.'

'If you say so.' Kimberley smiled, taking a mouthful of her drink.

———

The following day, Lamont chilled in Roundhay Park. The area was quiet, save for the usual visitors to the park. Everyone in his community-minded their business. It was easy to lose himself, to blend right in amongst the doctors, solicitors and bankers he had for neighbours. To them, he was another smiling businessman they saw on their way to and from work.

'Why do we have to meet here?'

'Because it's nice,' said Lamont.

'You live like five minutes away, though. We could have met at your place, or you could have driven to the Hood.'

'I didn't want to drive. Enjoy the weather and relax.'

Shorty plopped down on the grass, yawning so hard that Lamont almost copied him. He had bags under his eyes and looked irritable.

'What was so important?'

'I heard there was trouble.'

'I was chilling in one club; couple' girls started with Kim, so I pulled them off her.'

'Which Kim? The one you used to grind?'

Shorty grinned. 'Yeah. This big bitch tried hitting me, so I sparked her. A couple of Manny goons got involved, but Marrion squashed it.'

Lamont didn't like this. He wondered if it was coincidental that guys from Manchester had started with Shorty, only for Marrion to play the saviour.

'You need to chill,' he warned. 'Scrapping in town is short-sighted. There's CCTV and snitches everywhere.'

'Just leave it, L. I'm not feeling a lecture right now. My head's banging, and I'm stressed.'

'Fine. Did you sleep with her?'

'Who?'

'Don't play dumb.'

'Who, Kim?'

'Yeah. I remember how loved-up you were.'

'Fuck off; you're the master of being pussy-whipped. Look how open Jenny's got you,' said Shorty.

'Whatever. Still haven't answered my question, though.'

Shorty grinned. 'She tried playing hard to get, but after that hero shit, she was all over me.'

'You seeing her again?'

Shorty shook his head. 'She knows how it is. She said some slick shit about Amy owning me.'

'So? She's not lying.'

'Amy can fuck off. I dropped Grace off yesterday, and she had that prick Chris answering the door, playing daddy,' said Shorty.

Shorty had mentioned Chris before. Lamont hadn't met him, but respected the man's bottle. Shorty had intimidated more than a few guys who had stepped to Amy. Chris seemed immune to it.

'You can't get mad at her for moving on. She's waited years for you. What did you think would happen?'

'What the fuck did I say about a lecture!' Shorty exploded, causing people to stare in their direction. Lamont didn't flinch.

'I'm always gonna keep it real with you,' he said, meeting Shorty's angry eyes. 'You've taken the piss. Step up, or let her go.'

Shorty sighed, the anger abating. He was right. Amy had given him plenty of chances to commit, but he'd assumed she would always be around. The thought of them playing happy families sickened him to his stomach.

'Did you know Levi was back in Leeds?' Lamont sensed he didn't want to talk about his love life anymore.

'Yeah. He's living up Seacroft sides.'

'Why didn't you tell me?' Lamont couldn't believe Shorty had kept it from him.

'For what? So you could play hero like you did with Terry and put him in our thing?' Shorty made a face. 'He's a gimp, and he's on that stuff. He's done with.'

Lamont said nothing. Even in their younger days, Shorty had despised Levi. It had been foolish to bring him up.

'Speaking of fiends; everything is sorted. All the work has been distributed.'

'How many paid upfront?' Lamont asked.

'The dudes you'd expect. Have to admit, you planned this nice, L. I thought you might have ordered too much.'

'I anticipated the drought when I spoke to the man,' said Lamont. He had ordered far more product than normal. It was harder to get drugs at this time of the year, and he had contingencies in place. Not only was he putting out the best product, he was making it available at the time when it was needed. If all continued to plan, he would profit hugely for only two days' trade.

'I feel you. Can't imagine there'll be much spillage. Streets are fucking hungry.' Shorty looked wistful for a moment. 'Guess this is the last time we do this shit.'

Lamont watched him, but said nothing. Shorty stood.

'Gonna jet anyway. Business.' He slapped hands with Lamont and walked off.

MARRION SAT OUTSIDE MARIKA'S. Brownie and Antonio were with him, drinking and watching the world coast by.

'We all sorted then?' Marrion asked Brownie.

'Shorty's people dropped off the work this morning, so we're chopping that up. We should be ready.'

Marrion shook his head. '*Should be* ain't good enough. I need more than that. This is the chance to make some fucking real money. Antonio, make sure we can place everything. At a profit.'

'On it. What was happening last night, though? Solly was vexed.'

'He needs to calm down. The guy stepped to Shorty like he was gonna fight.'

'Solly's crazy. All that sniff has messed up his head,' said Brownie.

'Damn right. About to fight over Jasmine of all people.'

TARGET

'*Big Jasmine*? Why would she need anyone to fight over her? She's a fucking monster,' said Antonio.

Marrion gave him the low down on the fight from last night. Antonio chuckled again when he described how Shorty had knocked her out.

'About time. She's a lairy bitch.'

'Solly's girl instigated, trying to get Shorty rushed. He backed it, though,' said Marrion.

'Shorty's fucking proper. We could work with him. He's legit.'

Marrion frowned. He didn't like the way Brownie was fawning over Shorty. His pride was still hurt from the way he'd dissed him. Marrion had stopped him from getting jumped, and he hadn't appreciated it in the slightest.

'Look who it is,' said Antonio. Marrion glanced up at a tracksuit-clad Timmy Turner. The youngster touched fists with the three of them, then handed Marrion a bunch of notes.

'That's everything. Stevie tried running his mouth, but he paid up.'

Marrion smiled, handing him five crisp twenties. He gave the rest of the money to Brownie.

'Good lad. You're a fucking asset, Tim. I mean that.'

Timmy beamed with pride at his praise.

'I'm happy to help, fam.'

'Hopefully, people will realise it in time too, and the next bump will be yours. It was close this time.'

Timmy's eyes narrowed.

'What bump? Who got promoted over me?'

'Can't remember his name. Some young dude whose hustle Shorty liked. I thought for sure he'd pick you.' Marrion saw from Timmy's body language that his story had worked. 'Don't worry, though, kid,' he continued, hiding his smile. 'Stick with me, and I'll make you rich.'

Marcus pulled to a stop in his 4x4 but kept the engine running. He could see the Jaguar X-Type parked in front of him, and he waited for the man to get out.

Chink oozed from the car in a dark blue suit, salmon-coloured shirt and tan shoes. As he sauntered towards Marcus, he resisted the urge to shake his head. Chink was cool, but nothing ever came simple with him. Similar to Lamont. He shook hands with Marcus and handed him a leather case.

'There's twenty there, and one hundred in an account in your name. The details are all inside.'

'I only asked for one hundred,' replied Marcus, frowning. He put the case in the back seat.

'The extra cash will tide you over. I'm good for it. After this weekend, I'll eclipse that.'

Marcus smiled. 'Carnival weekend's always a big one.'

'Why don't you get involved? We can front you a box, and you can get paid.'

Marcus shook his head. 'I've survived this long without shotting. I can survive a bit longer,' he motioned to the money. 'Safe, Chink. When I've paid off my debts, I'm gonna spend the rest on Georgia.'

When Marcus said her name, Chink's insides turned to ice. He hadn't spoken to Georgia since they had spent the night together. He hadn't meant to fall in love with Georgia, but years ago, she was upset with Marcus over some fuckup. They had slept together in secret a few times before she ended it. Now, she had done the same thing again.

'You gonna buy her something nice then? I can get you a line on some jewellery.'

Marcus shook his head again.

'She's got fuckloads of jewellery from me for every time I've fucked up over the years. I'm thinking something different. I'm gonna take her away somewhere hot. Bahamas or summat. She'll like that.'

It almost hurt to keep the fake smile planted on his face. He wanted to reach across and strangle Marcus where he sat, but that would be suicidal.

'I'm sure she will. I need to go, anyway. Loads of last-minute meetings.'

'Cool. Thanks again, Chink. You're a good dude.'

Chink's bad mood lasted all the way back to his house. He parked up, slamming the car door with more force than necessary and headed into his building. When he entered his apartment, Naomi slouched on the sofa, watching television. She sat up, her eyes widening. She had been like this ever since he had to discipline her over her friend's behaviour.

'Get me a drink,' he said.

'What do you want?'

'Surprise me.'

Naomi hurried to the kitchen, returning with some lemonade. Chink sipped it and made a face.

'I don't want this.'

'What do you want then?'

Chink sat up in his chair. His eyes on Naomi the entire time, he poured the drink on the floor, dropping the glass with a resounding crash.

'Clean it up.'

She glared with traces of her old defiance. Chink hid a smile. He could almost see the gears turning in her head; the tug of war between standing up for herself and remaining subservient. She mumbled an apology. He grinned, the smile almost reaching his ears. Padding to the kitchen, he saw her on her knees under the sink, looking for a cloth.

'I like you on your knees,' he said, causing her to jump. 'Sorry babe, did I scare you?'

Naomi looked away from him, then tried returning to the living room.

'Where are you going?'

'I'm gonna clean up the drink before it sets.'

'Forget the drink.' Chink looked her up and down. Even with

her spirit crushed, she remained still spectacular. The skimpy shorts she wore highlighted her bronze legs, and the sleeveless top showed off her toned arms. 'Have I ever told you how sexy you are?'

Naomi didn't speak. Ever since Chink had struck her, she wondered how she had ever given him the time of day. He had seemed so harmless. Beneath that veneer, though, he was a monster.

'I asked you a question.'

Naomi recognised the danger in his voice and planted a smile on her face.

'Yeah, you've told me. I like hearing it, though,' she said.

'Ricky tell you how sexy you were? I bet he did. I bet you did whatever he told you to do whenever he told you to do it.'

Naomi rubbed her hand on her shorts, ignoring the prickling of her scalp.

'Am I right? Did you run around cleaning up Ricky's messes too? Did you fetch him drinks?' A creepy half-smile appeared on his lips.

'I—'

'Forget it. It's not important.' Chink looked at the rag in her hand. 'Put that down.'

She did it without thinking.

'Go upstairs and get in bed. Take all your clothes off. I'll be there in a minute.'

She left the room, hoping that Chink couldn't see her knees shaking. He watched her totter away. The control aroused him more than she ever could. Grin etched on his face, he sauntered upstairs to have his way with her.

―

IN A DINGY SPOT on the outskirts of the Hood, three rough-looking goons sat around, poring over a coffee table laden with guns. The crime film, *Rollin' with the Nines* played on a widescreen TV, but the youths paid no attention.

'It's going down tomorrow,' one of them said. 'Our guy will be at the park. The job needs doing then.'

'Won't the park be busy?' Another goon said.

'Doesn't matter. We've already got half the funds, so we're doing it tomorrow.'

'Why's this guy getting dropped?'

'Who the fuck cares? We're getting a shitload of cash to handle it, so that's what we're gonna do. Get ready.'

CHAPTER NINETEEN
MONDAY 26 AUGUST, 2013

CARNIVAL ROLLED AROUND in a flurry of good weather and great cheer. It first took place in Leeds in 1967. Forty-six years later, it was still going strong, holding its own against other large bank holiday events such as Notting Hill Carnival.

The main event was the parade, where dance troupes made their way through the streets of Leeds, playing music and steel pans. Huge, garish floats moved along at a slow pace with people aboard, drinking and dancing. The parade would proceed to Potternewton Park, where a stage was erected for artists. The card was typically made up of local performers, but the organisers would sometimes book a superstar.

Lamont and Jenny strolled through the park. Apart from some out-of-town goons and a smattering of hard-faced local youths, everyone was in good spirits. They had eaten fried fish and drunk bottles of Guinness punch. He'd enjoyed talking about the event's history, telling Jenny tales of going to the park with his family years back. They were debating whether to take another lap of the park or sit down when someone called his name.

'Lamont! Lamont Jones!'

He turned, spotting a figure from the past striding towards him.

He was an elderly black man with salt and pepper hair and powerful-looking forearms displayed in a bright, short-sleeved shirt.

'How long has it been?' The man asked, growing closer.

'A long time. Too long. How have you been?' Lamont shook his hand.

Nigel Worthington was a local coach from his football days. A talented player, Lamont had used the pitch to display the confidence he didn't have in the rest of his life. Nigel brought him back to earth by teaching him to play within the team, rather than on his own. They learned to work together and developed a mutual respect.

'I'm thriving. My son has brought the kids up to visit. I'm on my way to see them,' said Nigel. 'Is everything going well?'

Lamont assured him he was fine, introducing him to Jenny. He made small talk, then turned back to Lamont.

'Can I speak to you?'

They walked a short distance away and stood close, wanting to hear one another over the pulsating calypso beats.

'How are you really doing?

'I told you. I'm doing well.'

'Are you still doing that drugs stuff?' Nigel lowered his tone.

'I do what I need to do. Same as ever.'

Nigel closed his eyes, slowly shaking his head. His clear disapproval bothered Lamont far more than he wanted to admit.

'Do you need to do it? Even after all this time.'

'I don't need a lecture.'

'No, you need a beating. You were one of the most promising talents I ever trained, Lamont. You instantly picked up things it took the other kids weeks to learn. To watch you settle for this half-life? It's a waste. A complete and utter waste.'

'It's my life.' Lamont had heard similar sermons from Nigel before and didn't want them again.

'I know it's your life,' said Nigel. 'I walked in your shoes a long time ago. I did what I needed to do when I was broke, but you made a career from it. That's the part that sickens me.'

'I told you already; I do what I need to do. No matter the circumstances, I stick with my decisions. Sorry if you can't accept that.'

'You suffered with your Auntie, L, but you're a bigger man than that. That beautiful woman waiting for you,' Nigel jerked his head towards Jenny, who had her back to them, watching the stage, 'focus on her. Don't define yourself by hatred for your past, or you'll never be happy.' Nigel held his hand out, regret clear on his face. Feeling almost childlike, Lamont shook, and he left.

Dazed, Lamont walked back to Jenny.

'Are you okay?' she whispered.

'I'm fine, Jen.' The mask was back up now.

———

Shorty, K-Bar, and Timmy chilled at the top of the park, near a group of large music tents. People were out in force, dressed in colourful outfits. Carnival was a day for everyone to show off and out-stunt each other, rocking their best gear and jewellery. Dressed in a sweat suit and fresh trainers, Timmy nodded his head to the beat as he sipped from a bottle of Coke mixed with Disaronno.

K-Bar was all business with a phone glued to his ear. Most of the time, he nodded as someone on the other end updated him, but occasionally, his voice rose when he received news he didn't like. After every call, he would whisper in Shorty's ear.

Timmy scowled. He wanted to be part of whatever the plan was. It was definitely big. There had been rumblings of hot product hitting the streets, but he wasn't in the loop. Scanning the crowds as a distraction, he grinned when he saw Marrion and a large crew heading towards them. One, a stocky man Timmy hadn't seen before, glared in Shorty's direction. When Shorty noticed, he mugged the man right back. Marrion sensed the tension and nodded at Shorty, who reciprocated. After touching Timmy's fist, he kept it moving. K-Bar hung up, eyeing the Manchester contingent as they continued past.

'Was that dude eyeballing from the other night?'

'Yeah.' Shorty's eyes also followed the crew. 'He was the one acting like Nino Brown because I sparked that bitch.'

'Why's he with Marrion then?' K-Bar's instincts told him something wasn't right.

'Fuck knows. I don't give a shit, either. Focus on business, not those small-timers. They'll be gone by tomorrow.'

'True. We're solid anyway. I'm getting good news back. A few people have sold out. Everything's lovely.' K-Bar gave him the latest.

Shorty grinned. Lamont's planning was perfect. Even with the police presence and undercover officers masquerading as civilians, everything had gone off without a hitch. He was about to speak when a gunshot ripped the air, followed by another. Screams resounded in all directions, unable to drown out the claps of more gunfire. Shorty was low now, as was K-Bar.

'K, can you see anything?' He shouted, scrambling back to his feet. Their people were looking in all directions, trying to determine who was shooting. Timmy's eyes were wide, his lip trembling.

'Can't see a fucking thing. Too many people running about,' K-Bar yelled back.

Shorty saw a cluster of people gathering around the grassy section ahead of them. Police were there. With a sickening feeling nestling in his stomach, Shorty hurried towards the crowd with K-Bar on his heels.

LAMONT AND JENNY walked through the park. He was deep in thought, wishing he had told his former coach he was walking away instead of letting his remarks affect him. Nigel had given him structure when he'd needed it, and he would always be thankful for the attention the coach had shown him. He wished Nigel had more faith in him. He was successful, after all.

They were close to a smattering of funfair rides above the

embankment in the park now. Lamont was about to ask if she wanted to move closer to the stage when a small figure hurtled themselves at him.

'Uncle L,' screamed Bianca, as he picked her up and twirled her in the air. Marika headed towards him, flanked by Keyshawn and, to his surprise, Lorraine.

'Princess Bianca.' Lamont kissed the little girl on the cheek and set her down. He hugged his sister, touched fists with Keyshawn, and nodded to Lorraine.

'You okay, sis?' he asked Marika, who sighed.

'I'm knackered, and these kids are stressing me. Wanna take them for a bit?'

'I would, but we have somewhere to go after this.' Lamont put his arm around Jenny. 'Rika, this is Jenny. Jen, this is my sister Marika, my niece Bianca, nephew Keyshawn, and Rika's friend.'

'You gonna pretend you don't know my name?' said Lorraine.

'Don't start,' Lamont's voice hardened. Lorraine grumbled and turned away. Marika hadn't taken her eyes from Jenny.

'So, you're the one who has my brother whipped?' she said to her. Jenny smiled.

'We're whipped over each other.'

'Make sure you take care of him. You mess him around, and I'll deal with you. Got it?'

'Rika—'

'Your girl can speak for herself, L.' Marika cut Lamont off.

'I can, and I like that you're looking out for him. I love Lamont, and he loves me. We don't need to mess each other around,' said Jenny. Lorraine snickered under her breath, but she ignored it. Her eyes were fixed on Marika as the two dominant females sized one another up.

'I'll see you later, L. Come up, and I'll cook you dinner,' said Marika.

'I will. Here, take this for the kids.' Lamont handed her twenty pounds.

'What about me?' she made a face. He shook his head and

handed her two more twenties, then walked away arm in arm with Jenny.

'So, that was your sister,' remarked Jenny.

'Yeah. I hope she didn't upset you.'

Jenny glowed. 'She didn't. She cares about you. You can tell. Your niece is gorgeous too.'

'She takes after her Uncle,' said Lamont.

'She has another Uncle? I want to meet him.'

They were both giggling. Fifteen yards away, Jenny spotted Marcus and Georgia. Marcus had his arm around her, and they seemed more content than they had previously.

'L, Marcus is over there. Shall we go over?'

Before Lamont could reply, a scuffle broke out nearby. Some local youths were tussling with each other, but Lamont recognised none of them. Marcus noticed. He locked eyes with Lamont, his eyes then narrowing as he focused on something beyond his friend. Turning, Lamont froze, seeing a familiar face holding a gun. Maverick raised it in his direction, his bruised face twisted with hatred. Lamont heard Marcus's voice, then the crack of gunfire.

―――――

MARCUS AND GEORGIA roamed the park. Victor was nearby, giving them enough room to breathe. The day so far had been uneventful. He'd been with Georgia since the night before, and they were getting along better since sitting down and talking.

Marcus was taking it slow. Chink had loaned him enough to clear his debts, with some left to tide him over until his next hustle. It wasn't the first time he'd been broke, but this latest encounter had shown him he needed to put something away for the future.

'Are you okay?' He asked Georgia. She averted her gaze, biting her lip. Marcus had made such an effort to straighten out, and the guilt of sleeping with Chink was eating away at her. She'd enjoyed the sex, but felt dirty. Marcus wasn't Mr Sensitive, but she had known from the get-go, and it was no excuse for being unfaithful.

'I have to tell you something,' her voice shook. Marcus looked at her, distracted by angry shouts as some kids fought. Lamont was watching the brawl. With a jolt, Marcus saw the kid he'd beaten stalking towards his friend. He reacted and knocked Georgia to the ground, reaching for his gun. Someone spotted it and screamed. People ran, impeding his vision.

'Move!' He roared. It was too late. A bullet thudded into his stomach. He stayed on his feet, kept upright by his massive size, and fired once, watching with painful relish as Maverick fell to the ground, just behind Lamont. It was short-lived; one of the scuffling youths sprayed a Mac-10 that cut him down. All around, people were panicking, tripping over themselves to escape.

'MARCUS!'

Lamont tried running to his fallen friend, but Marika grabbed his hand, stalling him. He hadn't even seen her approach.

'Let me go!' he shouted, watching in terror as Maverick struggled to his feet and limped towards Marcus, who tried to sit up. Maverick smacked him across the face with the gun, then held the weapon to his head.

'I fucking told you. Your time is done,' he said, his finger tightening on the trigger.

Before he could pull it, another shot rang out. Maverick dropped, dead from the headshot. Victor tried shooting the second gunman, but he dropped the machine gun and disappeared into the wild crowd.

'Marcus!' Lamont wrenched free of his sister and charged towards him, grabbing his hand. 'Marcus! Fight! C'mon! Stay with me!'

Marcus couldn't speak. He was gasping, his tongue lolling out, blood dribbling from his mouth as he tried to breathe. His eyes dimmed. The crowd watched in horror. Jenny held Keyshawn's hand whilst Marika wrestled with a hysterical Bianca, fighting to get to her beloved Uncle. Georgia was on her feet, rooted to the spot as she watched Marcus take his last breath. His grip slackened in Lamont's hand, his eyes half-closing.

'NOOOOOOOO!'

Lamont's moan of anguish rent the air, mingling with the piercing noise that erupted from Georgia's mouth. Victor stared at Marcus, tears filling his eyes, smoking murder weapon in hand. He hadn't been quick enough to save his boss.

'Armed police! Nobody move!'

As the police converged on Lamont and Victor, Georgia fainted.

CHAPTER TWENTY
WEDNESDAY 28 AUGUST, 2013

LAMONT SLUMPED IN DARKNESS, drinking. The situation felt surreal, like something from a movie. One minute he was sauntering around the park with the woman of his dreams. The next, he was surrounded by armed police and covered in the blood of his best friend. Marcus had always lived his life a certain way, but it still shocked him that he'd died so brutally. He couldn't help but think if he had been swifter, Marcus might still be alive.

Lamont had been lulled into a false sense of security, and he had been unprepared for the ferocity of the gunmen. He saw with complete clarity how lax he had been, walking around as if retired, with no protection. It was his fault, and Marcus had paid the price.

On the vintage coffee table were two empty bottles of gin. Ever since the police had let him go, he'd confined himself to this room. He hadn't eaten, turning off his phone when it wouldn't stop ringing, wanting the anguish to disperse. He wanted the liquor to blot everything. He had asked Jenny to give him space, not wanting to suck her into his depressive vortex.

Amid his mourning, Lamont heard a rapid knocking on his door. He lurched to his feet and let Marika in. She glanced at his appearance and shook her head. He could tell by her blotchy face she had been crying. They sat in silence. She sighed when he made himself a fresh drink, but held her tongue, seeming to understand.

Lamont's stomach churned, but he didn't care. He wanted to be free of his burdens. Marika made a sudden movement as if about to pick up the remote next to her.

'You seem nervous.' He broke the silence.

'I'm not sure what to say. You must be fucked right now.'

He didn't reply. The gin tasted disgusting now, but he wouldn't let that stop him.

'How are the kids?' he asked, realising they weren't with Marika.

'Keyshawn hasn't stopped bawling. Bianca thought you had been shot. And then the armed police . . .' She trailed off.

Lamont understood. The police had flung him to the floor, their weapons inches from his body, screaming at him to stay down. None of it sunk in at the time, but he could understand his niece and nephew's reactions.

Victor had been detained and would undoubtedly face murder charges. Lamont retained multiple solicitors, but everyone had seen him shoot Maverick. He was protecting Marcus, but that wouldn't matter to the police. Victor would stay loyal as long as his family was taken care of. As a soldier, he knew the risks, and if he stayed quiet, the people he loved would be bereft of financial responsibility.

'The police questioned everyone nearby,' Marika continued. 'They asked if I recognised the shooters, but I didn't.'

Lamont didn't say anything.

'Did you recognise them? I mean, they were looking right at you. Did you lot have beef?'

'Yes, I recognised them,' admitted Lamont.

'Did you tell the police that?'

Lamont shook his head.

'Why not, L?'

'You know why.'

'Because of a code? L, Marcus was a brother to us. Don't you want to see his killer get what he deserves?'

'It's not that simple.'

'They killed him, L. That's as simple as it gets. One of them is still out there. Aren't you worried he'll come for you?'

Lamont had been mere yards away from Marcus. If the shooters had wanted him dead, they could have done it with minimal effort.

'Auntie's upset too,' said Marika, not waiting for Lamont to reply. 'I stopped by before I came here.'

Lamont's temper flared at the mention of his Auntie.

'Who cares?' He slammed down his drink.

'Don't start, L. She's an old woman. She raised him.'

'Like she raised us? Marcus was nothing but a cheque.'

'Auntie didn't have to take us in, L,' said Marika.

'She got rich off us. She screwed us over, yet you still want to love her. Why can't you see it?'

Marika's eyes widened. Lamont was drunk and overcome with grief. The last thing he wanted was a conversation about the woman who killed his childhood.

'You're hurting, but it doesn't give you the right to crap all over the only family we have left. Everyone can grieve, not just you.'

'Piss off back to her then! Fuck off out of my house and go be with your conniving bitch of an Aunt. You're just like her; a fucking leech! No wonder you're always defending her.'

Marika flared up, then softened. Her shoulders slumped. Watching, he saw the fight leave her. She gazed at him, then walked out. He started after her, but the door opened again, and Shorty stood there, red-eyed and defeated. Lamont sat him down.

'We need drinks.' The bottle of *Centaure de Diamant* caught his eye. It seemed like a lifetime since Akhan had gifted it to him. Shorty sniffed and looked up as he carried it over.

'You sure? That shit's expensive,' he said.

'I'm positive.'

Lamont poured them both a glass, and they toasted, then drank.

Straight away, the explosion of taste assaulted his senses. It was like heaven in a glass; a smooth, rich experience. He watched Shorty, who wore a watery smile. Shorty rummaged in his pockets for his weed bag and built a spliff, giving him a look to check it was okay before lighting up. Lamont topped their glasses up. He sipped his again, savouring the vintage liquor and taking a long burn on the joint when Shorty passed it to him.

'Fuck, I'm fucking done, Shorty,' said Lamont, later. The weed and liquor had him on another planet.

'We're just getting started.' Shorty's tear-stained face remained determined. He wanted to celebrate Marcus with the only other person who cared as much as he did. Lamont closed his eyes, taking deep breaths. His head spun. Shorty was right. This was their chance to reconnect. So they did. For hours, they told Marcus stories. Lamont recalled the money Marcus used to give him when he was broke, and the disastrous time he had gone on a robbery with him and Victor.

Shorty shared tales of missions he and Marcus had gone on, and how much he had learned. Both had heard the tales before, but that didn't matter.

'You saw him get shot, right?' Shorty asked. He nodded. All the alcohol and drugs hadn't removed the scene from his mind; the blood Marcus had coughed up as his eyes dimmed.

'People are saying it was a little dude called Schemes who popped off with the machine gun,' Shorty continued.

'They argued in town. Maverick was clocking Georgia, and Marcus didn't like it.'

'Marcus boxed him up a couple' days later. Victor told me,' said Shorty.

'Marcus fought him?' Lamont's eyes widened.

'Yeah. Didn't wanna take the disrespect.'

It seemed strange to Lamont, even in his befuddled state, for Maverick to retaliate by killing Marcus in a packed park. It was extreme.

'Schemes is dead when I find him. I'll rip him apart.'

Lamont bowed his head. He was as angry as Shorty, but as much as he desired revenge, he wanted to walk away, and he hated himself for that weakness.

'He's gone, L. They fucking took my brother.' Tears streamed down Shorty's face. Lamont gripped his shoulder, expecting him to recoil. Instead, he cried more. Lamont comforted him, now keeping his own emotions internal.

―――

Jenny unlocked the door early the following day, hoping Lamont would be in a better state of mind after some sleep. The first thing that hit her was the pungent smell of weed. She walked into the living room. Shorty lay on his stomach, snoring, almost cocooned by bottles of alcohol. She tiptoed past him, looking for Lamont. He sat in the kitchen with his head in his arms. A cup of coffee was in front of him, untouched.

'Hey, baby,' he murmured.

'How did you know it was me?'

'I smelled your fragrance.' Lamont lifted his head, his eyes sunken and drooping. 'Fuck, I feel rough.'

'I'm not surprised. How much did you drink?'

'Far too much. I need a shower.'

'Go get one. I'll make you some breakfast,' said Jenny.

Lamont stood, yawning and stretching.

'I'm not hungry. Don't go to any trouble.'

'Do as you're told.'

He complied and left the room as Jenny opened the fridge.

―――

'Fuck.' Shorty opened his eyes, sitting up. His head felt cleaved. He stood up, blinking his eyes to clear the cobwebs. He heard noises from the kitchen and headed to investigate.

TARGET

Jenny, Lamont's girl, was moving around, pouring orange juice into two large glasses. On the table were servings of grapes, strawberries and a medley of other fruit. She was putting the glasses on the table when she spotted Shorty.

'Morning. You're just in time. Lamont will be down in a minute. Have a seat.'

Shorty slid into a chair, sipping from a glass.

'Is this okay? I figured you would both want to eat something light.'

'Yeah, this is fine.' He popped a grape in his mouth. 'Thanks.'

'It's no problem. I'm sorry about Marcus.'

Shorty nodded, feeling the lump in his throat.

'Thank you,' he repeated, feeling a newfound affection for Lamont's lady. 'I'm glad you and L hooked up. You're the best thing to happen to him.'

Before she could reply, Lamont walked into the kitchen, looking refreshed. He slapped hands with Shorty, then greeted Jenny with a hug and a kiss.

'Finally, you smell human,' she said.

'Cheeky,' replied Lamont, a tired smile on his face as he sat opposite Shorty. 'This all looks good. Thank you.'

'It's fine. I have to go to work, but I'll finish early, and we can go out to dinner?'

'I'll book somewhere. What do you fancy?'

Shorty watched them interact. They were so in sync, so compatible with one another. Shorty couldn't think of any woman he had that connection with, apart from Amy. That was the difference between him and Lamont, though. Lamont could separate himself from his *Teflon* persona when he wasn't in the streets. He was always Shorty. There was no off-switch. Maybe that was the problem.

Maybe that was why Lamont was leaving.

'Shorty?'

Shorty snapped back to earth. They were looking at him.

'Yeah?'

'Do you want to come to dinner with us tonight?' said Jenny.

'I've got plans. Thanks for the offer, though.'

'It's fine. Speak to L if you change your mind.'

Jenny said goodbye and hurried out of the kitchen. They heard her fussing until she left the house.

'She's a keeper, L.'

Lamont smiled, wiping his mouth.

'She's not bad.'

'Is she living here now?'

He shrugged.

'She has a key.'

There was a moment's silence. Shorty nodded and struggled to his feet.

'I need to get shit in order with the crew.'

'I need to sort the funeral.' Lamont felt a fresh jolt of grief hit his stomach with those words. It was his responsibility, though. Marcus had no other family. Shorty headed for the door. Pausing, he turned back to Lamont.

'You can't leave now. You know that.'

Lamont didn't respond.

———

'CAN YOU BELIEVE HIM?'

Marrion listened as Marika raged. She had been in a bad mood the whole time he had been with her. From what he could gather, she and Lamont had fallen out big time. Marrion wasn't surprised. He'd met Marcus once, but knew of his reputation and how close Lamont was to him.

'He had the nerve to throw me out. I can't believe it. He's supposed to protect me, not mug me off because I don't agree with him on every little thing. It's bullshit,' Marika snapped.

Marrion kept his eyes on the TV. Keyshawn was plopped on the floor, watching a video on his tablet with his earphones in. Bianca sat between Marika's legs, wincing as her mother plaited her hair.

'This is it. He crossed the line. Basically called me a slag. And what he said about Auntie was unforgivable. I mean, she did everything for us. We would have gone into care if it wasn't for her. He's a fucking slanger who acts like he's *Martin-Luther-fucking-King* or summat.'

Bianca looked confused. Marrion didn't like Marika swearing in front of her kids, but couldn't say anything.

'It's all good. We're done with him. You kids don't have an Uncle anymore. He's dead to you,' she said to Keyshawn and Bianca.

The reactions were predictable. If Keyshawn heard, he pretended he didn't. Bianca burst into tears and ran from the room.

'Get back here,' Marika shouted. 'Keyshawn!' she said to her son. He continued to stare at the screen. Marika stomped over and snatched the earphones from his ears.

'What are you doing?' Keyshawn yelled. He received a smack that jerked his head. He looked up at his mother with a quivering lip, wanting to cry, but unwilling to give her that satisfaction.

'What have I told you about running your mouth? Go look after your sister before I kick your fucking head off.'

Glaring, he snatched his tablet, and stormed from the room. Marika stood in the middle of the room, panting. Marrion watched. The way she lived, she would make herself sick soon.

'So, you and your brother are really done then?'

Marika took a deeper breath. 'He's hurting over Marcus. I can't forgive him speaking to me like shit, though. He's done a lot for me. I'm not ungrateful, but still, he violated.'

'You know what the problem is, don't you?' Marrion picked his words, drawing her in.

'No. Tell me.' She sat next to him.

'He's jealous.'

'Jealous of what?'

Marrion paused for effect.

'You've got another man who can provide for you. Lamont's a controller. He liked having you in a position where you relied on him for money, and now it's shifting, and he's still trying to control the situation.'

Marika nodded along with what he was saying, just as he'd expected.

'You two should be pulling together now that Marcus is dead. Instead, he's picking fights, saying all kinds of shit to you. Because he doesn't like you being with me,' said Marrion.

'You're right. He said some nasty shit to Auntie too that time.'

'He's already turning the kids against you. Check Keyshawn's attitude.' Marrion didn't want to use her son as a tool, but the opportunity had presented itself.

'He's too smart for his own good sometimes, just like Lamont. I'm sticking with it. We're done. I swear down.'

Marrion held her close, kissing the top of her head. It was almost too easy.

Timmy Turner sat in his room, messing around with a plastic chessboard. After seeing Lamont with one at the barbers, he had bought one and often studied the pieces. He wanted to see what Lamont saw when he played. He had tried learning how to play, but it was a complicated game, and he lacked the patience.

Marcus's death had him reeling. Marcus had been a cornerstone of the Hood. He'd heard so many stories about him that he was invincible in his eyes. That was over now, though. Marcus was dead, and the streets grieved. He wanted to see Shorty, but his cousin was blanking his calls. Schemes was on the run. Shorty wouldn't sit back and let him get away with murder. As always, Timmy was out in the cold.

Lashing out in anger, he knocked all the pieces over and

reached for his PlayStation pad. The king piece shook for a moment, then tumbled.

———

Shorty stood in front of his crew. They were in the home of one of K-Bar's women, who had been told to wait upstairs while they spoke.

Shorty's face was lined, heavy bags under his eyes. He took a spliff that K-Bar handed him and inhaled, wiping his eyes. When he spoke, his voice was firm.

'I don't need to go into detail. People violated when they dared to touch Tall-Man. We're gonna rain down on them. I want the shooter. Alive.'

There were rumbles of approval from the crew. They all respected Marcus and wanted to make someone pay for killing him.

'Get the word out. It's ten bags for a location. Cash. I want everyone searching. Get on it,' ordered Shorty.

———

Schemes hurried along the streets with his head down. He'd been off the radar since the shooting, but had been summoned. His contact waited by an expensive motor.

'You're late,' The man barked.

'So what? You didn't tell me that fucking Marcus would be strapped or that he'd have a bodyguard. I lost my fucking boy behind that shit, and—'

The man tossed him an envelope. He thumbed through the notes, then stuffed them in his pocket without a word.

'Any job comes with risks. You knew what you were getting into when you took it on. Make sure you stay out of sight, and keep me updated of your location.'

Schemes nodded, realising that complaining wouldn't work.

'Don't spend too much in the same place. Don't flash it around either. Understand?'

'I'm not dumb,' said Schemes. The man glowered.

'Don't get lairy. You did a sloppy job, but it worked out. Don't ruin it by getting left in a ditch somewhere.'

Schemes stared at the floor, mollified.

'Get out of here. Marcus was just the beginning. I'll be in touch.'

CHAPTER TWENTY-ONE
MONDAY 2 SEPTEMBER, 2013

A WEEK after Marcus's death, a tribute took place at the West Indian Centre. An old building at the bottom end of Chapeltown Road, it had seen its fair share of memorial services. This one was no different.

People came from far and wide to pay their respects to a certified Hood legend and child of Chapeltown. Despite what he became, Marcus Daniels had still come from the absolute bottom, born to addicts who cared more about getting high than caring for their son. Marcus had been a menace. Despite his reputation, he was respected and, in most circles, loved.

Shorty brooded in the corner of the room, dressed in a crisp white shirt, black trousers and a cashmere overcoat with black Ferragamo moccasins. His eyes were blank. Mutely, he drank from the bottle of Courvoisier he was clutching. The devastation of his friend's murder sank in. Life would never be the same. He often chastised others for showing weakness, yet he could have cried and not stopped.

Marcus had lived life every day, knowing he might die. Many of them did. That didn't make it any easier.

Timmy stood with Shorty and looked around the room,

impressed at the turnout. Some heavy faces from other cities were in attendance. He'd seen Shorty shaking hands with them earlier and was irritated that he hadn't introduced him. With Marcus gone, he wanted his chance.

'Cuz, can I speak to you for a minute?' he asked Shorty, who kissed his teeth.

'I don't have time for your shit,' Shorty told him, just as K-Bar tapped him on the shoulder.

'Check who's here.'

Lamont was hand-in-hand with Jenny. He wore a flawless black suit and a matching tie, looking like a high-powered banker. People flocked like he was the Pope when they saw him. He addressed everyone, showing a politician's savvy and relating to each on a personal level. Almost twenty minutes elapsed before he made his way to Shorty. He saw the devastation etched on Shorty's face, aware the misery was mirrored on his own.

'How are you?'

Shorty took a swig of brandy. He swayed, but maintained his composure.

'Still standing. For now.'

'Relax. We need to keep our heads straight.'

'It's been a week, L. I'm not happy about this shit. I can't lie.'

Lamont didn't reply straight away. He focused on Timmy.

'Nice to see you, Tim. That's a nice suit.'

'Thanks, L.' Timmy was buoyed by the compliments.

'Don't mention it. Listen, can you take this beautiful girl of mine to get a drink? Get yourself one too.' Lamont handed him a crisp fifty-pound note.

Jenny glanced at him, but followed Timmy through the crowds.

'Where's that bitch that Tall-Man was grinding?' Shorty looked around the room.

'Georgia's in shock, Shorty. She's with her family.'

'What about Tall-Man's family? We're here. She should be too.'

'People grieve in different ways. She was right there. She saw him get shot.'

'How do we know she wasn't in on it?' Shorty's voice rose. People were staring.

'Shorty, calm down.'

'Fuck you.' The liquor had Shorty ready to fight. The other occupants watched, feeling the spike in tension. Lamont didn't react, gazing at him. A moment passed, then Shorty nodded, exhaling.

'Shorty, we'll find them. For now, we need to . . .' Lamont's voice trailed off. He had seen Marika. His heart soared when he saw the kids. Keyshawn held the hand of his younger sister. Their faces brightened, but they made no move toward him. He glanced over at Jenny, then moved towards his sister.

'Can we talk?' he asked. Marika's face tightened. Beneath the anger, he saw the pain in her eyes. He had said some harsh things. They were true, but he regretted them all the same.

'We have nothing to talk about,' said Marika. The hurt Lamont had just seen, dissipated in an instant.

'Rika, please—'

'No!' Marika shouted, drawing the attention of the room. 'You don't talk to me like that, then act normal. You don't.'

'There's no excuse. I'm not trying to hide from it, but you're my sister, and I love you.' Lamont ignored the room, focusing on her. He noticed people straining to listen, but blocked them out.

'Go to hell, Lamont. We are done. Stay away from me and stay away from my kids.' Wrenching Keyshawn's hand, Marika led the children from the wake.

Lamont watched them leave, his expression unreadable to the audience. Without missing a beat, he walked back over to Jenny and ordered a drink.

'Are you okay?' she asked. People spoke again now, likely discussing the argument they had witnessed. He forced a smile on his face and nodded, wondering if there was any way back for him and Marika.

Shorty staggered out of the wake, the heat killing him. For the past few days, the weather in Leeds had been crazy to where you couldn't stay outside for too long. Lamont had hung around for a while, then slipped out with Jenny, leaving enough money behind the bar to satisfy the crowd. Shorty had gorged himself on rum when his brandy had run out. He was now leaning to another level. He gripped the wall and tried to steady himself, needing fresh air.

'Shit,' he said. Before he knew it, he was on his knees, heaving. 'Never fucking drinking again.'

'That's what they all say,' a voice chimed.

Shorty was upright now. 'Who the fuck are you?'

'Sorry, didn't mean to startle you.'

Shorty wiped his mouth, thankful none of the sick had reached his clothes. He glared at the familiar man. He was average height, big-bellied, wearing glasses and rumpled clothing.

'Whatever. Dig up now.' Shorty didn't like looking weak.

'No need to be like that. I was just taking an interest.'

'I'm not interested, so back up,' Shorty told him. He was about to re-enter the wake, when the man spoke again.

'Franklin, you grew up big.'

Shorty froze, then whirled around.

'What did you say?'

'I said you grew up big. Look at you,' said the man. He was smiling now. He looked proud. Almost like a—

No

'Who are you?' Shorty's voice shook.

'I'm your dad, Franklin. It's been a long time.'

His ears were ringing. His knees weakened, but it wasn't from the drink. He stared at the man again, taking in his nose, eyes, cheekbones. They were Shorty's features. *It couldn't be, though.* His dad was gone. Long gone. A figment of his past.

'No,' Shorty spoke out loud.

'I've got a lot—'

'A lot of what? Catching up to do?'

'Son—'

TARGET

'You're not my dad. You're a mess.'

Trevor Turner was silent.

'What the fuck are you doing round here?'

'I was in Southampton. I came back and spoke to Serena,' said Trevor. Shorty's face tensed. He had spoken to his mother yesterday. She hadn't said a word.

'She tells me you've got kids of your own. I'm proud of you, Franklin. I didn't set a good example, but—'

'You didn't set *any* example. I wasn't even born yet when you ran off. Now what? You heard I'm rich, and you wanna creep up? Get out of here.'

Trevor took a step forward. 'Son—'

Unable to hold back, Shorty lashed out. Trevor took the shot on the bridge of his nose. There was a sickening crack, and he dropped like a stone. Shorty raised his fist to hit him again, but when he looked down at the pathetic excuse for a man, he changed his mind. Spitting on the floor next to his dad, he walked away, sobered by the experience.

CHINK KNOCKED on Georgia's door, checking his reflection in the window. When her sister, Angie, answered, he put on his nicest smile.

'Hi, Angie. I wanted to stop by and see how she's doing,' he said.

'Nice to see you, Xiyu. Come in. She's in here.' Angie led him to the living room.

Georgia was drinking a cup of tea and watching TV. She paled when she saw Chink.

'Sis, Xiyu's here to see you. Isn't that nice?' said Angie. She nodded, unable to speak. Angie appeared not to notice.

'I'm gonna go upstairs and finish sorting the washing. Can I get you a drink, Xiyu?'

Chink shook his head. 'Thank you for the offer, though.'

Angie smiled at the pair and headed upstairs, shutting the door behind her. Georgia broke the silence.

'What the hell are you doing here?' she hissed. Chink's brow furrowed.

'I came to see how you were.'

'You can't be in this house.' Georgia's voice was low, not wanting her sister to overhear the conversation.

'Why not?' Chink asked.

'Because, it's wrong. Everything that has ever happened between us is wrong.'

'I still love you, Georgia. I can be here for you now. We can be together.'

'No, we can't, Xiyu. You and I will never be together.' Georgia was trying to remain strong. Chink's shoulders slumped, but he needed to understand where she was at. When Marcus died, her entire world had crumbled. She couldn't eat, and she barely slept. He was the last person she wanted to deal with.

Chink sighed, his sadness evaporating.

'I don't accept what you're saying.'

'What are you talking about?' Georgia felt sick.

'I appreciate the convenience of copulating with you,' he said, each word a dagger. 'It's imperative you maintain your status as the *depressed wifey*. I can help. The alternative is everyone finding out you were cheating on the beloved Marcus Daniels.'

'I should have never done it. I won't do it again,' Georgia's words were said with a strength she didn't quite feel.

'I didn't come here to debate the finer points of our dalliance. I came because I want you.'

'You can't have me.' Her voice rose.

'Correction: I can, and I will.'

'Tell people what you want. I won't do it anymore.'

'You will.' He advanced on her.

'I'll scream. I mean it.'

Chink was already undoing the belt to his designer trousers. 'I wouldn't advise it.'

'Chink, I mean—'

He was on top of her now, forcing his tongue down her throat, yanking her black leggings down and pawing her body. His eyes were full of lust, but his face and movements were calm.

'Chink, don't—'

'I wouldn't recommend making too much noise. If Angie overhears, then I'll have to take measures to silence her.' He yanked Georgia's underwear to the side and entered her. She lay back, accepting his jerky thrusts as tears poured down her face. He didn't last long. After climaxing and pulling out, he pulled his trousers back up and resumed his seat. When Angie walked back into the room, she saw Georgia weeping.

'Sis, are you okay?' she asked.

'She's still struggling, Angie. I think she should have a bath and maybe try to sleep.' Chink's voice was full of false concern. He met Georgia's eye. About to throw up, she hurried from the room.

'I'm sorry,' Angie said to Chink. 'I don't think she's up for company at the moment.'

'No need for apologies. I'll leave her for now, but I'll be back soon. Give her my love, and keep up the good work,' Chink said, trying to hide his smirk. 'You're doing a stellar job.'

MARRION WAS at Marika's place, lying on the sofa with her. A few nights had passed since the wake. He knew of Marika's argument with Lamont, but she'd said nothing else, and he hadn't forced her. In the streets, the grief over Marcus's murder was giving way to anger. Shorty had his people out, doing what was necessary to get answers.

Marrion knew of at least three people who'd been beaten and interrogated. It made the hustle harder, but no one complained. Everyone knew what the stakes were. Until Marcus's killer was located, people would have to cope.

Over the bank holiday period, Marrion had done well with the product he had received. After paying Shorty and Lamont their end, he was now waiting for the rest of his money to come in. When it did, it would be the most he'd made in a single flip since coming to Leeds.

'Do you want a drink?' he asked Marika, her head resting in his lap. She shook her head. Marrion was about to make himself one when suddenly, gunfire erupted.

'Marika!' He pulled her to the floor as the windows shattered, bullets pumping into the walls and furniture.

'Keyshawn! Bianca!' Marika screamed, trying to break free of Marrion's strong grip to get to her children. He held her down until, after an age, the bullets subsided.

'Let me go.' She wrenched free and vaulting upstairs. They were both in Keyshawn's room, quivering under the quilt.

'Mummy,' cried Bianca. She smothered them with hugs as she wept with relief.

―――

'DO YOU WANT A TOP-UP?'

Jenny smiled up at Lamont, holding out her glass. They sat in the garden, enjoying the remainder of the sun. Lamont had foregone his usual routine and spent the whole day with Jenny. Earlier, they had gone to a museum, then for some food. Now they were sharing a bottle of wine.

He refilled their glasses and took a seat. He didn't spend much time in his garden, but had a decent table and chairs set for when the weather was good. There was also a football, and various bikes and toys that the kids would use whenever they were around. Jenny liked the garden, but it needed work. It was too impersonal. Nothing made it Lamont's.

'Thank you,' she said.

'You're welcome.' Lamont held his glass, watching the darkening sky. He felt at ease. The dark cloud that had hovered over him since Marcus's murder hadn't evaporated, but was becoming easier to deal with. He would always miss his friend, but the best way to remember him was to work hard at leaving the life behind. He would make his friend proud, and then he would solidify his legacy.

'I've been thinking,' he started. Jenny looked up.

'What about?'

'What to do with my life.'

'Have you come up with anything?'

'I want to travel and have a break from Leeds. When I was little, I dreamed of journeying to places like Japan, Argentina and the West Indies. I told myself that I would go if I had the money. He paused. 'I have the money.'

Jenny quietly watched him speak, moved by his passion. Like most things he did, he appeared to have given it serious thought.

'That sounds great, L,' she said. He smiled back.

'Would you like to come with me?' Lamont surprised Jenny.

'What?'

'I want you come with me. Wherever I go, I want you there.'

'L, I have a business to consider. If you're suggesting a holiday, I can arrange cover, but I feel you're thinking longer than a two-weeker.'

'I don't know.' Lamont lowered his head, deflated. The last thing Jenny wanted was to stand in his way, but she had to be honest. How long they sat silently contemplating, neither knew. When his phone rang, it startled the pair.

'L? Where are you?' Shorty said.

'Home. Why?'

'Get down to your sisters. Now.'

'Marika and me aren't—'

'Someone shot up her fucking house.'

Lamont hung up.

The street was packed with people as Lamont strode up, having parked his car on the next street. He spotted neighbours mingled around, and the flashing blue lights of police cars.

Marika sat in her garden, her arms around the children, who looked petrified. When she saw him, her eyes flashed, and she leapt to her feet.

'What the fuck are you doing here,' she said. 'Feel good, do you? Getting people to shoot at my fucking yard!' She tried lunging at him, but Marrion held her back.

'What are you talking about?'

'Don't play dumb. You wanna put my kids' lives at risk, you piece of shit?' Marika still tried to break free.

'Rika, let me handle this. The kids are scared,' said Marrion. Marika heeded his words and dragged the two children inside. Before the door slammed shut, Lamont glimpsed Bianca's confused little face, and felt something twist within him.

'What is going on?' he asked Marrion.

'They're coming to stay with me. How could you put your niece and nephew's lives at risk? Are you that desperate to control your sister?'

'I don't know what you're talking about.'

'I don't believe you, and neither does your sister. Rika picked me. She doesn't need you anymore, and you need to accept that,' said Marrion.

'Are you done?'

'You what?'

'I said, are you done.' Lamont's face shifted, eyes cold. Marrion took a step back.

'I don't know what—'

'I had nothing to do with this shooting, and you're an even bigger fool than I thought if you think otherwise.' Lamont paused, looking Marrion in his eyes. 'If I were you, I would think long and hard about who my enemies were, and which ones I owed money to.' He noted how pale Marrion looked after hearing those last few words. He glared one final time, then left.

CHAPTER TWENTY-TWO
FRIDAY 6 SEPTEMBER, 2013

TIMMY SAT in the passenger seat of Shorty's rented Mercedes and stared from the window.

After hearing nothing, he'd been surprised when Shorty rang and told him to get ready. Now, he was keeping his mouth shut, wondering what he wanted him to do and if he would get paid for it. He wanted Shorty to realise he was there for him. Shorty and Marcus had been tight, and Timmy knew the death was hitting him hard. Every time he tried to start a conversation, though, the words wouldn't come out.

After a while, they were in Huddersfield. Timmy hadn't been to the town for years, and when they drove to the affluent Fixby area, he sat up and paid attention.

Shorty pulled to a stop outside a semi-detached property and signalled for him to get out. He looked around, taking everything in. The garden was well-tended, with a new model Audi in the driveway. Timmy figured they were meeting the connect, so he was shocked when a beautiful woman strode out.

'What are you doing, Franklin?'

'You know why I'm here.'

'You should have called first.'

'Is he in?'

'Yes. He's in. That's not the point.'

'Stace, I'm in no mood for your mouth. Did you hear about Marcus?' Shorty asked. Timmy realised why she looked so familiar. She was the mother of Shorty's first child. No one had heard from her in years. He hadn't realised Shorty knew where she was.

'Stacey?' he blurted. Shorty glared at him.

'You've grown up, Tim,' said Stacey, smiling. He'd always fancied her. She had been stunning back then, and age didn't hadn't slowed her looks down.

'Forget him,' Shorty said. 'Did you hear?'

Stacey's eyes glistened. 'I'm sorry, Franklin. I know how close you both were. But, Marcus dying doesn't mean you can swan back into my life. Things are different now.'

As she said this, both Shorty and Timmy noticed the ring on Stacey's finger. Shorty kissed his teeth.

'I don't care about your life. I wanna see my boy.'

Timmy hung back, still confused by the whole situation. *Why were they here? And why had Shorty brought him along?*

Stacey folded her arms and frowned. 'You can visit for a few minutes. He's just come back from football training.'

She led them both into the house. Timmy took everything in as he walked through. There were neat paintings and immaculate, snow-white furniture. He stuffed his hands in his pockets and followed the others to the kitchen, where a tall boy hunched over a book. He looked up when the adults entered.

'Dionte, there's someone here to see you,' said Stacey.

'You're massive, son. You take after me,' Shorty broke the silence, his tone heartier than usual. Dionte stared, not saying a word.

Timmy was shocked at the similarities between them. Dionte had to be eleven or twelve years old, and was big for his age. Timmy hadn't seen him since he was a baby. One minute, Shorty was driving him and Stacey around, showing off his son. The next, they were both gone, and no one spoke of it.

Stacey cleared her throat.

'I'll leave you guys to talk.' She walked from the room. Timmy started to go with her, but then Shorty stepped further into the room.

'This is your cousin, Timmy.' Shorty pointed at him, and he nodded at Dionte. 'You kick ball too then? I used to play. What's your position?'

'Up front,' said Dionte.

'Me too. I bet you're banging in bare goals,' Shorty laughed. He stopped when neither of the others followed his lead. He scratched his temple, then, seeming to come to his senses, reached for his phone.

'Dunno if your mum ever mentioned your little sis, but here she is.' He brought up a picture of Grace, and showed it to Dionte, who displayed no reaction.

'Yo, what's wrong with you? I'm trying to show you your sis, and you're acting like a fucking retard.'

'Shorty—' Timmy spoke up, noting the bulging veins in Shorty's neck.

'Shut up, Tim. I'm talking to my son. D, what the fuck is up?'

'You're not my dad, and she's not my sister.' Dionte faced him.

'You little punk. Who do you think you are? I dunno what your mum told you, but there are two sides to every story.'

'What's going on in here? Why are you shouting?' Stacey hurried back into the room.

'Kill that. What have you been telling my son about me?' Shorty turned on her.

'I haven't told him anything.'

'Why's he so damn rude then? I tried showing him his sister, and he's running his mouth. You must have told him something. Don't lie.'

'Don't shout at my mum,' Dionte told Shorty, who looked stunned.

'Oh, so now you wanna talk?' His eyes narrowed. 'Don't be

pushing your chest out like you're gonna do summat. I'm talking to *mummy* now, so sit down and read your fucking book.'

Dionte held his ground.

'I said, sit down,' Shorty's voice rose, but still, he didn't move.

'Did you hear what I fucking said?'

'Franklin, it's time for you to leave,' said Stacey.

'I'm talking with my son.'

'If you don't leave, I'm calling the police.'

'You'd call police on me, Stace?' Shorty's voice was low now, his eyes wide.

'I would do anything to protect my son. Think about why he might not want to talk to you, or why he might not want to see a picture of the little girl you clearly love more than him.'

'I don't—'

'It doesn't matter. Don't you see? You swan back after years, and expect your son, who doesn't know you, to jump into your arms. Would you have done that if it were your father?'

'Tim, we're gone.' Shorty stormed off, not wanting her to realise how much her words had affected him. With a bewildered expression, Timmy followed.

OUTSIDE A HOME IN THE ST. Martins area of Leeds, Lamont steeled himself to do something he didn't want to do. He sat in his ride, gathering his courage. The meeting he was about to have was necessary, and with that in mind, he climbed from the ride, his legs heavy. He knocked on the door.

'Lamont,' Auntie said his name with her usual malice, tinged with a hint of curiosity.

'Hello, Auntie.' He went going to great pains to keep his voice level.

'Marika isn't here.'

'I came to see you.'

Auntie studied him, trying to gauge his reason for being on her doorstep. Curiosity won over, and she stepped aside. He stood in the living room, feeling ten years old again. Apart from the TV, everything seemed the same as it had the last time. Auntie took a seat, waiting for him to talk.

'You need to take care of Marika.'

Auntie blinked.

'What are you talking about?'

'We've parted ways. If I can't be there for her, then you need to be.' Lamont's words were more lucid than he expected. He was shocked at his composure around a person he loathed.

'*Parted ways*? I didn't invite you in so you could talk a load of nonsense.' Auntie's words were laced with intense dislike. She coughed then, a hacking cough that seemed to disappear only when she put a cigarette to her mouth and lit it.

'We fell out. Properly this time, so Marika needs you. She's always needed someone.' Lamont hated the smell of smoke but had become used to it over the years.

'Why did you fall out?' Auntie seemed chipper now, her eyes glittering.

'I said things in anger that she took to heart.'

'She told me that someone shot at her house.'

'I heard that too.'

'She told me you did it because you were jealous over Marrion.' Auntie dominated the conversation now, and knew it.

'She *thinks* I did it. I would never harm my sister, or her kids.'

'You've been harming her since day one. You never saw it, did you? Marika had a twisted dependence on you, and you revelled in it. Now, it's blown up.'

'Someone had to support us. You were never going to.'

'That's crap. You liked the control. You were always a messed-up child. I tried straightening you out, but couldn't.'

Lamont's blood boiled. He was allowing her to get to him.

'You're a horrible woman,' he started, taking a deep breath. 'You influenced my sister more than I ever could. Now, though, it's all on you; you and Marika no longer have me to unite against.' He hesitated, letting his words sink in. 'I wonder how long that will last.'

Auntie didn't reply. He looked at her, trying to see past the hatred and view her as a human being. He remembered her beauty, the guys she made jump through hoops. He felt sad, thinking about how life might have turned out had she only loved him.

'Why do you hate me?' The words were suddenly out before he could stop them. Auntie didn't hesitate.

'Because, you should have died. Out of the three people in that crash, it should have been you.'

Lamont allowed her words to wash over him, finding they didn't hurt as much as they should.

'You have a good life, Auntie. I don't imagine we'll see each other again.'

Back in the car, Lamont found he was smiling. He felt a certain clarity after speaking to Auntie. He didn't resent her as much as he had. She was an unhappy woman, but no longer would he be influenced by her loathing.

His phone rang as he pulled away from the curb.

'Lamont?' Georgia blurted.

'Hey. How are you?' Lamont asked. He was surprised when she burst into tears down the phone.

'Georgia, what's wrong?'

TIMMY SAT in a house in the Hood, watching Shorty chain-smoke and mutter to himself. The drive from Huddersfield was tense. Shorty had almost started a fight with a driver whom he had cut in front of. After being threatened with more police action, he'd driven off, swearing.

Timmy didn't know what to say, knowing Shorty was furious at how things had turned out with Dionte. He wanted to leave but couldn't. Instead, he sat and scrolled through Instagram, hoping for a reprieve.

TARGET

'Where've you been?' The door opened, and K-Bar sauntered in, drinking a bottle of Magnum tonic. He nodded to Timmy and took a seat.

'Away,' said Shorty.

'Where d'you go? I was looking for you.' K-Bar either couldn't tell Shorty was in a mood, or didn't care.

'I was busy, okay?'

'Whatever then. I handled it anyway,' K-Bar turned to Timmy. 'Were you with him?'

Timmy nodded. Shorty jabbed his cigarette into a chipped ashtray.

'What's up with him? 'It's only women that can get him this worked up,' said K-Bar.

'It's not a girl,' Timmy said before he could stop himself. Shorty turned on him.

'Shut your fucking mouth.'

'Shorty, chill,' K-Bar defended Timmy.

'Stay out of it, K. I'm dealing with my family.'

'I didn't do anything. Don't take it out on me because your—'

'Watch it,' Shorty pointed a finger at him. 'Don't say summat that will get you fucked up.'

'I'm not the enemy. I'm family. Why do you always treat me like shit?' It was out now, and Timmy was taking it all the way.

'You're a fucking worker,' Shorty said, laughing. 'How do you think this shit's supposed to go? You think because we're blood, you should get a treat? You little dudes kill me.'

'Steady on, Shorty. You're going too far now.' K-Bar spoke again, seeing how livid Timmy was.

'You're never gonna grow, Tim, and do you know why? It's because your mind ain't right. You're a fucking follower. You're not built to lead. That's why you get nowhere.'

Timmy jumped to his feet.

'What? You wanna go?' Shorty noted his clenched fists. 'I'll give you one free hit, and then I'm gonna put you in the hospital.'

227

Timmy glared at his cousin, seconds away from attacking him and taking the swift beating that would follow.

'Fuck you, Shorty.' Timmy stormed away and slammed the door behind him.

———

Chink was reading a newspaper in his kitchen when there was a hammering at the front door. He answered, surprised to see Lamont.

'L? Is everything okay?'

Lamont's face twisted into a mask of anger as he struck him in the face. Falling to the ground, he tried to rise, only for Lamont to boot him in the ribs.

'You piece of shit.'

'What the fuck, L?' gasped Chink, trying to catch his breath.

'Get up. You either get up, or I'll stomp on you. Get the fuck up. Now.'

Chink clambered to his feet, trying to get his bearings.

'What's this about, man? What's happened?'

'You raping piece of shit.' Lamont swung for him again. This time he ducked and tackled Lamont to the floor. They grappled, Lamont trying to damage, Chink trying to survive. Lamont brought his head back and caught him on the bridge of his nose with a stiff head butt. His nose exploded. Instinctively, he covered his face. Lamont smashed him in the ribs, feeling something shift as he grunted in pain.

He hit him again and leapt to his feet. He tried kicking him in the face, but Chink tripped him, determined to keep the brawl on the ground.

'L! Calm down.'

Lamont wasn't listening. His eyes blazed, fists clenched.

'Marcus was our boy. He dies, and you think you can rape his girl?'

Chink kicked out, catching him in the groin. He fell back with a grunt, allowing Chink to scramble away, leaning against the wall, panting.

'L, it wasn't like that. She came onto me. I'm weak, but I'm not a rapist.' Blood streamed from his nose. Lamont was also on his feet now, breathing hard but in better shape than Chink.

'You're a liar. You've always been a twisted fuck, but even this is beneath you. I swear, I'm gonna kill you.' Lamont tackled him to the floor again, throwing punch after punch at his former friend, Chink's hands by his side. Lamont was enraged. Never had he felt such anger. Chink's eyes glazed over. He cocked back his fist to hit him again when a scream startled him.

Naomi stood trembling in the doorway, watching the scene with terrified eyes. Lamont remembered she was once Reagan's girl. He was moments away from killing another person. The anger left him. He let Chink go and stood up.

'You and me are done. I never want to hear from you again,' Lamont told his old friend before leaving.

SCHEMES WAS a man on a mission as he stalked the streets of Harehills, searching for a phone box. He'd done well to stay under the radar, but it was driving him crazy now. The money he had been paid for the shooting was almost finished, and he was tired of being patient. Locating a phone, he dropped in some change and punched in a number.

'It's me,' he said when his contact answered.

'I told you I'd be in touch. You better have a good reason for calling.'

'I'm struggling, and I need to leave Leeds. That's my reason. I need more money.'

'You were given enough money. What you did with it is your problem.'

'My girl is pregnant. I can't be a fucking dad if I've got people shooting at me, can I?'

'Don't ring me again.' The contact hung up.

'MOTHERFUCKER!' Schemes slammed the phone down. He glanced around and saw a young black kid staring at him. 'What the fuck are you staring at?'

Mollified, the kid turned and scurried off. Still smarting, Schemes threw his hood up and stomped off back to his nearby hideout.

It never occurred to check if he was being followed.

Marrion was lounging at one of his spots. Since the business with Marika's house, he had moved her and the kids into his place, and he had his team watching his back in case there was another attempt on his life. His place was designed for one person, so it was a tight squeeze at the moment.

When he got his funds up, he would move them to a bigger place.

'Whoa,' he said, surprised by who had walked in, 'what happened to you?'

'It's not funny,' Chink glared at Marrion. He was flanked by Polo.

'The bruising gives you some character,' Marrion sniggered. 'Who put their hands on you? Shorty?'

'Lamont.'

'Lamont did that to you? I thought he was a talker.'

'Not important. What's important is getting things in place. People need to be removed. First up, Shorty. You need to handle it.'

'You sure you can't get him in line?'

'He's a thug, and he is dangerous. I won't have him or anyone else jeopardising my plan.'

'Get your boy there to handle it.' Marrion motioned to Polo, who scowled.

'I'm getting you to handle it, unless you want to go on that list too?' Chink asked. Marrion raised his hands in mock surrender.

'Okay, okay. I'm only playing. I'll get on it.'
'In the meantime, I will lock down our supply,' Chink told him.
'Have you got anyone in mind?'
Chink nodded.
'I have a meeting in place.'

Brownie entered then, holding two containers of food. He passed one to Marrion.

'I'll leave you to it.' Chink left without uttering a word to Brownie.

'What did he want?' Brownie said to Marrion. He didn't like Chink, and knew the feeling was mutual.

'We've got a job to do. Get Antonio in here.'

———

LATER THAT DAY, Chink climbed from his car, heading to his next meeting. Touching the bruises on his face, he frowned, unhappy at his looks being marred. It wasn't ideal, but he needed to handle this situation. Shown into the office, he stood in front of Delroy Williams, who appeared larger and more impassive than ever. Winston sat in the corner, watching him with intense dislike. Chink focused on Delroy.

'Thank you for seeing me.'
'What does Tef want?' Delroy ignored his pleasantries.
'I'm here of my own accord. We've gone our separate ways.'
If Delroy was surprised, he didn't show it.
'What does that have to do with me?'
'I want us to work together. I'm going into business for myself, and a supply such as yours will help me grow.'
'What happened to your face?' Winston spoke.
'Just a misunderstanding.'
'Yeah, I'll bet,' Winston chuckled. Chink pursed his lips. He didn't have time to dwell on the fight, but he was irritated with Winston for drawing attention to it. The last thing he needed was to appear weak.

'It's not important. What is important is the two of us making money together.'

Delroy scratched his chin with a chunky finger.

'You remember my prices?'

Chink nodded.

'Well, they've gone up. By two grand a box.' Delroy observed him, impressed when he didn't even flinch.

'Money is no problem. I'll want five for starters.'

Delroy almost smiled. 'Winnie will be in touch.' He nodded over at his son, who crossed his arms and scowled. Chink beamed, shook his hand and glided from the room.

'What the hell are you playing at?' said Winston as soon as the door closed.

'Have you forgotten who you're talking to?' Delroy gave his son a thunderous look.

'I mean no disrespect, Pops, but Chink is a snake. You can't trust him.'

'I don't.'

Winston's eyebrows rose. 'Then, why would you agree to a deal?'

'So I could see his cards. Get Teflon on the phone. I think he needs to hear what his little lackey has been up to.'

―――

MARRION STILL SAT in his base, drinking a beer. On the coffee table, his phone vibrated. Eventually, it stopped, but then it started again. He knew who was calling, but he couldn't talk to them yet. He didn't have control of the situation.

Back in Manchester, he'd been affiliated, but he didn't stand out. He was a rung above street dealer and resented it. Before moving, he had borrowed a lot of money from the wrong people. He'd had every intention of paying the money back, but upon arriving in Leeds, he burnt through the money, flossing to build up his profile and woo Marika Jones. Now, he was in a bind.

TARGET

Marrion needed a saving grace. He needed to deal with Shorty, then he could ask Chink for a loan to pay his creditors. The shooting had been a warning. Next time, they would take his head. He rubbed his eyes and looked up as Antonio and Brownie traipsed in.

'Well?' he demanded.

'Boss, he's too fucking para.' Antonio threw his hands in the air. 'Our guys can't keep up with him. He's always switching cars, or he's running red lights.'

'Fuck!' Marrion pounded his fist on the table. He hadn't expected tracking Shorty to be easy, but this took the cake. It had been twenty-four hours since Chink had given his orders. Marrion needed Shorty dead. He needed Chink's goodwill. It was his only way to win.

'Yo, we can get him, but it'll have to be some guerrilla-style shit. You'd have to get someone to run up on him and blast him,' Brownie pointed out.

'That's suicide,' said Marrion. 'No one's dumb enough to roll on him like that. Not in Shorty's own city, anyway.'

'Well then, tell Chink you're not doing it,' Brownie said. 'He wants him dead anyway, not you.'

Marrion didn't reply, rubbing his chin. There was a bang from outside, and Timmy burst in.

'What the fuck are you playing at?' Marrion had jumped up, thinking his debtors had found him.

'Sorry. I'm just stressed.' Timmy slumped down.

'Why? What's happened?'

'I'm not working with Shorty anymore. He's a dickhead. I wanna work with you.'

The final straw had come when Timmy turned up for work today, only for K-Bar to tell him he wasn't needed. Shorty was behind the demotion. Marrion spotted the anger and realised Timmy could solve his problems. He planted a contrite expression on his face.

'I've been waiting for you to step up and join my squad,' he

233

said. In reality, he had him at arm's length since Shorty had spoken to him. 'I need loyal people, though.'

'I'm loyal,' said Timmy.

'Are you ready to prove it?'

———

SHORTY LAY IN A DARK ROOM, messing on his phone and trying to avoid thinking about his issues. He was still angry at his dad for trying to creep to him. The anger Dionte had shown him mirrored the way he had greeted his own old man, and he didn't like that.

Shorty had been locked up when Dionte was born, and his son's birth hadn't deterred him in the slightest upon release. He had carried on partying and giving Stacey money every time he made a raise. She soon saw the light and moved away. He'd been relieved, even helping her pay towards the mini-mansion she was swanning around in. It had all backfired. Dionte had outgrown him, and that hurt. Amy was moving on, Stacey already had. Shorty had been crushed when he saw the ring on her finger. He hadn't even known she was involved with anyone. There had been no hint of the affection she had once lavished on him, and it hurt.

Shorty sat up when his phone rang. He glanced at the screen and answered.

'What, Tim?' he said. He didn't have time for his whining.

'I need to see you.'

'What's going on?' said Shorty. Timmy sounded panicky, and that wasn't normal.

'Marrion's up to summat. I overheard him talking about you and L.'

'Not over the phone. Where are you?'

———

SHORTY SCREECHED to a halt outside a spot in Seacroft. If Marrion was moving against them, he would kill him, no questions asked.

'Tim, where the fuck are you?' he called as he climbed from the car. The street was deserted, and his instincts were going haywire. Something wasn't right. He rang Timmy's number again, which went straight to voicemail.

'What the fuck?' He murmured. The hairs on the back of his neck rose as he heard a shuffling sound, spotting a flicker of movement to his right. He ducked, a hail of bullets hitting the spot he'd stood in. Shorty popped back up, gun in hand and fired twice, hearing a scream as he hit one of his attackers. There were more of them, though, and they continued firing, keeping him pinned down.

'Oi badman. Why are you hiding?' a voice taunted.

Crouched behind a car tyre, Shorty recognised the Manchester accent as Marrion's idiot friend from the club. With a sickening feeling, he realised Timmy had set him up.

Even coked-up out of his head, Solly was amazed by Shorty's reflexes. They'd had the drop on him, but he'd not only avoided the trap, he'd taken out one of the two gunners Solly had brought along. Solly had assumed Shorty was all talk, but he had never seen anyone move like that.

Signalling to his remaining hitter to flank him, he watched the goon hurry forward. Shorty was ready, ventilating the man's head with another bullet. He was amped, eyes alight with rage. Solly was out of his depth, and he knew it. He dropped the gun and put his hands in the air, standing by a streetlight so the surrender could be seen.

'Chill! Chill! I don't have a gun,' his voice shook. Shorty stalked over, eyes flitting in all directions. He pointed his gun at him, his finger caressing the trigger.

'Marrion send you?'

Solly nodded, sweating and scared.

'Thanks.' Pulling the trigger three times, Shorty watched Solly's body drop, then hurried to his car and sped off.

CHAPTER TWENTY-THREE
WEDNESDAY 11 SEPTEMBER, 2013

LAMONT SLOUCHED IN HIS GARDEN. He had been here for hours, watching the dark sky lighten and the sun rise. His sleep pattern was picking up, but last night's events had him wired.

There had been a shooting near Shorty's, and three people were dead. Associates of Marrion. Lamont hadn't heard from Shorty yet, and that worried him. He was hard enough to control, but if someone had attempted to take his life, he wouldn't rest until he'd had his revenge.

Lamont had also received a phone call yesterday from Winston Williams, informing him of a meeting that Chink had with his father. He was surprised at Chink's swift manoeuvring, but going to Delroy had been a foolish move. He'd never shown much love for Chink, and as he'd shown in past dealings with Lamont, he was all politics. Even armed with this knowledge, Lamont did nothing. As badly as Chink wanted to be his enemy, his plans were unchanged. The meeting with Akhan was in place. Lamont would plug in someone to take over distribution for the team and then go.

He needed to clear his head. The tickets to Uruguay had been purchased. He hoped Jenny would agree to come. He was banking on the trip, convincing her they should travel. It was selfish to

TARGET

expect her to put her business on hold, but he loved her and wanted her around him. He checked the time and wondered if it was too early to call her.

K-Bar stood in the middle of a dank cellar. Known as *The Dungeon*, it was a secluded, soundproofed spot where violators were punished without the risk of interruption. Grimer, a brawny associate of Shorty's who loved dealing with the heavy work, was with him. K-Bar had called him especially. The streets were red-hot. Shorty was off the grid. K-Bar was a loyal soldier, but even he didn't understand half the things that were going on. Chink had split and was doing his own thing. People said Lamont had ordered a shooting at his sister's spot. It was ridiculous.

He assessed their battered victim, slumped against the cellar wall with his arms tied above him. Naked from the waist up, his torso and chest were covered with burn marks and various cuts.

'Where were we?' Grimer asked the victim with an evil smile. He was old school and couldn't believe the little shit in front of him had gunned down Marcus Daniels.

'Please, I don't know anything,' said Schemes through cracked and bloodied teeth. They had caught him slipping after someone tailed him in Harehills, then dragged him to the dungeon. So far, the youngster had held firm, but it wouldn't last long.

'You know how to squeeze off a fucking Mac, don't you?' K-Bar stood in front of Schemes. 'Our people spotted you in the park, spraying bullets at fucking Tall-Man. You thought you were a bad man, didn't you? Well, now I'm gonna show you how a real bad man rolls, unless you talk. Who hired you to do Marcus?'

'Nobody! I told you, he jumped Maverick. We were coming back on him.'

K-Bar turned to Grimer. 'Get your tools.'

Grimer reached into a nearby leather bag, removing a battered mini-sledgehammer. He swung it, testing the weight. Grimer delved into the bag again and pulled out a selection of nails. Turning to the kid with a smile, he walked towards him. Schemes tried to rear back, but there was nowhere he could go.

'No. Don't!' He screamed.

'Talk then. If not, it's gonna get biblical. We're gonna nail your fucking feet to the floor, and that's just for starters,' warned K-Bar.

'All right. All right!' Schemes shouted, as Grimer raised the hammer.

'Stop stalling. Spill.'

'I don't know who ordered it,' said Schemes. 'Wait! I met one of his people—Always the same dude; white guy, big, flash whip.'

Bored, K-Bar signalled for Grimer to begin.

'Wait,' Schemes yelled again. 'The guy, he was a Brummie.'

K-Bar halted Grimer.

'What did you say?'

'The guy was from Birmingham! I recognised his accent.'

'You better not be lying.'

'I'm not! The numbers in my phone. Ring it! It's the last one I called.' Schemes sobbed with fear.

K-Bar found the phone and rang the number, holding his breath.

'Yeah?' said Polo. K-Bar closed his eyes.

'Oi, you little prick. I told you not to fucking ring again. You'll get the money when I say so.'

K-Bar froze and dropped the phone, cold fury engulfing him.

'What's up? Do you believe me now then?' Schemes asked. K-Bar smacked him in the mouth, causing Schemes to hit his head against the wall.

'Shut the fuck up. Tell me everything, and I mean fucking everything.'

———

'Yo, it's crazy. They're saying that Shorty blazed some dudes from Manny.'

'Why, though?'

Ben and Jerome were chilling. Ben's mother was comatose somewhere, meaning they were free to raid her liquor stash. Jerome was filling Ben in on the situation with Shorty. He'd tried ringing Timmy, but he wasn't answering.

'There was beef at Carnival. Shorty beat up one girl, and she must have been linked to these Manny goons, because they ran up on Shorty. They flopped, and he dropped them.'

'Shit. That's heavy. They'd never have tried that if Tall-Man was still alive.'

Jerome snorted. 'Fuck him. He was all hype. He got fucking riddled. No one was scared of him.'

Ben shrugged, helping himself to more rum and mixing it with the bottle of Lilt resting between his legs. Jerome was knowledgeable, so he took everything he said as gospel.

'Yo, try Tim again.'

As Ben pulled his phone out, there was a loud crash from downstairs and footsteps trudging towards them.

'What the fuck?' Jerome jumped to his feet. The bedroom door burst open, and Shorty stood there.

'Yes, Shorty. What's—'

There was a sharp crack as Shorty hit him in the mouth with a left hook. Jerome talked a big game, but he crumbled like pastry from the blow. Petrified, Ben tried running to the door, but Shorty stood in his way. He raised his hands, but he stood no chance. Shorty hit him with a ferocious two-hit combination, and he slid to the ground.

'You little bastards better start talking.' Shorty pulled a gun. 'Where's Timmy?'

'W-We thought he was with you,' said Ben, moaning when Shorty smacked him with the weapon.

'I said, you better talk,' Shorty repeated. 'Oi, big man,' he kicked Jerome in the stomach. 'You think you know everything. Where's Timmy?'

The pair lay on the floor in a terrified heap. Shorty had always scared them, but as Timmy's close friends, they thought that gave them a pass. They realised now how wrong they had been. Shorty's eyes popped, his nostrils flaring. He pointed the gun at them, shaking with rage.

'We haven't seen him, I swear! We tried ringing him, but he didn't answer,' Ben gibbered.

'You expect me to believe that?' Shorty laughed. 'You two are his fucking bum boys. He tells you lot everything. You probably knew all along.'

'About what?'

Furious, Shorty hit Jerome with the gun.

'Tell me where he is!' he roared, but Jerome was unconscious. He stalked toward Ben, who had urinated out of sheer terror.

'Your turn,' he said, raising the bloody gun again.

―――

Grim-faced, red-eyed and unshaven, K-Bar climbed from a car and hurried into a house. Lamont waited. He took in his comrade's unkempt appearance and sensed that it was serious. His first thought was that K-Bar would announce Shorty was dead, and he braced himself.

'We've got big problems.'

'People have been calling. Have you heard from Shorty?'

'No,' K-Bar wiped his forehead, 'It's about Chink.'

'Chink?'

'He paid for the hit on Marcus.'

It was like a ton of bricks had toppled upon Lamont. Of all the things K-Bar could say, few would have had more impact. He closed his eyes, knowing why Chink had done it.

'Georgia,' he whispered.

'You what?'

'Chink is in love with Georgia. He took out Marcus because he wanted her to himself.'

'Snake,' K-Bar spat. 'He can't live. You know that, right?'

TARGET

Saddened, Lamont nodded.

'I know.'

———

Shorty put his hood up as he crouched across the road from Amy's. He knew she was in. He needed to see her, and more importantly, he needed to see Grace. He still clutched the blooded gun. Despite wanting to hide it, his street senses screamed for him to keep it.

Family had betrayed him. Timmy had lured Shorty to a meet, knowing he would be killed. He would never forgive that, and once the heat died down, he would end both Timmy and Marrion.

Shorty hurried across the road and knocked on Amy's door. He looked around, scanning for nosy neighbours.

'Shorty?' Amy was startled to see him standing on her doorstep. He gazed. In his fatigued state, she seemed more beautiful than ever.

'I wanna see Grace.'

'Is that a gun?' Amy noticed the piece in his hand.

'Amy—'

'You need to leave. Police have been by twice already. They're saying you killed three people.'

Shorty kissed his teeth. He didn't have time for this.

'I wanna see Grace.'

'You're holding a bloody gun. Is that how you want her to see you? She's asleep. It's late.'

'Just move! I have to hide, but I need to see her,' Shorty was almost pleading. Amy felt his sorrow and her heart went out to him. She was about to speak when another voice interrupted.

'What the hell are you doing here?' Chris Hart appeared at Amy's side. Shorty's eyes narrowed.

'I'm here to see my kid. Stay out of it.'

'No, I bloody won't. Do you have any idea the aggro you've

caused? Police went to Amy's work. They've been here twice because of you.'

'Chris—' Amy tried to speak, but he waved her off.

'He's a murderer, Ames. He killed three people, and now he's trying to implicate you and Gracey.'

'Get out of the way, or I'm gonna pop you too.' Shorty raised the gun. Chris looked scared now, but didn't move.

'Just leave. They're coming for you.'

'Who's coming?' Shorty asked, his question answered by sirens and flashing lights. Chris smirked, so he clocked him with the gun, turned to vault a nearby fence, and took off running.

MARRION HUNG up his phone and slammed it down. Everything had gone to shit. The hit on Shorty had gone awry, Solly and his guys were dead, and Shorty had to know he had been behind it. Now he would have to deal with the vengeful thug who had eluded the police so far.

Brownie was handling the latest mission, but Antonio was waiting for Marrion at the spot, and would guard him. Worst was the news he needed to give to the woman he loved. Marika was cleaning in his front room when he approached.

'Sit down a sec, Rika. I've got summat to tell you.'

'What is it?' Marika asked. She would kill him if he was about to say he was leaving her. She knew he'd been seen with other girls in town, which was bad enough.

'It's about your brother.'

'What about him?' Marika hadn't heard from Lamont since he had turned up at her house after the shooting.

'I'm only telling you this to prepare you, but I've got confirmation Lamont was behind the shooting at your place,' said Marrion.

'That fucking prick!' Marika couldn't believe he would put her kids at risk like that.

'Yeah. He's a cunt,' said Marrion, launching into the next phase. 'That's why he's getting taken out.'

'W-What?'

'My people are on it. It'll be quick, and I promise he won't suffer.' Marrion held her close. He was startled when she wrenched free.

'No. Stop them.'

'What do you mean? He tried to kill you.'

'If Lamont wanted me dead, he would have made it happen.' Marika shook her head. 'He's my brother. Just because we're not talking, doesn't mean I want him to die.' She clutched Marrion's front, tears in her eyes. 'If you love me, then you'll call it off.'

'For fuck's sake, Rika.' Marrion pulled away and stormed from the house. Chink had been insistent that Lamont had to die, but he loved Marika. It was early evening now. Brownie would already be en route. He climbed into his Mercedes, dialling Brownie as he started the engine. Before he could move, a tinted ride screeched to a halt alongside him. The windows wound down, and automatic gunfire erupted, spraying the Benz with bullets. As the car sped down the street, Marrion slumped over in the driver's seat, bleeding.

———

POLO SAT in his car across the road from Naomi's place. Chink had been holed up for hours, and he was irritable. He couldn't even turn the radio on, and the battery on his phone was low from the silly internet videos he had viewed.

'He's taking the piss now,' Polo said to himself. When his boss emerged from his bird's house, he decided they would talk. He'd decided to risk urinating in the street when he spotted something. A man darted across the road heading for Naomi's. Polo reached for his pistol. Before he could grab it, a gun pressed against the back of his head.

'Don't move.'

Polo froze, feeling a devastating pain as the gun smashed into his kidney. He fell onto the pavement, bile rising in his throat.

Arms grabbed him, relieving him of his gun and a knife, dragging him into a nearby garden.

'I thought we would have to do you in the car, mate,' said K-Bar, attaching a silencer to his weapon. Polo stared at him, steeling himself to meet his fate like a man.

K-Bar aimed the gun, tilted his head, then pulled the trigger.

———

'I'LL BE BACK LATER.'

Naked on the bed, Naomi nodded at Chink's words, returning to messing around on her phone. He was tempted to knock it from her hands, but didn't have the time. There were still details to sort, and he didn't think Polo would wait outside forever. Chink was waiting for confirmation that the job was done on Lamont. After failing to take out Shorty, Marrion was on his last chance. If he messed it up, he was finished. Chink had no time for fuck ups. Shorty had escaped for now, but he couldn't hide forever.

When everything was done, he could focus on wooing Georgia. Only Lamont stood between him and the woman he loved. He smiled to himself as he buttoned his silk shirt.

'Clean this place up when I'm gone too. It's a mess,' he added. Naomi glowered. It was her house, and yet he saw fit to tell her what to do in it. Not liking the way she was looking at him, Chink glared at her.

'Is that a problem?'

'No.' Naomi stood up. Chink stared at her naked body, feeling himself grow aroused again. He was about to tell her to lie down when he heard a noise.

'What was that?'

'Shut up,' said Chink. The noises grew louder. He hurried to the window. What he saw made his heart race.

K-Bar crept through the garden with a gun in his hand, his face full of resolve. Chink felt his bowels churning as he rushed downstairs, sprinting through the rooms and lunging for the back door. Before he could flee, Grimer appeared at the door. He backed him into the room as K-Bar charged in, his face resolute.

'Going somewhere?'

Chink raised his hands.

'What's going on, K? Is there a problem?' He tried talking his way out of the reaper's hands. He didn't like K-Bar any more than Shorty, but he knew what K-Bar could do. He was a killer, and if he was in the house, that meant Polo was dead.

'I think you already know,' said K-Bar, letting him know his words wouldn't cut it. There were more footsteps, and Naomi stood next to K-Bar. She wore a dressing gown, a hateful expression on her face, and the penny dropped for Chink.

'Why?' He said to Naomi, eyes blazing.

'You should never have hit me, rapist,' she told him.

'You told them where I was?' he was flabbergasted. 'Fucking ungrateful—'

'Forget this,' said K-Bar. His gun was raised.

'K, I have money. I'll make you a wealthy man. All you need to do is walk away; pretend you never saw me,' said Chink. He was terrified but didn't want to show weakness in front of Shorty's pet wolf.

'I know all about what you did,' K-Bar's voice was low, tinged with controlled anger. 'You killed Marcus.'

'That wasn't me. Marrion did it. He was behind the whole thing. He tried killing Shorty too. I swear!'

K-Bar fired his gun, hitting Chink in the thigh. He screamed and fell to the floor, clutching his leg and moaning.

'W-Whatever happens, Lamont dies too. You can't stop it, unless you let me go,' said Chink.

K-Bar, Grimer and Naomi stared at him with disgust, lying on the floor in his expensive clothing, pleading for his life.

'Hold these for Marcus.' K-Bar fired at Chink until his clip was spent.

'We need to go.' Grimer glanced at Chink's body.

'You're right.' K-Bar turned to Chink's girlfriend, who looked shaken. When he had contacted her through a third party, she had agreed to set him up for free.

'Do it.'

Naomi realised what was about to happen and screamed. The bullet smashed through her right eye, causing her to sink to the ground. Grimer took two steps forward, looking at her prone form.

'No witnesses,' he mumbled, firing again.

'Let's go! L's in fucking trouble.' K-Bar was already by the back door. 'Call Maka and tell him to go to L's bird's house. I'll give you the address.'

―――

Lamont was outside Jenny's place. He had gone home hoping Shorty would contact him. He left it as long as possible before heading out with a travel bag.

Jenny waited in the garden as he pulled up. Even in the night, he saw her eyes sparkle with a happiness that made his heart almost burst from his chest. She beamed, and he returned the grin. He was so engrossed that he didn't see them approaching until the last second.

'Jenny! Get inside,' Lamont said, a tremor of fear cascading down his spine when he saw the guns. *Not now*, he thought. His eyes widened when he recognised one of the men.

'Timmy?'

―――

'Shoot him!' Brownie shouted Timmy, who trembled, his eyes wide. It was bad enough he'd set up Shorty, but now he was about to shoot the man who had employed him for years.

The gun Brownie had forced on him was heavy, almost burning

in his palm. He tried raising it, but when he saw the terror in the eyes of Lamont's girl, lowered it again.

'Useless little shit,' Brownie pushed him aside, aiming at Lamont and firing.

Time slowed. Lamont was aware of Jenny's screaming before he felt the fiery pain as the bullet slammed into his chest. The second shot tore into his stomach, sending him tumbling to the pavement. He gasped for air, panicking as the blood billowed beneath him. Jenny knelt over him, covered in his blood. He tried reaching for her, but his arms wouldn't respond.

Brownie moved forward to finish him but was distracted by the screech of tyres. Maka jumped from the Renault Clio, firing, missing him but catching Timmy in the neck and chest. The kid crumpled in a heap, and Brownie turned tail, running for the car. He jumped in and sped off, bullets whizzing around him.

JENNY . . .

NEVER IN HIS *life had he experienced such pain. His body felt like it was on fire. He couldn't move his limbs, but his eyes were wide open, staring at her.*

She was still with him. Saying words he couldn't understand. Tears streaming down her perfect face. His blood staining her sweater.

Neighbours converged. One of them clutched a phone.

He tried to speak, but his throat didn't work. Maybe he was already dead. He could feel the darkness coming. He tried to fight it, but it was futile.

MEETING JENNY'S dark eyes one more time, Lamont succumbed to nothingness.

EPILOGUE
WEDNESDAY 24 SEPTEMBER, 2014

AKHAN SAT IN HIS OFFICE, staring into space, enjoying the quiet. Outside the window, the trees slowly lost the green leaves for another year. Akhan was checking the time on his watch when Saj knocked and entered.

'He's here.'

'Show him in.' Akhan sat back as Lamont Jones entered.

Lamont had recovered from the worst of his injuries, but moved slower than before. The bullet to his stomach had gone straight through, missing his vital organs. It had taken over a year for him to function, but now he perched opposite Akhan.

'You look well.' Akhan poured him a glass of water.

'I've been worse.' Lamont sipped his drink and focused on Akhan. 'I received your gift. It was thoughtful of you.'

'You seemed pleased with the first bottle, so I thought more might suffice. How are you?'

Lamont shrugged. 'Day by day, I guess. It's all I can hope for right now.'

Akhan nodded. 'When will we be able to resume business?'

Lamont looked him in the eyes. 'Never.'

Akhan didn't speak straight away. Standing, he stared out of the window as if Lamont wasn't there. He recognised the strategy. It was designed to make him uncomfortable, to make him talk first. He didn't take the bait. Instead, he sipped his drink and stared at the unread books on Akhan's shelf.

'Why, Lamont?' We have done well together. Look how much we made over the Bank Holiday period. Imagine that over a year? Imagine it over ten?'

'Some things mean more.'

'Such as?'

'Such as life.'

Akhan rubbed his eyes. 'How much do you want to leave this life?'

'More than anything.'

'Then, are you willing to pay the price?' said Akhan, his words cold.

'I paid the price. I was shot.'

'You also survived.'

'What's the cost then?'

'Everything, Lamont,' said Akhan. He paused, waiting for his words to take effect. 'The cost is everything. That is the cost of leaving for good. You must ask yourself now, how much she is worth to you.' He smiled at the surprise on Lamont's face. 'Don't look so shocked. A man talks like this; It can only be because he is in love. Is this woman worth it?'

'Yes,' Lamont said without hesitation.

'So, your mind is made up then?'

Akhan was shocked at the intensity that appeared on Lamont's face. He was reminded of the powerful young man who had sat in his office over a year ago. There seemed to be no trace of his injuries as he stared him down and spoke.

'There's no choice to make. I see this life for what it is; you have power, wealth and status, but you're a slave to the game. The choices you make are not your own, just like my choices weren't mine. You're not playing the game; the game is playing you.'

Akhan was silent. Lamont continued.

'It's lonely. This life. Never relaxing. Doing business with people you don't like, all to keep the wheel spinning. You have to put on an act. You can't do what you want.' A wistful smile appeared on Lamont's face. 'I've sampled another world, and I'm ready to immerse myself in it.'

Akhan shook his head.

'You're an impressive speaker. It's one of the things I admire about you, but you will do as I say.'

'No, I won't.' Lamont was on his feet now.

Akhan smiled.

'I heard a story . . . Over a year ago. A story of a struggle in a barber's shop.' He paused, watching it dawn on Lamont's face. 'A man ended up dead. It was covered up, but I recall everything about this story.'

Lamont couldn't speak. His throat constricted. He sat back down without even realising.

'Lamont . . . Sorry, *Teflon*. I know what you did to Ricky Reagan. I understand why you did it, but it becomes my gain. If you leave this life, you will go to prison. It's as simple as that.'

Lamont felt faint as he groped for the glass of water and guzzled the clear liquid. He couldn't believe this was happening. He was so close.

'Let's talk no more of you walking away, Teflon. For you, this game we're both being forced to play is just beginning.'

DID YOU ENJOY THE READ?
YOU CAN MAKE A HUGE DIFFERENCE

Reviews are immensely powerful when it comes to getting attention for my books.

Honest reviews help bring them to the attention of other readers.

If you've enjoyed this I would be very grateful if you could spend just five minutes leaving a review on the book's Amazon page.

Thank you so much

TARGET PART 2 PREVIEW

Check out the first chapter of Target Part 2, book 3 in the Target series

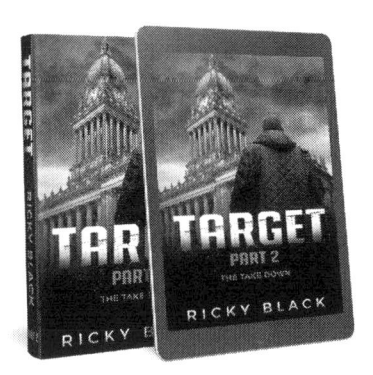

PROLOGUE

TUESDAY 15 OCTOBER, 2013

THE STREETS OF HULME, Manchester, were deathly quiet, a rattling wind shuffling the sparse tree leaves. Only a few faces were out; kids in parkas and hooded tops mooching around, spitting on the floor and talking in loud voices. They were unaware they were being watched.

A car at the bottom of the street idled with its lights off. The passenger, a brawny dark-skinned man with closely cropped hair and scarred features, turned to the driver.

'Are we gonna have a problem?'

The driver shook his head. He was a dreadlocked killer known as *K-Bar* on the streets of Leeds. He tugged on a pair of weathered leather gloves. Both criminals wore black jackets, combat trousers and plain black trainers. He stifled a yawn, a gun resting on his lap. In the dark car, it was hard to see the livid bags under his eyes.

'The right people know what we're doing.' K-Bar cocked the gun. 'We're gonna go through the back, nice and quiet.'

Grimer nodded. Black balaclavas securing their faces, they moved. The youths glanced at them but didn't speak. In silence, they made their way to the back of a terraced house, Grimer keeping a lookout while K-Bar broke in. They checked their weapons and padded through the living room, silenced guns at the ready.

Grimer approached the stairs, K-Bar covering as he tested the steps for any noise. They ascended, searching each room. Approaching the master bedroom, they saw a flash before gunfire ensued. K-Bar ducked, Grimer following his lead. The gun smoke made it hard to see, but they had been in similar situations before, and their movements were fluid. The shooter's aim was off, but they needed to be quick. Police were likely en route.

'Cover me!' K-Bar yelled, rolling into the bedroom. Grimer rose from his position, firing multiple shots in the shooter's direction. K-Bar spotted the muzzle spray and picked his shots carefully. He hit the shooter, who dropped with a scream. Hurrying towards the prone frame, he kicked the gun away, training his own on the shooter. The shooter wheezed, staring up at the figures, unable to recognise them.

Grimer moved to flick on the bedroom light. They surveyed Brownie, gritting his teeth in obvious pain. They hadn't seen him since he'd fled Leeds after almost killing Lamont. His frame remained stocky, but his face seemed thinner. Living on the run hadn't agreed with him.

'You're lucky we don't have time to get deep,' K-Bar snarled. 'We took out your shit crew. Marrion's gone, and Antonio squealed like a bitch when we put him down. You're the one we wanted, though.'

'I don't give a damn. I ain't a punk,' growled Brownie, eyes watering from pain, blood trickling from his shoulder down to his t-shirt.

'Yeah, you are. You tried getting a kid to do your runnings, and you really thought you and that clown you worked for were gonna run our thing?' K-Bar laughed, Grimer chuckling in his booming voice.

'Fuck you. Go to hell.' Brownie spat on the floor.

'Let's forget the talking then. You can hold this for *Teflon*.' K-Bar fired, shooting Brownie twice in the head.

READ BLOOD AND BUSINESS

Tyrone Dunn wants to take over Leeds, and he is willing to battle anyone who gets in his way.

Even family.

Will it be settled by blood . . . or business?

Order now, and find out.

ALSO BY RICKY BLACK

The Target Series:

Origins: The Road To Power

Target

Target Part 2: The Takedown

Target Part 3: Absolute Power

The Complete Target Collection

The Deeds Family Series:

Blood & Business

Good Deed, Bad Deeds

Deeds to the City

ABOUT RICKY BLACK

Ricky Black was born and raised in Chapeltown, Leeds. He began writing seriously in 2004, working on mainly crime pieces.

In 2016, he published the first of his crime series, Target, and has published four more books since.

Visit https://rickyblackbooks.com for information regarding new releases and special offers and promotions.

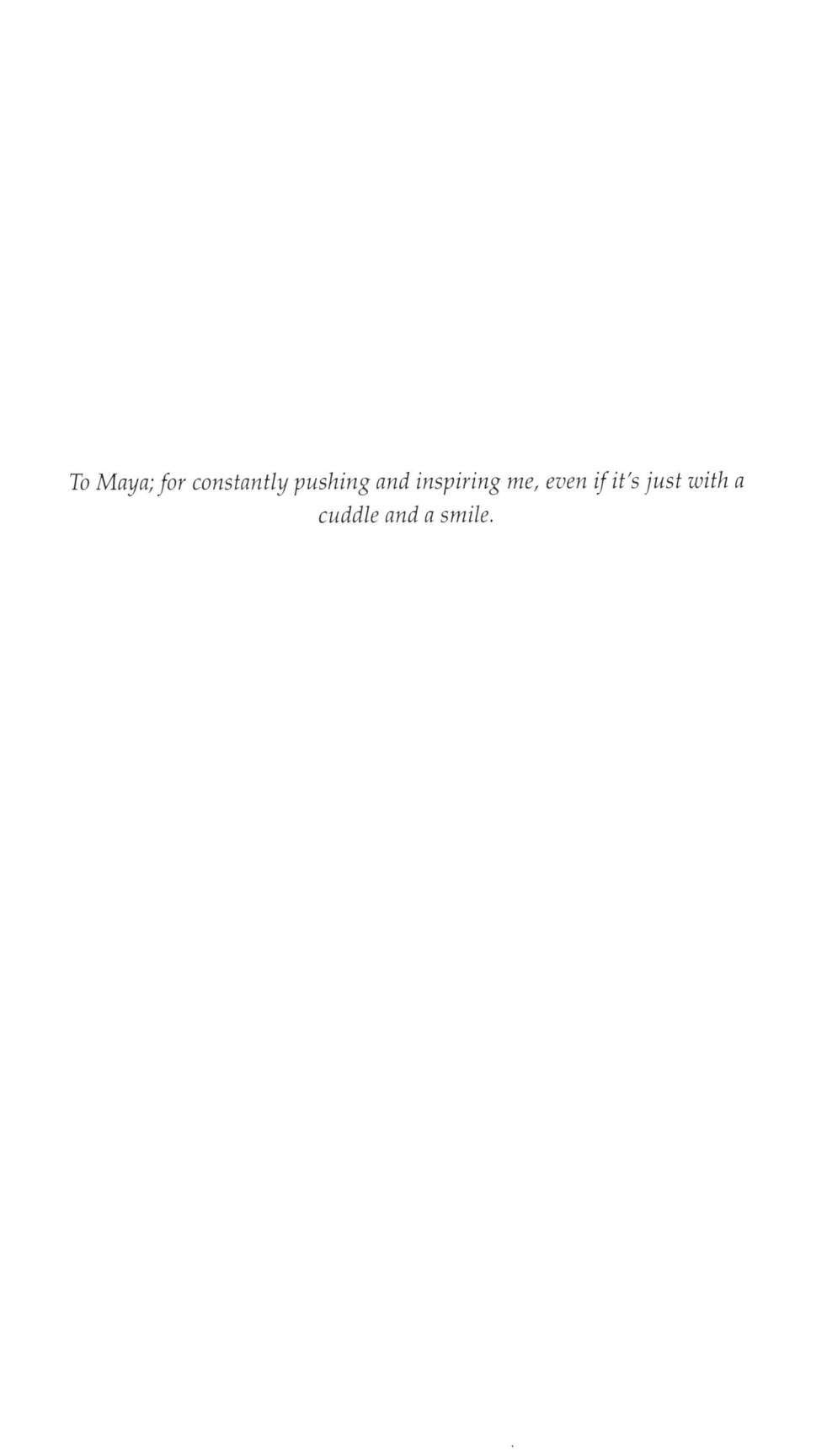

To Maya; for constantly pushing and inspiring me, even if it's just with a cuddle and a smile.

Copyright Notice

© Ricky Black 2018 All rights reserved worldwide. Except as provided by the Copyright Act. No part of this publication may be reproduced, stored in a retrieval system or transmitted in any means without the prior written permission of the publisher

This book is a work of fiction. Characters and events in this novel are the product of the author's imagination. Any similarity to persons living or dead is purely coincidental.